ITCHY FEET

ITCHY FEET

by

Jane Stickland

The Intrepid Traveller

Regency Press (London & New York) Ltd
125 High Holborn, London WC1V 6QA

To my late husband, a Gemini and a traveller,

ISBN 0 7212 0886 X

Printed and bound in Great Britain by
Buckland Press Ltd., Dover, Kent.

Contents

The author expresses her sincere thanks to:–

Mrs Joan L. Grahame, *The Lady,* for permission to reproduce two articles which she published.

The editor of *The Sunday Times of Malta* for permission to reproduce articles published in his newspaper.

John Kenyon, writer, of Malta, for his help and encouragement with my manuscript, *The Maltese Islands.*

Lt-Col P. J. Emerson, Hon. Secretary of the Indian Army Association, for checking my drafts on India and *The Bridge over the River Kwai,*

Mr David Ambrose, editor of *Guide to Visitors* on Maseru, Lesotho, South Africa, for permission to use his article.

British Airways for checking *A Transatlantic Experience,* Concorde.

Frances Bondi of North Carolina, USA, for checking my manuscript on *Staying on a Marine Base.*

Mr Sidney Smith of Wales for his help with my Nigerian manuscript.

Miss Geraldine Gordon of Vancouver, Canada, for reading my manuscript on *Canada Again.*

The late Major Charles Risdon, Sussex, for reading my manuscript on Cairo.

Mr Scott Kinsey, Shore Excursion Manager of the P&O Shipping Line, for his notes on Acapulco.

Lastly, to my editor and the manager of Regency Press for their patience and endurance in reading, correcting and editing my script which I hammered out on an old manual portable typewriter. With their co-operation, this book came into being.

CHAPTER ONE

1932 – On Foreign Soil

Landfall and departure mark the rhythmical swing of a seaman's life, and of a ship's career. From land to land is the most concise definition of a ship's fate.

Conrad, ' The Mirror of the Sea.'

Often I have been asked which, of all the countries I have visited, do I like the best. This question I find very difficult to answer as each country had a special appeal at the time. Perhaps China was the most impressionable, with its ancient civilisation.

Armchair travel has never been my scene. As the great philosopher, Dr Samuel Johnson, said, 'The use of travel is to regulate imagination and, instead of thinking how things may be, to see them as they really are.'

In the early twenties I had 'itchy feet' to see the world. Some years later my dream came true, and I realised my ambition. To be hooked on travel for travel's sake is like an incurable disease; it never lets go!

Born on a Thursday (*Thursday's child has far to go*), I am also a Gemini under the auspices of Jupiter, one of the planets ruling travel, pursuing my desires by my own go-getting. Now in my eighty-third year I still have the urge to 'get up and go'.

I first set foot on foreign soil as far back as 1932 from John Brown's vessel mv *Ormonde* which was subsequently taken over by the P&O line; it was one of four liners on the Mediterranean run. Thomas Cook were my travel agents and they have since organised some of my tours; the remainder I have done under my own steam.

Cruising in the early thirties was considered an adventure as few people could voyage abroad. There was no need for security as there is today and everything went according to plan. Cruise fares were ridiculously cheap being no more than we pay for travel insurance now. A tourist-class cabin on the *Ormonde* cost £14 for fourteen days – just a pound a day! The optional seven shore excursions, at Cadiz, Ceuta, Malaga, Casablanca, Gibraltar, Lisbon and Vigo, cost £5. 1s. 6d. in old money.

Our first port of call was the old city of Cadiz, built on a narrow isthmus with a network of long and narrow cobbled streets. The houses were built so closely together they almost seemed to be touching.

At one time Cadiz was one of the wealthiest cities in Europe. In the sixteenth century it had been Spain's great distribution port thronged with merchandise from Genoa and the Netherlands. Since those days the old walls and fortifications have crumbled, revealing tunnelled galleries, breached in many places.

With only a few hours in port, Mary, my sister, and I set off for the town in search of Spanish leather shoes. Wandering down the aviendos and along the narrow little streets, we soon had a trail of curious and poor-looking locals following us, including a mob of piccaninnies. One of the men had a smattering of English; he became our guide, and led us to a shop crammed full of shoes. We tried on a few pairs, squeezing our feet into the narrow fittings; I bought a pair, but could never wear them when we reached home. Cosmopolitan dancing was in full swing in the cafes; in the past the city was famous for its ancient dances. Cadiz was the centre of music with Italian opera companies regularly visiting Madrid.

With my five-shilling box camera, snapshots were taken of the Spaniard; we sent copies of the photos to him and back came blown-up pictures together with a photograph of his sister.

We docked in Ceuta, a Spanish enclave in Morocco. The Romans called it the city of the seven brothers or hills; the highest hill, Monte del Hacko, is one of the ancient Pillars of Hercules.

We drove out to the Berber town of Tetuan, meaning 'eyes'. The Moors certainly lived up to that name; everywhere we went the veiled white-clad women watched us with their staring eyes through the maze of streets of dead-white walls, until they reached their sealed doors where they disappeared into a world apart. Tetuan is a land of mystery, brothels and gypsy camps.

In Casablanca, the major port of the kingdom of Morocco, there were hordes of beggars. Morocco was at one time one of the most primitive countries in the world, even wild at times. The country is imbued with the fascinating mysteries of the east, mystic songs and dances told of wars, of saints, of the land, even of love!

Hidden in the valleys, sheltered the strange Berber and nomad tribes with their ancient customs. Often they would trek over the magnificent Riff mountains.

In the souks (bazaars), craftsmen were at work as their ancestors before them. Nothing was created hastily, the passage of time bringing perfection to their work. Some were weaving carpets by hand; others were etching copper or decorating pottery. On show and for sale were exquisite Berber jewellery, embroidered clothing, tooled leather and inlaid work; it was all there for the bartering.

The Arab in his loose djellaba (gown) and sandalled feet harmonised with the surrounding architecture of domes and minarets and the glamour of the sultan's palace. The scene was like a fairy tale from the Arabian Nights with its medieval sights and strange customs.

Malaga is a characteristic Mediterranean city with broad avenues and symmetrical streets, palm trees, airy cafes and pleasure parks; there were even trams. The city is a winter refuge for all those whose lives are fog-bound. Consequently, Malaga is adorned with every kind of villa that the imagination of sun-seekers from Northern Europe could devise. At the beaches, there were bathing huts for hire for 1.25 pesetas (one peseta equalled about fivepence halfpenny in old money. In the empty bullring, one of our party, Charles, gave a matador demonstration.

An excursion to Granada was to see the exquisite fourteenth century Alhambra Palace, the old summer residence of the Moorish kings, and one of the most beautiful sights of the world. It stands in a forest of green, high up on a hill like a great giant casting a shadow over the city below. A towering fortress by the remote inaccessible snowy mountains with their delicately tapering peaks glistening in the sun.

The exterior of the Alhambra has red walls and towers. On either side are elegant pavilions around which is the most dainty filigree work of the Moors. I particularly enjoyed the Court of the Lions where twelve perfectly carved stone lions surround a fountain and, inside, the Hall of the Two Sisters and the Hall of Abencerrages.

Leaving the Alhambra, down the hill we came to the majestic cathedral of Granada, conceived and planned by architects who moulded their lives to a rigid pattern to complete their task. The cathedral is the work of Diego de Siloe, one of the greatest plasteresque artists. The Royal Chapel is a fine specimen of fifteenth century plasteresque architecture by Eurique Egas, combining the rich imaginative qualities of late Gothic with the elegance of Italian Renaissance.

Sailing to Gibraltar, the great rock loomed in the distance, a promontory stretching south into the Mediterranean Sea from the Andalusian coast. A little over two miles in length, it tapers in width to Europa Point, the southern tip. The name Gibraltar is derived from Jebel Tariq (Mount Tariq) named after Tarik ben Zaid, who invaded the Rock in 711 AD.

With few cars at that time, we were able to amble down the main street and its environs with ease. The weekly ceremonial Changing of the Guard outside the governor's residence, known as the Convent, attracts a large crowd with the governor taking the salute from the balcony.

On the Rock are the legendary Barbary apes whose ancestors have lived there for centuries. What happens to them when they die is a mystery as no skeleton has ever been found. It is thought that the Romans or the Moors brought the apes to Gibraltar. The Moors occupied Gibraltar for over 700 years from 711. The earliest written record of apes in British Gibraltar dates back to 1740 when some were brought over from Morocco. These were the tail-less Barbary ape, *Macaca sylvana,* identical to the Gibraltar ape which originally came from the Atlas Mountains across the Strait in Africa. It is said that as long as the apes are on the Rock the British will remain. The colony of apes at the Apes Den has been guarded by the army since 1915. Hordes of tourists ignored the notices asking them not to feed the apes so the animals have now been enclosed in the Apes Den and tourists have to pay to see them.

Since the Rock was taken by the British in 1704, the keys of Gibraltar have come to be regarded as the seals of office of the governor. The Ceremony of the Keys is a fitting occasion performed with dignity by any regiment stationed on the Rock.

The upper galleries, hewn out of solid rock, were eerie with dummy service men popping up in places. The caves were hewn out of solid rock in the eighteenth century at the time of the great siege. There was a fine view of the Spanish mainland from the turrets, including the Gibraltar's airport and the frontier, closed and re-opened over the years.

We arrived at the great port of Lisbon. It became the Portuguese seat of government in 1422 and reached the height of its prosperity in the sixteenth century through the riches of the Portuguese empire pouring in. A century and a half later, the flood of newly discovered gold and diamonds from Brazil raised more splendid palaces and one of the finest opera houses in Europe. Much of this splendour disappeared for ever in 1755 when the city suffered a severe earthquake and tidal wave.

Lisbon today is not a city of grandeur, but of charm, of graceful facades, gentle colours and enchanting corners. From the river Tagus, it opens like a fan of pink-pearl and ochre houses, churches and palaces jutting from a dozen hills. To the east, the ancient houses of the Alfana quarter reach up to the castle walls with streets too narrow for a car to pass. Old house-fronts tower like white cliffs and sparkle with carnations and geraniums, with washing fluttering in the breeze. At night the scene was gentle with gaslight from wrought-iron brackets.

We drove out to Cintra to see the fairy-like castle, Palacio da Pena, perched on the highest point of the Serra and built on the site of a convent in the nineteenth century by Ferdinand of Saxe-Coburg who married Queen Maria II of Portugal. From the terraces there were superb views of Lisbon. In the town itself is Cintra Palace which was the summer palace of Lisbon's Moorish rulers in mediaeval times. It was extended by ex-King Manoel who died while we were in Lisbon on 1st August, 1932. Thousands of mourners flocked into Lisbon.

Our last port of call was Vigo, a seaport in the province of Pontevedra and standing in the Bay of Vigo on the Atlantic coast. It was attacked by Drake unsuccessfully in 1585 and was plundered by him in 1589. In 1702 a British and Dutch fleet, under Sir George Rooke, sank Spanish and French ships in the bay, capturing treasure worth a million pounds. Vigo is the principal port of Spain for Atlantic traffic, and now a well-planned city with important fisheries, ship-building and metallurgical industries. Paper, sugar, leather, soap, brandy and flour are produced in Vigo; it is also noted for its luscious eel pies.

CHAPTER TWO

1933 – The Med. Again

In 1933 my itchy feet found me cruising again in the Med with a friend, Freda, on the turbo electric P&O *Strathnavar* chiefly cruising on the Indian and Australian run; it was one of the Strath class of that era, of 32,000 tons and launched in 1931, the first P&O liner to have a white hull. I was to join Freda on board, but just before Watford Junction an axle of the train broke. I had to walk along the track to the station with other passengers and then took a taxi to the docks. The ship was held up for the boat train. Three hundred first class and over six hundred second class passengers were booked for the cruise. Our first class cabins were more than adequate. The fare was £22 each for the round voyage of two weeks. We were pampered by the ship's company on this luxury air-conditioned liner.

As the cruise took place over fifty-five years ago my recollections of the ports of call are somewhat dim. I recall docking at Naples where Freda and I engaged a guide to take us to Pompeii to see the well-preserved remains of this Samnite city which came under Roman rule in the first century BC and was buried by the eruption of Vesuvius in 79 AD. Survivors were able to tunnel down and remove many objects of value, but the city then lay forgotten. It was rediscovered when the architect Domenico Fontana was building an underground aqueduct in 1594-1600. Only when this aqueduct was inspected in 1748 was the full extent of the city discovered and excavations have proceeded periodically since then, particularly under Mussolini before the second world war. Now two-thirds are revealed showing how the people of the first century AD lived. Wandering along the little cobbled alleyways and footpaths we could visualise where shops and houses once stood. For a little 'something extra', our guide was intent on showing us the brothels, frowned on at that time, which were still covered with an unrivalled series of vividly coloured sexy frescoes and wall paintings.

Docking at Athens, Greece's sprawling capital, we climbed a number of steps to the towering rock of the Acropolis with a view of the Parthenon, 447 to 432 BC.

In the Principality of Monaco, looking out on to the Mediterranean, I had a flutter at the gambling tables of the world-famous Place de Casino. I recollect winning a few pounds. Freda tried her luck at the nearby Sporting Club set in picturesque surroundings. In 1967 the casino was taken over by the principality.

CHAPTER THREE

1947/8 – My Passage to India

In August 1947 I sailed to India to be married. Earlier in the year I met my future husband, an army officer, when he was on sick leave. On his return to India he cabled to me to go out and marry him.

Sea passages at that time were difficult to come by but there was a chance to fly to Karachi. My shipping agents did all they could to obtain a passage and eventually there was a chance on s.s. *Cilicia* of the Anchor Line. Forms for Egypt and India were endorsed and I attended the Resettlement Bureau. As clothing coupons were still in use I applied to the Board of Trade for supplementary coupons.

On 29th July a small pebble was thrown up at my window by a representative of the shipping line. 'There's a passage to India on 30th August,' I was told. By coincidence, it was the troop ship on which my fiance sailed on its maiden voyage after World War II; in the June I had seen him off from Liverpool.

On 31st July I received definite instructions to embark on 30th August, arriving Bombay 17th September, single fare eighty pounds. I was to share a two-berth cabin on B deck. After visiting my bank manager, I had a shopping spree – first for a strong tin trunk, then tropical kit.

The Passport Office wanted evidence of my forthcoming marriage, and names and address of my future husband. I said my farewells and was set to sail, but not without opposition from my family and friends; they were aghast at my going to India during the country's unrest at the time of independence.

On embarkation day I arrived at Liverpool docks. My friend of *Strathnavar* days saw me off, but was not allowed on board owing to tight security.

My cabin companion, the wife of a tea planter, was on her way to rejoin her husband. There were five other brides-to-be, a number of clergy, missionaries (including Judy, a member of the Salvation Army, who, it was rumoured, was going out to marry a bandmaster), Indians of all denominations, and about forty schoolchildren who were to spend their holidays with their parents.

With the usual allocation of tables on board, two bachelors asked me to join them, together with Judy. They were ideal companions with Judy taking charge in her officer's uniform.

On 10th September we docked at Port Said. Boys dived in the harbour for coins, and gippies came on board selling their wares. One had a live canary which he used to do disappearing tricks up his sleeve, to the amusement of some passengers.

In Port Said I made my way to Simon Artz, the bazaar. My travellers cheques were refused, Egyptian money only. Thomas Cook's offices were empty, so I returned to the ship. On the way an undesirable gippy followed me; a policeman kept a close watch on him until I reached the ship. The next day, all shore leave was cancelled as there was trouble in Suez. We sailed through the narrow neck of the Suez Canal; there was barely room for the ship to manoeuvre. On the bank on either side there were little settlements and, beyond, the ageless Egyptian desert, backed by a glorious sunset.

Through the Gulf of Aden, we reached the Arabian Sea en route for Bombay. I had a jab for yellow fever which gave trouble as I had had a drink!

On 17th September the *Cilicia* sailed into Victoria docks, Bombay. A representative of Thomas Cook saw me through customs. At the dockside, there was chaos with hordes of beggars, including women with their babies carried on the left hip, partly supported by a cloth under their bottoms and looped up over the mother's right shoulder. The baby is shown as hungry, ill, under-nourished, or just to elicit pity from the westerner. There was the continual cry of 'baksheesh' (alms) from the beggars. My cabin companion located my fiance by his photo in the cabin and off we went in a taxi to the Taj Mahal Hotel.

After obtaining the marriage licence and buying the wedding ring, we arrived at Victoria Railway Station. A burly coolie insisted on carrying all my kit to our first class carriage. This daily mail special travels between Bombay and Poona (now called Pune) along a scenic route. The line rises a thousand feet in sixteen miles, winding its way up the hillside through twenty-five tunnels and eight viaducts. The *Deccan Queen* is known as the *Drunken Queen* as it rolls and hurls along the incredible single gauge track with twists and turns as it climbs the Western Ghats, the mountain wall. It operates in the coastal strip and up the Western Ghats to the Deccan plateau two thousand feet up. It was a hair-raising experience.

After a five-hour journey from Bombay a hundred miles away, we arrived at Poona Cantonment station to be welcomed by army officers and their wives, including my host and hostess, Colonel and Mrs C, who were arranging our wedding.

At the Club of Western India, affectionately called the CWI, quarters were loaned to me by my hostess until the wedding day three days later. I slept under a mosquito net. Chota hazri (early morning tea) was brought by Aziz, my host's bearer on loan to me; he wore a white starched uniform with puggaree (turban) and cummerbund (waist sash). In the house his feet were bare, as was the custom. The customary footwear for officers was chaplis (sandals).

I was taken to a derzi for two of my long cotton dresses to be copied in other colours. The derzi, after working all night, arrived next morning on his bicycle, carrying the dresses shoulder-high on hangers! They were indeed identical.

Our wedding day was 20th September. According to tradition, a bride in India has a six-month honeymoon, and becomes a mem-sahib. The service was at noon and my host gave me away. The wedding breakfast was held at the temporary home of my host and hostess.

Then we set off by car to the hill station at Panchguani (meaning five hills), eighty miles from Bombay and 5,000 feet above sea level. Driving through shanty villages, native children welcomed us.

India is well-known for its 'Indian summers', periods of dry, unseasonably warm weather in late October or November in the central, eastern and western states.

At the Prospect Hotel there was only one other guest. Shortly after our arrival, the monsoons broke, and the rains descended in torrents all day, for several days, thundering on the corrugated iron roof. The bearer unpacked the sahib's bistra (bedding roll) and filled the drawers with the contents. There was no room for my clothes so I kept them in my suitcase. The bearer had to dry our clothes with the aid of a small primus stove as shoes were going mouldy. Most of the week we were confined to the hotel, but there was a well-stocked bar, and the curries were all to be desired. When the rains eventually ceased, we toured the countryside which was covered in red sand.

On our return to Poona we were temporarily housed in a large bungalow in the cantonment. My husband then left for Delhi as his leave had expired. Through a pair of sandals I had bought in the bazaar, I contracted impetigo. For several days I had to visit the British Military Hospital by tonga for treatment. As I was on crutches my bearer brought my meals to the bungalow from the officers' mess.

Poona lies on a plateau two thousand feet up in the exposed brown hills; the colonial rulers used to escape to Poona from the searing heat of the plains. In late September and October, the 'fishing fleet' arrived as the P&O steamers brought out from England girls on the look-out for husbands. They went to all stations in India depending on where and with whom they were to stay. If unsuccessful they returned to England at the beginning of the next hot weather.

The Club of Western India was founded in the early part of the nineteenth century, one of the oldest European clubs in India. In 1948, I was the first woman member in the club's history to be permitted to live on the station while my husband was at headquarters – an honour I appreciated.

The club area was walled and manned by sentries. Outside the military area, families and the children's ayahs lived. The grounds extended to sixteen acres of land, tended by a fleet of malis (gardeners). Colourful trees lined the walks – frangipani, jacaranda, bougainvillea, flame of the forest and cassia. The club house contained an officers' mess with khitmagars waiting at table. After siesta, tea with the traditional cucumber sandwiches was served in members' quarters, followed by golf or tennis. Sundown was chota-peg time.

The club house contained an officers' dining room with khitmagars (butlers) in white uniform waiting at table. Dining at night meant formal dress, the ladies in full-length dresses, the men in mess kit. Those going on to the cinema after dinner would 'dine dirty' in less formal dress but would not be allowed to dine with those in full evening dress. The club also contained a lounge with dance space, a bar, reading and writing room and well-stocked library. With the hand-over, voluntary help was sought for the sale of books etc. I was appointed assistant librarian, and later co-opted to the club committee.

Poona in 1947 was a delightful station, away from the city riots. Petrol was rationed, and the bicycle came into its own, though there were a few cars for senior officers.

The employment of servants was cheap. My bearer received fifty rupees a month; one rupee was then worth 1/3d, or sixpence in decimal money. The sweeper kept the house clean with his long locally made broom. The dhobi earned ten rupees a month. At night the 'Bombay milk-cart' would go his rounds emptying the 'thunder boxes' (earth closets) – unfortunate for anyone on the 'throne' at the time!

In October 1947, the CWI hosted distinguished guests at a gala ball. The mess and grounds were decked out in bunting and lights. I was invited to join an IMS party. Afterwards, I was escorted back to my quarters. The front door was open, the lights were full on, but nothing had been taken – a hoax which I never solved.

The Sunday morning church parades were well supported. A general used to take me in his car and he read one of the lessons.

In January 1948 we left Poona for HQ in Delhi, travelling by Frontier Mail. Delhi is a city steeped in three thousand years of history, with marble pavilions and inlaid domes, congested traffic, with the sacred cow allowed to roam at will.

While stationed in Delhi, we received two invitations to Government House, the viceregal lodge designed by Sir Edwin Lutyens and then the official home of the Earl and Countess Montbatten of Burma; Lord Mountbatten had served as the last viceroy up to independence in the previous year and was then the first governor general of India. The first invitation was cancelled due to Mahatma Gandhi's assassination; the second came as we were leaving India. Nevertheless we toured the beautiful grounds and landscaped gardens.

In the bazaars, craftsmen carried out their ancient skills with tools of bygone days; wood and ivory turners, gold beaters, blacksmiths and coppersmiths, carpet makers – all working with delicacy and precision. The smell of ghee, a kind of clarified butter, seeped into my nostrils. Fair and dark haired children played together in the gutters. Dignfied old men played chess, oblivious to the traffic noises.

The 30th January, 1948, was a day to remember when the Hindu Mahatma Gandhi, prominent leader of Indian nationalism, was shot by a Hindu fanatic whilst on his way to a prayer meeting. The news caused great consternation in India. We had planned to go to Agra to see the Taj Mahal mausoleum; instead we watched the funeral procession.

The cortege left Birla House with the body on an army weapon carrier. Slowly it made its way along the Mall, where a million people watched in silence. We could see the half-draped body of Mahatma Gandhi lying on the raised dais, his face serene and peaceful. There were shouts of 'Ki Jai!' (long live Mahatma Gandhi!). The multitude broke into sacred chants, while overhead a Dakota aircraft dipped in salute. Thousands of soldiers, airmen and sailors marched along the route; mounted lancers bearing aloft red and white pennants while armoured cars maintained order. In charge of the parade was Major-General Roy Hughes, chosen by the Indian government to be the-commander-in chief. As the procession reached the last resting place at Rajghat where the funeral pyre was ready, the family waited in silence to honour their beloved leader.

After the funeral, with the coolies back in service, we left for Agra. The city lies on the bank of the sacred Jumna river; it is a handsome town, noted for its fine handicrafts. The Taj Mahal is known as 'the Jewel in India's Crown', rescued from neglect by the late Lord Curzon. It is a magnificent monument, built by the Moghul Emperor Shah Jehan as a token of great love for his wife who died after giving birth to their fourteenth child. During the construction of the tomb, artists were employed who adorned the building and the tomb with precious stones.

In Agra, one of India's best known cities, people of different religions work together in harmony. Among the great city buildings is the Agra Fort, within whose walls Hindu and Muslim architecture merge in splendour. Sikandra, the burial site of the great Moghul Emperor Akbar the Great, has a handsome gateway leading to the mausoleum. Fatehpur Sikri, south-west of Agra, is now a deserted sandstone city; once a complex of forts, palaces and mosques, it is a ghost town haunted by memories of a resplendent era.

Back in Delhi, General W invited us to tour the old city; he was a great authority on its history. Eight previous cities have existed near the present Delhi. There is conjecture about the first, believed to have been founded in 326 BC when fact blends with legend. Some authorities talk of King Delhu of the Morya dynasty as the founder; others believe that it was called Indraprastha founded by the Pandava brothers, the mythical heroes of the *Mahabharata,* the national epic of India. Excavations confirm that the oldest habitation in the Delhi area dates back to the third or fourth century BC.

After over a century of service, and the end of the Raj in 1947, the Club of Western India was taken over by the Indians, and the great exodus of British expatriates from India began. Administrators, soldiers and missionaries appeared for the last time in passenger lists of west-bound liners from Bombay – the advance guard of the home-coming army divisions whose careers ended when the British had to quit India by June 1948. They ranged from the empire's highly-regarded civil service, the ICS, to fitters and engine drivers recruited from England for the Indian state railways. In between were forest officers, mining engineers, educational, agricultural and veterinary experts and a small army of customs officials, post and telegraph and civil aviation officers.

Outnumbering these was the army contingent, including General Slim's Forgotten Army in which my late husband served as lieutenant colonel with the Chindits. He was awarded five medals for his services. Patrolling the jungle in Burma, the army had to contend with steaming heat and torrential rain, tropical disease, insects and reptiles. The Fourteenth Army had about a million British and Commonwealth troops.

From the time of the partition of India, troopships maintained a regular service between India and England. The majority of homecomers (including my husband) regretted the severance with India. Many were attached to the country and its people among whom they had spent the greater part of their lives. In November 1947 many battalions were split, with the Hindus remaining in India and the Muslims being sent to Pakistan. As British officers became redundant, many booked passages to the UK.

On 8th March, 1948, we boarded mv *Amra* for England; we were guests at the captain's table. Our ports of call included the Seychelles where we dropped off six cows for breeding purposes. On to Mombasa and Nairobi for the game reserve where the back axle of the car broke leaving us stranded in approaching darkness. Luckily, a party spotted us and took us back to the hotel. Later a gang of Africans were driven out to the spot and retrieved the car. Docking at Beira in Mozambique we boarded the train for Salisbury where we saw bales of tobacco being auctioned. We reached Zambia in the tropical belt of south-central Africa, a plateau and the birthplace of the great Zambesi River, and saw the magnificent falls from the Victoria Falls Hotel; the Africans call them 'the waters that thunder'!

Just north of the falls is Livingstone, named after the famous Scottish explorer. We travelled to Bulawayo and Pretoria, the administrative capital of South Africa, and had a day in Johannesburg. At the end of June we were on the last lap of our journey home, embarking on ss *Warwick Castle.* At Port Elizabeth, an important commercial and industrial centre, we took advantage of a coastal tour. The city remained a struggling settlement until 1820 when four thousand British settlers started a new life on the frontiers. Reaching Durban by train we made family contacts before sailing for Cape Town. Sailing up the west coast of Africa, we arrived at Madeira, our last port of call before docking at Southampton.

CHAPTER FOUR

West Africa in the Fifties

Life in Nigeria was bearable in the fifties, although it was a far distant outpost of the British Empire. At one time the area was known as the 'white man's grave' on account of the tropical diseases prevalent at the time, such as sleeping sickness and malaria, the scourge of Africa, for which we took a paladrine tablet every day. Quinine made one a yellow colour.

The first Europeans to venture into this part of Africa were Portuguese explorers in the late fifteenth century, sailing into the Gulf of Guinea. Two centuries later there was a demand for slaves for the cotton and sugar-cane plantations of America and the West Indies. Traders came to West Africa for slave labour. Nigeria was known as the Slave Coast of Africa.

In the nineteenth century Great Britain and Denmark endeavoured to end the slave trade. England then traded with Nigeria for a new commodity – red oils from palm trees for industrial purposes, such as making soap and candles. Explorers, missionaries, traders and ships came up the Niger River with its trading stations. In 1900 the British government took over the administration of the area.

The twentieth century saw advances in mission work, commerce and administration. Nigeria became independent in 1960 and elected to be a republic within the Commonwealth in 1963. In 1966 the army seized control and there has been a succession of coups alternating with democratically elected governments. In 1967 the Ibos broke from the federation and formed the Republic of Biafra in the east and Nigeria became involved in a civil war. Originally regional in structure the Federation was divided into twelve states. In 1976 it was divided again into nineteen states and a further two were created in 1987.

After serving in India we were posted to Nigeria through the Crown Agents. The Elder Dempster Line dominated the West African sea-route with their coastal vessels, *Apapa, Accra, Aureol* and *Empire Bure.* A shuttle service plied back and forth from England to Lagos, the voyage taking two weeks, calling at Madeira and Las Palmas en route. Many a gamble was had on the ship's run by the colonials serving in West Africa.

We lived in the European quarter of Ikoyi outside Lagos where we were allocated a quarter. The rooms were spacious, light and airy. Our ground-floor flat had a garden patch where marigolds grew especially well in the sandy soil.

At first we had one servant, Momo, a Hausaman who wore a long white gown and round skull cap. He was not the best of servants, neither was he honest – he liked his perks! We replaced him with three servants, Yorubas and Ibos. They wore khaki shorts and shirt. The head steward, when waiting at table, wore white uniform. They lived with their families in a nearby compound. I had to dismiss the small boy, Sylvanus, as he developed a severe cough and would not see the medicine man. The servants spoke some English.

Nigeria was subject to incidents, thieving, fighting and being involved with witchcraft. Witch doctors have many roles – they cure the sick, make rain, ensure success in warfare and in the hunt, exorcise demons and smell out evil. Their power is believed by fellow tribesmen to come from evil spirits that are feared, revered and placated by every member of the community.

The nineteenth century judu hat is shaped like a skull cap, fashioned from cork, and covered with the cowrie shells that serve as money. Two antelope horns suggest that this animal was the totem or guiding animal spirit of the tribe. Adding horns made the wearer seem less human and more frightening to the rest of the clan.

Food in Nigeria was not always hygienic, especially salads – permanganate of potash was recommended. Taking over the cooking I invested in a Baby Belling cooker. We drank mineral water or the local brew in place of tap water. The locals drank palm oil wine; I used to watch them scamper up the tall trees to obtain the sap in cans.

We shopped chiefly in Kingsway Store, signing for our purchases. The larger items were delivered, and if meat was ordered it came in a refrigerated van.

The local markets were a colourful sight, surrounded by a maze of dilapidated mud-wall shanties. The women wore baggy brightly-coloured blouses and skirts. They sold 'mammy' cloth, dyed in smelly vats in Kano, Northern Nigeria, a town of flat-roofed pink earth houses. The native dress is indigo and white, or gay jungle prints. The women carry enormous calabashes on their heads filled with fruit, vegetables and other commodities. The camel-caravans, taking salt to market, block the way for cars. Wooden carts are stacked with sacks of groundnuts, the staple diet, by half naked chanting work forces.

Nigerians have a good eye for business, especially the women; many are wealthy traders selling rice, cocoa pods, yams, cassava, palm-wine and palm-oil. A good sideline is women's hats, The local women love dressing up for weddings, naming ceremonies, festivals and church-going. Whole families are attired in similar mammy cloth as a sign of prosperity.

A car was a necessity in Nigeria – Europeans did not use public transport. During harmattan time (sand from the desert) the car-roofs are covered with a thin layer of red sand, which penetrates into one's nostrils. Walking was very refreshing in the cool of the evening. In Ikoyi, a popular stroll was by the coconut palm-fringed lagoon. Often there was the odd snake, but we were never bitten. It was fascinating to watch big orange-coloured lizards on the low walls of the houses. My cat one day came in with a huge lizard in her mouth. Small transparent lizards lived behind pictures and I found one in our radio. There were plenty of stray cats, one of whom produced her off-spring in the club rafters, bringing them down to ground level one by one. The first was deposited under a tree and one was planted outside our third-floor flat door. Cycling around Ikoyi, I found homes for the rest.

A menace was the mosquito. We slept under nets and burned Japanese 'moon tigers' to keep away the pests. The cockroaches were huge and appeared from nowhere; they could fly too! Periodically the Public Works Department would spray the rooms with DDT. Flying ants came in their thousands and gathered around street lamps where the locals collected them to eat as a great delicacy. The very small ants were a problem, favouring sweet things. Standing the legs of tables in small containers of water kept them at bay where food was concerned.

Many wives were bored living in the tropics. Some sought outside interests in offices. The *Lagos Times,* the daily paper, filled five of my mornings each week. A driver was engaged to take me to the offices, with my typewriter, for which work I received a weekly salary of £26, plus £2 for the use of my machine. One day I came face to face with a car accident. I phoned a reporter and the next morning I was congratulated. A full page picture of the incident was plastered on the front page of the paper with a report that a European judge had collided with a local car, prior to his home leave. A court case ensued.

We rose at seven o'clock. Offices opened at eight and closed at two o'clock for the day. About four o'clock, after siesta, the steward served tea; then it was time for a game of tennis or golf, and a sun-downer (gin-and-it). Saturday night was dance night with a band at the Ikoyi Club on a circular parquet floor.

Our first tour of eighteen months was extended by a month. I developed a severe cough and a tape-worm! Whisked off to hospital, a purgative kept me in for three days.

On Sundays we lunched at the club, relishing the traditional ground-nut stew. Nigeria being a major producer of the South American ground-nut or peanut, and chicken being cheap, this stew was very economical.

Local leave was spent at Jos, a hill station. The plateau, five thousand feet above sea level, lies in the middle belt of deciduous woodlands graduating to open rolling landscapes. In this region were pagans, the women wearing just a bunch of leaves hanging from a thong at the waist, with a 'plate' at the back. On their heads they carried their wares. The men wore leather aprons or jock straps. The semi-nudity was in keeping with the surrounding countryside. For threepence they would let us photograph them.

We drove for miles through barren and isolated land, often not seeing a human being for hours. A lion once crossed the road in front of us. One year we drove to the northern state of Kaduna, the seat of the administrative government, for the opening of parliament, staying with H.H., a barrister friend. The emirs in their traditional colourful robes were a picturesque sight. We were photographed with them by the National Geographical Society; a copy was sent to us.

Keeping cool in Nigeria was a problem with one hundred per cent humidity.

Cotton dresses were worn by the European women by day, and khaki shorts and white shirts for men. In the evenings women donned long skirts, and often mosquito boots to keep the pests at bay.

Swimming at Victoria beach was dangerous as there were treacherous seas and pounding waves on the shore but we used to go down and join parties for a swim, heeding the danger. Fatalities often occurred among the Europeans. Decades ago, natives were hanged there for their crimes.

The Nigerian people are said to come from the Upper Nile, migrating to the grasslands and dark-green forests of West Africa, inter-marrying with the original negroes and extending their power. Messages were carried by bush telegraph, the beating of drums from one village to another.

The Yorubas are a friendly race, and like visiting and entertaining; families live together in the same compound. The Ibos are a vigorous and go-ahead race. They live in the region bounded by the rivers Niger and Benue. The Hausaman are great traders and very apt at handicrafts, peddling their wares from house to house. Time was no object and a Hausaman would sit endlessly on my veranda waiting for Madam to bargain. In exchange for a handicraft I would give him a dress, three of the master's cigarettes and the usual tip. Then he would go away happy, only to return a few days later.

Life in Nigeria in the fifties was memorable for its simplicity. Today, with the discovery of oil, Nigeria has become a modern and thriving state.

CHAPTER FIVE

1959 – Living on the Maltese Islands

Since Lord Nelson's day, there has always been a strong British link with the Maltese people.

Set in the Mediterranean, the archipelago consists of three separate islands, Malta, the sister island of Gozo, and tiny Comino. The coastline is well indented with harbours, creeks, rocky beaches and caves. No mountains or rivers exist on the islands; a series of low-terraced hillocks are tilled by farmers.

I first set foot in Malta in 1959 when the British fleet was much in evidence, with Grand Harbour chock-a-block with naval shipping. We were on a three-year contract with the Admiralty. Malta became independent under the crown in 1964 and a republic member of the Commonwealth in 1974. Since independence the islands have attracted tourists like many other Mediterranean countries.

We had a flat in the residential part of Sliema overlooking the sea. In 1966, when I became a widow, I returned to Malta as a sixpenny settler (taxwise) and lived in the same area for many years.

The climate of the islands varies from season to season; summers are hot and sticky, in July soaring so that even the sea is warm. August is sirocco time with sandy winds from the African desert. Winters are mild. The rainy season is November to January. I have known December when the sea had been warm enough for a dip. I have also known Malta when it has suffered whirlwinds causing damage to property and trees.

The Maltese people are a friendly race, proud, thrifty and shrewd; they do not take kindly to criticism. On Commonwealth Day at Westminster Abbey in London, Chris Grima proudly carries the Maltese flag alongside forty other countries represented.

The old Maltese houses still retain the British-style parlour, but villas and high-rise blocks of flats are gradually taking over and many hotels have sprung up. The leading one, the Phoenicia in Floriana, Valletta, caters for the discriminating guest, being long-established and central.

Maltese is a mixture of semitic and romance languages. For centuries it was a spoken language only but a written language was constructed by Maltese scholars using modified Roman characters. In Maltese schools today English is taught and they are the official languages of the islands. Italian is spoken by many educated Maltese for contact with Italy only fifty-eight miles away.

Malta was in turn held by the Phoenicians, Greeks, Carthaginians, Romans and Arabs. In 1090 the crusaders conquered it and in 1530 it was handed over to the Knights of St John who made it a stronghold of Christianity. It survived the great siege by the Turks in 1565, but the knights were expelled by Napoleon in 1798. The people rebelled against the French garrison and the British fleet blockaded the islands. The people requested the protection of the British crown in 1802 and they were annexed in the peace settlement of 1814. Malta was again besieged from 1940 to 1943 and suffered a great deal of damage and many casualties; for their courage the islanders were awarded the George Cross by King George in 1942 and this still appears on the flag of independent Malta.

When the British fleet was in the Mediterranean, Valletta became the rendezvous for sailors. Their retreat, Strait Street or 'The Gut', hemmed in by buildings, was patronised by sailors in the bars, dance halls and brothels. When the fleet was recalled, this notorious quarter lost its notoriety, but the alley-ways still retain nostalgic memories.

Pubs have always been part of the island life and relics of war days. Many have English names among the twenty licensed houses between Sliema Ferry and Gzira. One well-known bar patronised by locals and visitors is the *City of London,* prominently sited on St Julian's corner. First established in 1914 at the outbreak of the first world war by the late Carmelo Borg, it has been carried on by the Borg family ever since, celebrating its seventy-fifth anniversary in 1989. No-one really knows why it has been called the *City of London – The City* for short.

Valletta is the hub of the business world, and the main shopping centre. The Sunday market always attracts the tourists who flood in from outlying areas searching for hand-made woollen goods and the odd bric-a-brac. The streets run parallel to each other and with many steps. The street signs during British rule were in English; they have since reverted to their original Maltese names.

Among Valletta's prominent buildings is the ornate St John's Roman Catholic Cathedral built by Gerolamo Cassar and his Italian assistant, Laparali. Cassar also designed the seven auberges or lodges of the Knights of Malta, but only three remain. The Magisterial Palace in Republic Street, also of Cassar design, was built by the great master's nephew, Eustachio del Monte. One of the rooms houses armour worn in the great siege, and lining the walls are fine, if worn, Flemish tapestries. On show is the Spitfire *Faith,* a relic of World War II.

To gain an insight into the history, *The Malta Experience,* a multivision show in Valletta, depicts Malta from neolithic to present times. The building used was formerly the hospital of the knights, one of the best in Europe at the time; food was served to the patients on silver plates by the knights.

Valletta's charming Manoel Theatre, once a doss-house, is Malta's national theatre for staging classical productions. It was built in 1711 on the lines of a theatre in Palermo, Sicily, with tiers of painted boxes and adjacent salons.

Near the theatre is St Paul's Anglican Cathedral. The foundation stone was laid in

1839 by Queen Adelaide, widow of King William IV, the sailor king.The dowager queen paid for the building from her private purse. Fortunately this cathedral escaped the ravages of wars and it is now visited by people from all over the world.

Mid-winter carnival creates a carefree atmosphere among the young-at-heart who tour the streets in decorated floats making a tourist attraction. Fiestas also play a vital part with images of patron saints being hauled through villages. Petards (fireworks) blast through the air, the louder the bang, the better.

Historical sites can be reached by bus in Malta, like Hagar Kim, Tarxien and the Hypogeum of Hal Saflieni. The privately owned bus service covers the islands. At one time the buses on Malta were of different colours; now they are all green.

A traditional dress was the 'valdetta' worn by peasants, consisting of a black wired head-dress and a long black gown. This conspicuous costume has disappeared from the streets, and is now a museum piece.

The local vendors still peddle their wares, except for the goat owner (the animals were 'shoats') who milked his goat at house doors until early in the 1900s it was discovered that the organism responsible for Mediterranean sickness was carried in the milk of Maltese goats.

The horse-driven hooded karozzin cab is dying out, but the occasional one can still be seen trotting along streets taking tourists for rides. The vegetable and fruit seller meanders along side streets with his horse (or donkey) and cart and a load of produce. Baskets are dropped from high windows and hauled up full by the housewife. People congregate for a refill of oil from the kerosene man as he ambles along with his horse and cart, calling out 'Oil!'.

Among the industries, pottery has been a tradition for decades. In the late fifties Peter the Potter was at his wheel in Mdina, the silent city. moulding clay with his hands as did his ancestors. A glass-blowing factory produces delicate glassware. Mdina, a mediaeval city, once the capital of Malta sits on a hill overlooking surrounding countryside. Close to the imposing cathedral in the square is the Sanctuary Museum housing treasures of a thousand years. Alley-ways lead off the square where it is easy to be temporarily lost.

The island's fishing industry is important, bringing in lampuki, dentici and swordfish for the luxury trade. Other favourite dishes are the pastas like tagliatelli, lasagne and spaghetti. Rabbit, which is cheap, is the staple diet of the Maltese who concoct dainty dishes for the family. Their sweet tooth has resulted in shops being crammed with richly-decorated cakes and sweetmeats, especially at the festive seasons. Due to the influx of British visitors, bacon and egg and fish and chips are on the menus, accompanied by a local cisk or hop beer.

Two indulgence stand-by flights to England came my way. One by Comet (two shillings for lemonade and sandwiches) which took me to Lyneham airport where I stayed overnight with dinner, bed and breakfast for five shillings. My return journey was overland taking three days through France, Italy and Sicily. The second flight was on a Beverley and return on a Hastings for thirty shillings for the return journey.

Gozo, The Sister Island

Three miles north-west of Malta lies the tranquil agricultural island of Gozo, a patch of green in the azure blue of the Mediterranean, and my spiritual home.

A ferry service plies back and forth from the mainland, hugging the coast, then past the tiny Comino Island (Greek for 'Refuge'), with its one hotel and sweet-smelling herbs. Tourists are ferried to Comino for the day for a dip in the clear-as-crystal waters of the Blue Lagoon. Nearby is the uninhabited islet of Cominotto.

The first landmark on Gozo's horizon is the tall-spired Church of Our Lady of Lourdes atop a hill towering over Mgarr harbour. Painted fishing boats in the harbour complete the scene. As the ferry docks the harbour comes alive as passengers disembark for taxis, local buses or footing it with a choice of seventeen walks.

Gozo is a haven of simplicity and charm, where the world stands still. Its image would be lost for ever if the bulldozers were to encroach on its shores, building high-rise hotels as in Malta.

The Gozitans are a very friendly, independent, hardy and self-supporting community, producing vegetables, fruit, flowers, wine, olives and peppers. The queer-looking 'shoats' (half sheep, half goat) live on farms. The yellow flowered oxalis grows wild and is called 'English Lady' as it was brought from England by an English lady; it spreads like a carpet over everywhere. The sweet-smelling narcissi bloom in January. In February come the chrysanthemums and the red poppy. Many blooms are ferried to Malta's shops and to the flower-sellers' baskets.

Buses on Gozo are not as frequent as on Malta, especially in winter. From the harbour a bus used to go to the capital, Victoria, for six cents. My favourite walk from the *Duke of Edinburgh* is to Marsalforn Bay. In the hollow is the Marsalforn Hotel, run by Maria and her family and famous for its pastas. Gozo wine is very potent. Along the beach is the modern Calypso Hotel where I have also stayed.

A hike to the village of Zaghra is rewarding for its country lanes and the Xaghra wine is even more potent! On the plateau are two neolithic temples with sixteen-foot limestone slabs. The cave, with its stalagmites and stalagtites, is worth a visit to see the lace-effect tracery. A popular walk from Victoria is to the pretty inlet bay of Zlendi. Once a quiet resort, it has been taken over by hordes of tourists in the summer months.

Gozo's traditional industry is lace-making. Local women sit with their bobbins clicking away on a 'stump'. It takes a day for two women to make a lace edging for a handkerchief.

Victoria's main interest is the citadel though only ruins remain after destruction by the Turks. The cathedral in the market place has rich trappings and marble slats. Friday is market day when stalls are laden with produce.

Returning to the harbour, a stop should be made at the new Gozo heritage spectacle telling of seven thousand years of Gozo history.

A Mediterranean Exercise

In July 1963, my husband and I sailed out of Malta with the fleet on a Mediterranean exercise which included HMS *Ark Royal.* Our home for three weeks was on the Australian freighter *Tide Austral* for twelve shillings and sixpence a day for messing. We called at the ports of Palma, Alicante, Gibraltar and Haifa. One night, as part of the exercise, the freighter was blacked out.

In 1978, while wintering in Gibraltar, it was a coincidence that I should be on the Rock during the *Ark Royal's* last visit. The captain arranged for me to visit the warship. Over tea in the wardroom I was shown nostalgic photographs of the NATO exercise. Prior to the final departure from Gibraltar, I had a visitor's pass to the quay to see her off. Dressed overall, her crew manned the decks with the Marine Band playing her out. As a helicopter hovered overhead taking photographs, she slipped slowly out of the harbour – a sad spectacle. Later I received by post a blown-up photo of *Ark Royal's* last farewell.

CHAPTER SIX

1967 – An Educational Cruise to Turkey, Lebanon, Israel and Heraklion

In February, 1967, I sailed from Malta on ms *Dunera* (British India Line), together with a crowd of schoolchildren and their teachers, bound for the Middle East on a purely educational cruise with lectures by the teachers and entertainment by the scholars.

The most important ancient city in western Turkey is Ephesus. Driving south from Izmir we came to the Magnesian Gate with its Odeum. We were shown the Temple of Hadrian, the Library of Celsus, the Greek and Roman Agoras (squares), The Temple of Serapis, the marble street, the great theatre to hold twenty-five thousand spectators, the double church of the Virgin Mary, the gymnasium of Vedius, the Basilica of St John and then returned to Izmir.

Browsing around the souks in Izmir I came across genuine handicrafts like silver bracelets, necklaces of amber and turquoise, brocades and silks woven with gold thread, glassware and antique works of art.

The Lebanese capital of Beirut had broad avenues and fine architectural houses, part oriental, part Florentine, a city of cars, resembling a huge garage with no pedestrian crossings. It is a country of great cedar trees, the emblem of Lebanon, one of the country's most precious relics and represented in the national flag. From the trees Solomon obtained wood for his palace and temple, and the pharaohs used it to carve their sarcophagi and sun-ships. About four hundred of these venerable trees, some over two hundred years old, are spread around the slopes of Mount Makhaal at an altitude of more than four thousand five hundred feet.

Beirut was well-known for its fantastic night life with a hundred and fifty night clubs and two hundred restaurants. Forty miles out of Beirut was the casino of Lebanon at Maameltein with one of the largest and most modern forms of entertainment in the world. Drawn from east and west, a whole international world of people witnessed this spectacular show on a long, central stage with performers giving a breath-taking performance in exquisite costumes. Before leaving I had a flutter at the casino tables.

The Lebanese standard of living was the highest of any Arab state except Kuwait.

The principal exports included apples, figs, bananas, tinned fruit, oils, fats, textiles and cotton goods.

On a half-day tour we drove along the coast out of Beirut to Dog River and then on northwards to Byblos (now called Jubail), the most important of the Phoenician city states. In the excavations were the remains of every civilisation to touch the town from neolithic houses and graves of 4000 BC to a crusader castle and church.

Thirty miles out of Beirut stands the magnificent palace of Beit Eddine in a setting of orchards and cypress groves, surrounded by terraces and tree-shaded waterfalls. It was built by the Emir Beshir, who reigned over Lebanon for fifty-four years until deposed by the Turks in 1840, when he fled to Malta. This exquisite building is a model of eastern architecture with delicately decorated arcades and galleries, and rooms designed by artists of Damascus. The palace had a museum with weapons, costumes and jewellery belonging to the feudal era of Lebanon. It was often used as a summer residence of the president of the republic. In the romantic-looking gardens, a fairy-like setting, are ornamental bath-houses of great beauty.

Our next port was Haifa in the land of Israel, which I had visited on a NATO exercise in 1963. A small country of 8019 square miles, it stretches over a hundred miles along the eastern shore of the Mediterranean.

To the Jewish people, Israel is more than just a territory. Since biblical times, it has constituted an essential element of their faith. It is a land of contrasts where the east merges with the west in a thousand variations of race and colour. This land of the Bible, with recollections of past events, has shaped the history of the world; the cradle of civilisation from Genesis to the present day.

Israel's population when I was there was over two million and now has passed five million Jews, Muslims and Christians. Hebrew, modernised from the ancient language of worship in the synagogues, and Arabic are the official languages, but English, French, Yiddish and German are also spoken.

The people of Israel are home-loving. To know them you must meet them in the intimacy of their homes. On a tour of Jerusalem, 2500 feet above sea level, Israel's holy city and City of Peace, was crowded with many nationalities as in centuries past. For a sight of distant Bethlehem we visited Mount Zion, returning via the Hebrew University to the white-domed Shrine of the Book where the Dead Sea Scrolls, discovered by a shepherd boy in 1947, are on exhibition. Just outside Jerusalem on the way back to Haifa, we came to Ein Karem with its two lovely churches, one up a mountain commemorating the visit of the Virgin Mary to her aunt, Elizabeth, and the other recording the birth to Elizabeth of the baby who became John the Baptist.

Sunday was our day for Lower Galilee. In Nazareth, capital of Galilee and home of Mary and Joseph, we saw Mary's well, Joseph's workshop and the Grotto of the Annunciation. Leaving Nazareth, we set off for Cana of Galilee, the site of Christ's first miracle of turning water into wine at the wedding feast. On, via the Horns of Hittin where Saladin defeated the Crusaders in 1187, we saw Tiberias and on along the shores of the Sea of Galilee to Magdala, the Mount of Beatitudes where Jesus preached the Sermon on the Mount, Tabgha for the miracle of the loaves and fishes,

Capernaum with its ruins of a second century synagogue, returning again past the Sea of Galilee where Jewish girls were swimming and back to Haifa.

Our last port of call was Heraklion on the island of Crete where we anchored for twenty-three hours. Crete, a cradle of civilisation, is the largest of the Greek islands, dominated by three main mountain ranges which divide the island into two parts.

On a cold and wet day, we drove from the port to Knossos, the ancient capital of the kingdom of Minos. On a tour of the partly-restored palace we visited the living quarters of the royal family, the School of Fine Arts, the theatre, the store rooms and the lapidary and potters' workshops.

The museum in Heraklion contains archaeological findings and treasures from sites in Crete. There were idols made of terracotta, marble and alabaster, ivory figurines, golden jewellery, frescoes and the Kamares-style pottery, the so-called eggshell ware.

Sailing out of Heraklion, *Dunera* cleared the western end of Crete and set course for her return voyage to Malta.

CHAPTER SEVEN

1968 – The Austrian Tyrol

In August, 1968, I flew from Malta to London, picking up a coach for the ferry crossing to Ostende. After driving along the motorway via Brussels to Liege, regional capital of the Walloon province, we stopped overnight at Hotel l'Angleterre.

The next morning we drove towards the German border which we crossed on the way to Aachen where Charlemagne resided and where thirty-two German emperors and kings were crowned between the years 813 to 1531. On the autobahn we reached Cologne and visited the cathedral with its colourful stained glass windows before continuing to Montabaur. We reached Frankfurt before going on to Rothenburg ober der Tauber for an overnight stay at the Gasthof aum Rappen.

Rothenburg is a picturesque medieval town with well-preserved ramparts, towers and gateways, together with historic houses dating back to the fourteenth century. We travelled on via Ansbach to Nuremberg, the town of the *Meistersinger,* where we lunched before continuing on the autobahn to Munich, capital of Bavaria, and past Starnberg Lake to Garmisch-Partenkirchen, Germany's foremost winter sports resort where we stayed at Hotel Roter Hahn.

The next day, we drove through Mitterwald, which is well-known for the violins made there and for its houses covered with colourful frescoes, into Austria where we reached Seefeld.

Seefeld is fourteen miles from Innsbruck, the seven hundred year old capital of the Tyrol. We were booked in at the Glosterbrau Hotel for five nights. This delightful family-run hotel is well over a hundred years old and the name translates as 'monastery brew'. Our meals were served from a silver salver by the fourteen-year-old heir to the hotel.

We took advantage of the free chair-lift up the mountain, the sauna baths and a Tyrolean folk evening.

Visiting Salzburg, we travelled on one of the six famous mountain roads, which lead to various parts of Europe, by a 6500 foot mountain, a skiers' paradise and noted for its Nordic Games. By the closed salt mines, we came to a glass and jewellery factory. Then on to Schwan and the medieval town of Battenburg situated in the most beautiful part of the Tyrolean Lower Inn Valley; it was granted a charter as early as

1393. Its uniform architecture mostly dates back to Renaissance times.

We crossed the Austrian/German border several times during the day. We were shown the scene of the film *The Sound of Music,* with the summerhouse of the von Trapp family, the castle, the convent and church of St Peter where the wedding took place. Part of the film was shot along the road with trees which the children climbed and the lake on which they rowed.

Leaving Bavaria we travelled under the runway of Salzburg airport, and by Mozart's birthplace and Salzburg cathedral which gives open air concerts.

On the Olympic road to Munich, we passed the oldest house in Mittenburg, and the violin school where scholars attend from overseas, and on through a village where the monks make liqueur chocolates.

Making a special detour we reached the town of Oberammergau, about two hours' run from Seefeld, first visiting the Linderhof Castle where King Ludwig lived. We called at the grotto of Oberammergau to see the theatre of the well-known passion play which takes place every ten years. We were shown the auditorium, the cross which is carried, and the robes worn by the characters in the play.

This play was started in the seventeenth century when a serious disease affected the district. People suffering from it used to hide in the rocks to get away from others. A shrine was built to those who died in the epidemic.

Tickets for the passion play soon sell out though five thousand five hundred spectators can be seated at each performance. Many visitors from England and elsewhere pack the stands each decade when the play is performed, spending on average two days in Oberammergau. In May, 1990, I again visited the Austrian Tyrol, this time to see the passion play, but it was not to be owing to the duplication of tickets from which so many people suffered.

A two hundred and fifty mile tour of the Dolomites was a day to remember. We passed through Innsbruck, an important university centre, which in the middle ages had its own imperial court, then we went up into the mountains towards the Italian border and saw a superb view of these magnificent peaks. Back on the original route we climbed from 3,500 to 5,400 feet and passed through the eighth Tyrol Pass which belonged to Austria until the end of the first world war. Fortifications were visible across the border.

Driving on the Vienna road we passed by the prison where the inmates make bricks, a castle now a girls' school, and a hospital for injured tourists from the ski centre, complete with helicopter on the roof. We could see the Olympic ski jump and the pole on which the flame is lit for the games.

On the eleventh day we set off for Rheinfelden, driving down the steep Zirlen Berg to Zirl, then continuing along the Inn Valley via Landeck to the resort of St Anton, ascending the Arlberg Pass and driving via Bludenz through the province of Vorarlberg to Feldkirch where we crossed into the tiny principality of Liechtenstein. From there we continued into Switzerland via Sargans, and on the new road along the Wallen Lake; through Zurich, the commercial and industrial centre of Switzerland, to Rheinfelden for an overnight stay at Hotel Schiff.

The next day we went through Basle into France, past Mulhouse and over the

Bussang Pass in the Vosges to Epinal and Nancy, former capital of Lorraine. We continued via the old garrison town of Metz to Luxemburg, capital of the grand duchy, to Arlon which has a history reaching back to the Romans. Before stopping for the night at Hotel de l'Aubepine, we went through Beauraing where the Virgin Mary appeared to several children in 1932.

The last day we reached the banks of the River Meuse, noted for its trout fishing and strawberry farms. Then on to Brussels via Namur, before reaching the motorway to Ostende and back to London.

CHAPTER EIGHT

1969 – Cruising in the Baltic

From Malta in 1969 I boarded the P&O liner *Uganda* at Tilbury for a fifteen day scholastic cruise to the Baltic, covering three thousand miles calling at Lubeck, Leningrad, Stockholm and Copenhagen. Clearing the fifty-three miles of the Kiel Canal and passing south of Lolland Island, we sailed south for Travemunde and Lubeck, the most popular of all Baltic ports. Thick pine woods run down to the sand-dunes and a stretch of beach with a sheltered position in the Baltic Bay; it cuts in behind the long peninsula running north from this point.

About eleven miles from Travemunde is Lubeck, known in the middle ages as the 'Queen of the Hanseatic League'. It remains the site of a wealth of architectural monuments and art treasures. The old city is surrounded by water.

Lubeck's trade mark, the fifteenth century Holsten Gate, and the fifteenth and sixteenth century Salt Lofts are both along the embankment of the Am der unter Trave to Marlegrube. The frontier between east and west Germany was heavily guarded by a watch tower and the area was mined. It was an unnerving experience to stand so close to the demarkation line; one step over and a shot would be fired! Since then, of course, the Wall has come down.

Leningrad is one of the most beautiful cities in the world, the second city of Russia after Moscow. It is famous for its harmony, splendid embankments, and over three hundred and fifty bridges spanning the canals, channels and rivers, sixty of which are in the metropolitan area.

There are hundreds of industrial enterprises among which are metal-working and machine-building industries, dozens of scientific research institutes, a state university and forty colleges. The city covers 94,000 acres on a hundred islands in the delta of the River Neva.

As we sailed into port the town band struck up a welcome. Before sightseeing in Leningrad arrangements had been made for a railway excursion to Moscow for an adult fare of £18 return.

Just before midnight a party of a hundred passengers and four hundred students joined the overnight Red Arrow Express for Moscow. The station was spotlessly clean. I boarded a four-berth sleeper (called 'soft travel') where our bunks were already made up – they were as hard as bullets! An attendant brought round a basket of black woollen bedsocks which we declined at two roubles a pair. Our stewardess saw we had a spare bunk so rolled up the bedding and took it away. The loo was filthy! In broken English the stewardess offered tea. Three glasses of strong black Russian tea arrived in metal containers. At midnight, by the light of two guard lamps we left Leningrad and proceeded across four hundred miles of Russia to Moscow. Loud piped music roused us next morning with more black tea.

We were met by our Intourist guide, Vera, small in stature and well-dressed in western style. She spoke fluent English. On the way to the Okrania Hotel she gave a chat-up on Moscow. We drove past Red Square, Moscow's largest. Lenin's portrait was on hoardings in the main streets.

The hotel was massive and overlooked the Moskva River. Built in Stalin's time it is one of Moscow's sky-scrapers and the last of its kind on account of building costs. Breakfast was served in an outsize restaurant and we had the choice of glasses of fruit juice, boiled eggs, sliced black bread, tea and one small pat of butter – butter is expensive in Russia. Afterwards we were taken to bedrooms to freshen up.

Touring the eight hundred years old city, capital of the USSR, we drove along the spacious avenues with twelve lanes of traffic, to the massive walls of the Kremlin for a glimpse of the palaces and cathedrals before going to Red Square.

In bright sun we joined the one-mile snake-like queue. The square is so large that mobile toilets have been installed with flexible piping going down into a manhole. The square is marked out in red and numbered for special occasions. On one side is the sprawling Gum universal store (pronounced 'Goom'), the largest store in the Soviet Union, catering for 140,000 shoppers daily. It was built at the end of the nineteenth century by Trappist merchants, but time was too short for us to go inside where we might be lost.

We moved shuffle fashion along to the entrance of the Mausoleum of Lenin; the structure appeared low against the walls of the Kremlin as though the base had sunk under the weight of the stone. The top was tiered back to provide a platform for the Soviet leaders on special occasions. Across the front of the mausoleum was a black band of polished stone bearing the simple word 'Lenin'. Close by, young Christmas trees grew, softening the severity of the Kremlin walls. in the porch of the mausoleum was a large red-ribboned wreath of flowers vividly lightening the severity of the guard of young soldiers with their shining bayonets. Our parcels were scrutinised by the MVD in their colourful peaked caps, and we were asked to leave them outside.

Out of the bright sunlight, we entered the air-conditioned and somewhat eerie chamber. Then everyone straightened up and walked with solemn dignity. Against the dark marble was a hammer and sickle medallion worked in twinkling silver. Two abreast, we followed the queue, in dim light, down a flight of marble steps into the subterranean tomb. Spot-lit lay the wax-like body of Lenin on a catafalque with bronze banners and flowers as adornment. At each corner stood a young soldier, facing inwards. Lenin's body appeared to be almost transparent, encased under finely-polished glass. The lighting showed up his features which stood out clearly. Dressed in a black suit with breast pockets adorned with coloured braid, he lay with his arms out-stretched, the right fist almost clenched, the left hand open revealing strong, square fingers. The embalmed body was covered with thick shrouds from the waist down. Lengths of black crepe were at his feet. His bald head was neat, his eye-lids closed. On his cheeks, the beard receded. It was a gruesome sight, and I was thankful to return to daylight.

Inside the Kremlin we went to the Armoury Museum which contained richly adorned armour, gold and silver objects, precious stones, coronation robes, royal carriages and thrones.

The underground railway was a unique experience, shiningly clean with white marble walls and columns, cut glass chandeliers and ceramic bas-reliefs, some of them gilded. Vera escorted us down the great escalator to the tube station; we were to travel from one station to the next. No pin-ups or advertisements marred the walls. Some three million people use the metro every day paying five kopeks (fivepence at the official rate of exchange) to travel any distance on the six-line system. No smoking is allowed.

Back in the hotel, after buying Russian postcards, I was directed to the first floor for stamps. In a small room sat the attendant. 'I speakie de German; I speakie de German,' she said, thumping her fist on my cards. She then produced the necessary stamps for several countries, and posted my cards in a small wooden box on the wall. They all reached their destinations – *From Russia with Love!* Returning to the ground floor, I could not find my party but outside stood six Muscovites. 'Bus,' I said, but that did not register. 'Coach,' I said, and one put out his hand and pointed to where I found my friends.

We set out for the opera. *Iolanta,* a one-act opera and a ballet, *Francesca da Rimini,* both by Tchaikovsky were being performed at the Stanislavsky Theatre in Mayakovski Square. There are some thirty theatres in Moscow. A full orchestra accompanied the players with the conductor in full evening dress to give an uplift to the evening for a crowded house. A ballerina appeared on stage attired in a flimsy-looking dress. During her performance, the top of her dress slipped from one shoulder, revealing her bare bosom. Quickly she went off stage, returning draped in tulle, but this was unsatisfactory. After another exit, she reappeared with the adjustment made. At the end of the opera bunches of flowers were passed to the performers.

Leaving the theatre, we boarded the overnight train to Leningrad, arriving in time for breakfast on board. On a tour of Leningrad each coach contained Russian students as guides and they spoke excellent English. Through the dock area photographs were forbidden. We travelled along the wide boulevards to the bank of the River Neva for a view of the Peter and Paul Fortress. Decembrists Square contains a striking monument to Peter the Great, the founder of the city in 1703. During the years of Soviet power, the city was expanded with new boulevards and avenues reaching far into what was formerly suburbs. There are now new squares, parks and monuments. Many wooden buildings add to the charm of this great metropolis. The main thoroughfare of the southern part of the city is Moscovsky Prospekt. Lining the avenue were busts of heroes of the Soviet Union who were born in Leningrad. One of the many museums open to the public is the cruiser *Aurora,* the only Russian ship to survive the Russo-Japanese Battle of Tsushima in 1905, and which signalled by its gun the start of the 1917 Revolution in Leningrad.

Munching sandwiches in the gardens, I acquired a thirst. An ex-army passenger joined me in search of a refreshing drink. This resulted in a lot of queueing before we obtained our purchase – a sickly liquid which I gave to my steward on the ship. My best buy was a bottle of vodka, Russia's traditional liquor, which my friends in Malta well remember!

A visit to Leningrad would not be complete without a look at the Winter Palace of the tsars, now the Hermitage Museum, patronised by thousands of ordinary Russians and tourists every day. There are over three hundred rooms crammed with priceless art treasures.

All was agog on board and on shore as we made ready to sail. British students and Russians festooned each other with streamers and balloons. Notes were exchanged – even kisses! Cheers went up and there was a general air of goodwill between the *Uganda* and Russian students. As we slowly left the docks, the town band struck up with *Auld Lang Syne.*

Stockholm, the City on the Water

Docking for ten hours in Stockholm was like another world – Sweden's capital had a culture of its own. Touring the city by coach and water-bus, we entered the narrow streets of the Old Town connected by a bridge over the water. The royal palace faces the water and we watched the changing of the guard. This city, where the waterways of Lake Malaren meet those of the Baltic, is situated in a region of remarkable scenic beauty. Stockholm translates as 'defenceless wall island'.

The historic buildings and monuments are memorable. The vast City Hall on the water is famous for its architecture and treasures; in the museum there was the salvaged man-of-war Wasa, rescued after three hundred years a hundred feet down in the depths of Stockholm Harbour. Built in 1625, she mysteriously sank as she sailed out of Stockholm on her maiden voyage in 1628. In the seventeenth century several attempts were made to raise the *Wasa.* In 1959 the Swedish navy took up the challenge and raised the warship in 1961. The archaeologists recovered twenty-four thousand objects, mostly of wood, but including leather, textiles, gold, silver, copper. bronze, cast-iron, all in fair shape. The re-discovery and salvage of this ship is one of the most important events in marine archaeology.

Wonderful Copenhagen

We docked at Copenhagen, Denmark's capital, for fourteen hours. A cheerful and welcoming city of the Danes, in latter years it has been especially remembered for Hans Christian Andersen and the adaptation of his work into the song and film *Wonderful Copenhagen.* The writer of fairy-tales at times lived in the sailors' quarter but later he became a celebrity touring the capitals of Europe.

Over five million people live in Denmark now, a quarter of them in Copenhagen, in a country only half the size of Scotland. Denmark consists of a continental peninsula called Jutland. Of the five hundred islands in the archipelago about one hundred are uninhabited, many being just plots of land and sand. the largest island is Zealand with Copenhagen on its eastern side. Between it and Jutland is Funen.

Denmark is smaller and flatter than the other Scandinavian countries, with no mountains, but just a five hundred foot hill. This archipelago is a good base between Great Britain and the Baltic. The country has a strong monarchy; since 1953 there has been no upper house in the Danish Parliament, the Folketing.

A city tour starts from the red-bricked Town Hall, which has an astronomical clock, the life-work of a Danish clockmaker named Tens Olse; the clock is so accurate that it is not expected to lose one second in the next hundred years! It shows the phases and eclipses of the moon, and the position of the stars for the next three thousand years. The driver pointed out, on the top of a city column, a statue of two lur players; the lur is a pre-historic bronze instrument familiar to us as a brand insignia on Danish Lurpak butter packs; it used to be blown as a war-horn and at pagan ceremonies. The ones in the national museum are from the bronze age found in peat bogs dating back to 500 BC. The Rosenbourg Palace, once the king's summer residence, is now a museum housing the collected treasures of Danish kings, including the crown jewels. If a hand reaches out to steal them, the thief disappears into the floor as an electric eye beam is broken!

The royal residence is Amalienborg Palace, four identical eighteenth century buildings connected by colonnades in a square. Pacing up and down between sentry boxes are smartly dressed royal guards, their busbies being especially tall. The Danish sentries wear light blue uniforms but on the sovereign's birthday they are scarlet.

The Kongens Nytorv Square (King's New Market) in the centre of thick trees encloses a small park with a central statue of Christian V, mainly remembered for his wayward ways!

Boarding a launch we sailed by Edward Eriksen's bronze statue of Hans Andersen's character the Little Mermaid, sitting precariously on a rock by the seashore. The statue was donated by brewer Carl Jacobsen in 1913, one of many gifts to Copenhagen.

At Christiansborg Palace are the apartments of state, parliament, the supreme court, foreign office and the royal library of a million books recording Viking ships which sailed to North America hundreds of years before Christopher Columbus. In the gardens stands a statue of a religious philosopher, the father of existentialism and a loose liver!

In Copenhagen's old city we had a walk-about to see Hans Christian Andersen's home. His statue is of a tall, thin youth with an outsize nose! Hans was the son of a shoemaker in Odense. His grandfather was addicted to drink, an eccentric in his habits and the laughing stock of the town with his decorative hats. Hans struggled after the early death of his father, but eventually secured royal patronage, travelled extensively and published thirty-three books, though it is for his fairy stories that he is remembered. He was made the first freeman of Odense.

Frederiksborg Castle at Hillerod is one of the most beautiful pieces of architecture in Scandinavia, set in the heart of woodland scenery of North Zealand. Named after King Frederick II, the greater part of the present buildings is the work of his son, Christian IV in the period 1600 to 1620.

For years Frederiksborg was the favourite residence of Danish kings and the scene of many solemn ceremonies and royal banquets. To the Danish people, Fredericksborg became a symbol of Denmark's past.

We were invited to tour the Carlsberg breweries with a glimpse inside the largest beer house. The annual output then exceeded five hundred million bottles of beer and is now nearly double! One of Carlsberg's hundred and thirty storage vaults covers an area of nine and a half acres! The breweries were established in 1847 by J. C. Jacobsen, a benefactor of the city.

Carlsberg's picturesque Elephant Gate leads to the brewery, a unique industrial enterprise whose proprietors, the Carlsberg Foundation, contribute their profits to the development of science and fine arts.

Copenhagen's famous Tivoli Gardens are a rendezvous for visitors and locals. A stroll through these gardens, illuminated at night with firework displays, is a fitting climax to a day's sightseeing.

Re-boarding *Uganda,* we sailed out of Copenhagen for Tilbury Docks, London.

CHAPTER NINE

1970 – To the Orient by Freighter

Freighter travel to far-away places in the early seventies was an experience to seafarers in search of adventure, relaxation, unknown ports and meeting other nationalities. In April 1970, my four month round voyage to Japan cost £550, crossing the North Atlantic and Pacific Oceans with seventeen ports of call.

At Tilbury Docks, I boarded the Greek freighter mv *Eurymachus* (Great Warrior) of 19,000 tons, one of five vessels of the Marchessini Line, ploughing back and forth from London to America, Rotterdam, Antwerp, Panama Canal, Manila, Hong Kong, Kao'hsiung, Keelung, Pusan, Kobe, Nagoya and Yokohama. My home for the round voyage was a first-class double stateroom with every comfort. My meals were taken in the officers' mess at the captain's table.

The vessel carried up to twelve passengers. On board were Filipinos, Americans, Japanese, Koreans, Italians, Panamanians, Armenians and three British. At two stages of the voyage I was the only passenger. The ship did not carry a doctor – when an Armenian developed a boil on her neck, the cook lanced it. We did not have a lifeboat drill for the whole time I was at sea.

While I was unpacking, an elegant woman, clutching a bunch of daffodils, breezed into my cabin, followed by my steward with her cases. Introducing ourselves, 'V' said she was to share my cabin to Staten Island in New York after a short visit to England. She was an amusing character with many a tale to tell of her adventurous life. A professional pianist of Irish-Lebanese descent, she was born in Australia and became an American citizen. Two other personalities bound for USA and Australia were Derek Townsend, travel writer, and Jill, his wife, with her weight-watching chart and vitamin foods.

The 14th April was the Greek Easter Sunday, an important day in the Greek calendar, with carnivals and parades in cities and villages. Celebrations on board began at breakfast with coloured eggs. At lunch there was spit-roasted lamb, delicious sweets, and wine on the house. Tea and dinner called for more celebrations and presents. The next day we docked at Rotterdam, the largest European seaport, and the birthplace of the great philosopher, Erasmus.

Holland's industries include shipbuilding, diamond factories, Delft pottery, cheese-making and flower bulb growing. In spring public gardens and parks are turned into floral carpets. Motor barges cruise up and down the canals carrying tourists and V and I spent a day in the city sightseeing. There are fine buildings and unique are the houses called 'Ref Jan' owned by wealthy families of generations past.

We sailed to Antwerp with its Gothic buildings and countless port pubs. Antwerp is the centre of the Flemish School of Art where Van Dyck flourished.

Across the North Atlantic we docked at Baltimore, an city of charm and culture, and the original US border town, renowned for art. The city's attraction is based on the extraordinary scope of its activities. Baltimoreans become artists, writers, engineers, scholars and doctors.

An historical site is the Star Spangled Banner House. It became the home of Mary Pickersgill, who made the great flag, 30 feet by 42 feet, which flew over Fort McHenry when the British fleet was turned back in 1814. It inspired Francis Scott Key to write *The Star Spangled Banner.* Flag House is now an historical museum.

After docking at the cargo port, Staten Island, for five cents I ferried over to Manhatten. It was Ascension Day, and Holy Trinity Church was holding a special service. Two students escorted me in. During the service, riotous demonstrations could be heard in the direction of Wall Street. Demonstrators were opposing the invasion of Cambodia by US forces. There were many casualties; my good companions took me to Child's restaurant.

Our next port of call was Charleston, South Carolina. Walking around the old town was like being in bygone days, as so much of historic interest has been preserved. It was a Sunday, and the 'Mammas' were dressed in their Sunday best. An American passenger arranged for me to visit the Citadel, South Carolina's military college, where I saw a parade of the two-hundred-strong corps. On the campus was a colossal nuclear missile pointing skywards. When complete with warhead it becomes operative, firing forty-eight miles into space. Mark Clark Hall, the activities building, is named in honour of General Mark Clark, President of the Citadel.

Sailing through the Caribbean, we passed into the Isthmus of Panama at Christobal, the cross-roads of the world, and through forty miles of canal with nine locks, past jungle-clad shores of the Gaten Lake, with hardly room for *Eurymachus* to manoeuvre, towed by an electric locomotive running on railway tracks. It takes two hours for a vessel to pass through the locks at each end, and twelve hours for the whole of the canal. Going ashore at night was an experience. On the quay I met Viola, a Panamanian, with her black shiny face and mop of black curly hair. She took me to the YMCA for a drink where she had cocoa. A bunch of mixed customers cast glances in our direction; it was a relief to have the protection of Viola to the ship.

It was a non-stop run of twenty-four days across the Pacific Ocean to Manila. The only sign of life at sea was the odd bird in flight. One landed exhausted on deck; the first officer revived it and let it go. On the horizon, the lights of ships caused me to rush to the rails! We passed over the International Date Line (going west losing a day, gaining one on the return journey).

Manila, where three million souls lived and worked in 14.7 square miles, is a bustling oriental city, with ancient buildings dating back to 1571. The captain warned me about going ashore. I took a taxi to the bank to change travellers' cheques; my driver seemed a doubtful character and, taking his taxi number, I was advised to pay him off. Three teachers from northern Manila, bound for Hong Kong, showed me around the town in a hired 'teepney', a converted jeep, highly decorated with slogans. My companions came back to the freighter; the gangplank was up, but was soon lowered and, with the captain's permission, the teachers came on board till sailing time.

Hong Kong was fascinating; we anchored off-shore with 'walla-wallas' (water taxis) careering back and forth to the shore. Two resident friends boarded the freighter and invited me to stay with them. With sailing time uncertain, I spent the day ashore with Moira and Ted. First we went to the New Territories and the Chinese border passing duck and rice paddies. We lunched at the Royal Yacht Club and dined at a Peking restaurant, finishing up at the 'Poor Man's night Club', an open-air market which is a car park by day. On a choppy sea, I caught the last walla-walla to the freighter.

We sailed to Taiwan (meaning 'dais rising from the sea'), in the past known as Formosa. We docked at Kao'hsiung, a quaint port and a town rich in cultural heritage, with hospitable and friendly people.

Through Keelung Travel Service I took a tour by road to Taipei, the capital. The temperature was in the nineties and my driver and guide were in dark business suits. I was advised to wear old clothes, carry a small amount of money and to drink beer instead of water. We drove through countryside reminiscent of England, and on to the MacArthur highway. Eight thousand American personnel were stationed in Taipei. The city was crammed with traffic jams, an accident prone area. My guide suggested I visit the Lungshan Temple where the goddesses of Mercy and Matsu are worshipped. The interior was ornate, with a strong fragrance of incense. I was hoping to lunch at the Grand Hotel, famous for its gourmet international restaurants, designed by Madame Chiang Kai Shek, but in Hong Kong I had picked up a virus and the guide recommended the US military officers' mess. It was the 20th June and my birthday so I invited the two men to join me over a light meal. There followed a visit to the National Palace Museum, Taipei's extinct volcano, and the pottery factory, before driving back to the ship.

We sailed on via the Korean Straits to Pusan, the largest port in Korea, located at the southernmost tip of the peninsula, and one of the finest natural harbours in the Far East.

Korea, known as the 'Land of Morning Calm', is noted for its health-giving ginseng, a herb said to cure all ills. In a corner-shop window in Pusan were bottles of ginseng herb in roots, wine, packets of tea, and in tablet form. Korea is also known for its beautiful women.

We left Pusan and entered Japanese waters. The weather was poor. We reached Kobe, famous for its Kobe steaks for which the cows are rubbed down with beer to produce succulent meat.

It was Expo year in Japan. Leaving Kobe's Mayo Pier, I travelled by special train to Osaka and the site, accompanied by a Chinese couple. In the grounds I was besieged by school-children, in smart uniforms, for my autograph, for which they politely bowed and thanked me in English. There were dozens of stands but first I visited the English one, and then the Malta exhibition where I met Mr. Sammut, and signed the visitors' book.

I was recommended to see the Nagota Shrine and at a bus stop I asked a businessman the way. He offered to take me by taxi. On arrival a mob of children clustered round me as a token of welcome, while a priest gave me a sixty-year-old plaque, for luck.

On a couple of buses, I made my way back to Mayo Pier, But I alighted at the wrong bus stop! It was night-time, and the only contact I had was the freighter name in Japanese. Seeing a light in a window, I knocked at a door. A young Japanese appeared and I explained my predicament; he seemed to understand, and took me alongside a bridge over which traffic was passing. After what seemed a long time I spotted ships in the distance. With a thank you and a bow, I hurried back to Mayo Pier. I was told I was lucky to be back.

After twelve hours at sea we docked at Nagoya, Japan's third largest port. Booking a taxi, I was driven by uniformed driver with white gloves, to Nagoya Castle, 144 feet high, set in delightful grounds. Climbing the stairway, I was rewarded with a panoramic view.

We sailed into Yokohama harbour in torrential rain,with the threat of a typhoon. This was our last call in Japan and we would stay for seven days in port. As recommended by 'Sparks' the radio officer, I went to Kyoto on the famous bullet train, shaped like a bullet, and with sixteen coaches. Like a white snake, this super-express of the new Tokaido Line is regarded as the fastest train service in the world. On the way to the station, my taxi driver had to thread his way through river-like streets. With a return ticket to Kyoto I was off travelling at 130 miles an hour. If Japanese trains are late, a refund can be claimed. The interior of the air-conditioned coach was lush, with excellent service. A unique way of travel, but with a cocooned feeling, boxed in from the outside world by unopenable sound-proof windows.

Nearing Kyoto, the imposing Kyoto Tower Hotel, recommended by Sparks, came into sight topped with a candle-style white steeple which towered into the sky for a hundred metres. An observatory commanded a magnificent view of the outlying area as far as Osaka. The third highest tower in Japan, it is very strongly built to be safe from earthquakes. On the eighth floor of the hotel I booked in for two nights. There was everything for my needs, from kimono and slippers to toothpaste.

Kyoto is a city of historic associations and legendary lore, serving as a repository for the finest relics of old Japan, shrines, temples, palaces and elaborately-designed gardens. In the Miyako Hotel I met Mishko Sasaki; we dined together at a noodle shop over 'suviveri', a kind of stew.

In the old capital of Nara, the birthplace of Japanese art, one of the most popular places is Nara Park, a natural woodland, where many tame but timid deer roam freely. They come to the fence bowing and nudging for tit-bits from visitors. The belief is that the deer are messengers of goddesses enshrined in the adjoining Kasuga shrine.

Tokyo is only forty minutes by train from Yokohama. In this great metropolis, I gazed at the glittery shops and windows displaying samples of plastic food. The Japanese eat raw fish. The Marunouch Hotel was the starting point for a city tour, passing the parliament building and visiting the Imperial Gardens and National Museum. I attended a tea ceremony, an authentic bridal show, the Asakusa Kannon Temple dedicated to Kannon, Goddess of Mercy, the Ginza shopping area, and Tokyo's residential quarter.

Catching the evening train back to Yokohama. I sat opposite a young Japanese girl. I was counting my yen for my taxi fare, when suddenly she picked up her parcels, dropped a large slab of chocolate in my lap, and fled. I just had time to thank her before she disappeared.

The next day, in Yokohama town, I ascended to the top of the Marine Tower; at a thousand feet it was then and maybe still the tallest steel tower in the world. In the Silk Museum I saw silk being produced in all its stages. I read that a typhoon could hit Japan around Saturday. It was Independence Day, and Japan was celebrating with firework displays.

On a second visit to the town, I heard that typhoon *Olga* had passed us by. On the way back, I boarded the commuter train, the only Britisher, and was jammed in by 'pushers' in a crowded compartment.

We sailed away from Japan for a month at sea, passing through the Panama Canal at night, brilliantly lit. On through the Caribbean, we reached Staten Island. With two days in port, I retraced my steps to Manhatten, entering Trinity Church to find that the church magazine contained pictures of the recent riots. After shopping at Macey's department store, I reached the observatory of the Empire State building to see the magnificent views, after negotiating two elevators.

After sailing back to Tilbury Docks, *Eurymachus* had cruised thirty thousand miles in four months.

CHAPTER TEN

1971 – Snowed up in Andorra

It was not yet daylight as I left my hotel in the Costa del Sol on a warm February morning. Although I had been advised not to go in February, my destination was Andorra in the Pyrenees, via Barcelona.

At Barcelona airport I parked my luggage in anticipation of a pre-arranged taxi to take me up to Andorra la Vella, the capital; it was windy and very cold.

In the distance I could see Barcelona Cathedral, known by the locals as 'Le Seu'. With time to spare, I decided to visit the cathedral, and crossed the busy thoroughfare. To reach the outside of the cathedral I had to climb two hundred steps! There was no time to go inside as I was to be met at the air terminal in the afternoon by a taxi driver. At three o'clock there was no sign of him.

I approached one of the taxi drivers on the rank and enquired if he would take me to Andorra for two hundred pesetas, the pre-arranged fare. After much chatter in Spanish with other drivers, my man said, 'Si, si,' and my luggage was put into his taxi. We appeared to be on our way to Andorra! The driver suggested I sat in front, which I refused. After passing through the suburbs he suddenly drew up at the bus station. I followed him into the entrance and to the ticket office. I then gathered he was trying to fix me up on a bus to Andorra that day. 'Not posseeble,' said the man at the ticket office. 'Tomorrow at seven.' The driver and I went away. He tried the Iberia Lines office nearby, but no help. At a travel agent, the receptionist, who spoke a little English, endeavoured to assist. I said I would have to stay over night at an hotel and she recommended the *Messen* close by. I asked the taxi driver to take me there. 'Yes, there is a vacancy, room only,' said the proprietor. I handed over my passport and phoned the hotel in Andorra saying that I had been delayed as I was not met as arranged. I learned that a driver was in another part of the air terminal at Barcelona with a card held up on which was my name. The proprietor said there had been a heavy fall of snow in Andorra the night before. I asked to be met at Andorra bus station.

Receiving back my passport at the *Messen,* I was advised to buy a ticket at the bus station overnight. I found a restaurant and returned to the hotel.

My room was somewhat scruffy and cold. Looking up hot water bottle in my

Spanish/English phrase book, I asked for one. Up came a glass of hot water! I asked to be called at six next morning, not relying on my alarm clock.

I was already dressed when the night porter knocked at my door. My luggage was taken down and a taxi booked for the bus station, though I could have walked the short distance. The bus arrived at seven o'clock.

Ten minutes later the bus started to pile up with families and, shortly after, we left for Andorra; it was just getting light.

We drove through long palm tree lined boulevards and floodlit avenues. On the horizon was a glorious sunrise as we met the early morning traffic into the city. We reached the mountains; orange trees were in bloom in the passes. We came to hairpin bends and narrow roads which were unnerving. The wind whistled outside but later we stopped at a local bar for breakfast.

Ahead lay snow on the mountains, and then we saw the first signs of snow on the roadside and on the roofs of oncoming traffic. The weather was fast deteriorating. We reached the frontier where passports were checked and our luggage taken off the bus for inspection.

At one o'clock we reached Andorra la Vella. By now the snow was thick on the ground. We arrived a little early and there was no-one to meet me. I arranged for a fat sun-tanned local to take me to my hotel which was just around the corner, so we walked.

After meeting the proprietor and a line-up of agents anticipating I wished to buy a property, I relished a hot meal. It was impossible to explore the little town then or on the next day as snow was falling heavily. I was confined to the hotel.

The next day there was a lull in the blizzard; the sun shone and the snow started to thaw on the roofs and slither down to the pavement below. The roads became chock-a-block with cars. The snow and slush were fast turning into rivers. It was a toss up whether it was safer to walk on the pavements or on the road. I went in search of a pair of wellies, a godsend during my stay.

At last the blizzard abated, I was able to walk in the mountains and take the local bus to the villages.

For over five hundred years Andorra, a small tax haven, has been politically and economically stable with a very high standard of living. It is easily accessible from Barcelona, Paris and London by air, and is a skier's paradise.

Andorra has great physical charm and beauty with a hundred valleys. Four rivers water the country to Les Escaldes (the junction). They then become the River Balira. The water is cold, clear and unpolluted; it flows everywhere, producing crops of tobacco, vegetables, wild strawberries, roses and orchids. The mountains are as high as any in Central Europe, and the latitude is almost that of Rome. In January residents enjoy breakfast on their terraces surrounded by picturesque snow-capped mountains. I was taken by car to visit a friend who had been marooned in his home by snow.

The average number of sunny days between November and March are one hundred. There is low humidity and no extremes of temperature. I found the climate very invigorating. Andorra is particularly suitable for those convalescing, especially for respiratory troubles and rheumatism. in Escaldes there are excellent thermal springs and the Hotel Roc Blanc provides sauna baths, massage, gymnasium and swimming pool. Parts of Andorra are naturally very French as it lies next to France. The country currently has a population of about 40,000, though when I was there it was reckoned to be only 19,000.

The principal resources are tobacco growing, cattle and sheep raising, commerce and tourism. Andorra enjoys folklore celebrations.

According to legend, Andorra was founded in 784 by Charlemagne but its position was formalised by a treaty between France and Spain in 1278. Constitutionally the sovereignty of Andorra is vested in two 'co-princes' – the President of France and the Spanish Bishop of Urgel – who can veto certain decisions of the democratically elected council of twenty-four councillors, but cannot impose their own will without the support of the council.

French and Spanish are the usual languages but I found that my English was understood.

CHAPTER ELEVEN

1971 – Sojourn in Greece

As we touched down at Athens airport on Christmas Eve, the city was illuminated with twinkling lights which gave a message of goodwill; the atmosphere was even more impressive as the taxi wended through the artistically and well-decorated streets to the hotel.

On Christmas Day, Athens, the ancient and modern city capital was bathed in glorious sunshine; it was delightful to stroll down the wide streets and sip coffee at one of the open-air cafes in Constitution Square, the heart of the city, and watch the Greek way of life.

Athens has grown from ancient civilization to be a large commercial and tourist city with an excellent shopping area. Its people are friendly and helpful.

Greece is steeped in history. The Acropolis above the Agora is a masterpiece of classical architecture; it stands magnificently, high upon a rock overlooking the city. The Houses of Parliament attract crowds of visitors daily to watch the Evzones, soldiers of the royal guard, with their picturesque uniforms dating back to the liberation from Turkish rule.

Athens is a good centre and stepping-off ground for nearby attractions, the highlight being Delphi, sheltered by Mount Parnassus, with the Temple of Apollo. The ancients thought this to be the 'navel of the world'.

Another must is the rock promontory of Sounion in Attica on which still stands the fifth century BC Temple of Poseidon, the god of the sea, with its twelve erect Doric columns, on one of which Byron's engraved name can be clearly seen.

A tour recommended is to the Argolis region in the Peloponnese area, along the coastal road of the Saronic Gulf to the new town of Corinth with its deep-cut nineteenth century canal connecting the Ionian and Aegean Seas and running below railway and road bridges. This tour incorporates old Corinth, through hilly country to visit the Apollo temple and museum.

Mycenae was the next stop where I walked around the ruins of the palace and cemeteries, including a visit to the Lion Gate, standing over ten feet high, and the beehive-shaped tomb of Agamemnon.

Nauplia, in the province of Argolis and for several years the first capital of the modern Greek state, has the beautiful island of Bourdz and an ancient fortress, now a luxury hotel. The road leads on to Epidaurus where I could see the very well-preserved fan-shaped marble theatre with fifty-five rows of seating and accommodation for fifteen thousand people; it is famous for its acoustics. Each June and July the Greek National Theatre re-enacts in traditional costumes some of the ancient tragedies and comedies.

Another highlight is the day cruise from Athens on m.s. *Marina* to the islands nearby, passing close to the limestone island of Poros, said to be sacred, with its little pink and white houses scattered on the rocky hillside. The boat sails on to the Bay of Idhra, noted for its sponges, for a visit to the town with smart shops lining the quay, crammed full of local handicrafts. The island attracts artists and writers.

Last is a visit to Aegina Island, the largest in the group and with a variety of scenery; on Aegina stands Mount Oros, the holy mountain. A short trip up to the Temple of Athena, built in 480 BC, is well worth while.

This chapter was published in the Times of Malta *on 8th January, 1972. Permission has since been granted by the editor for its publication elsewhere.*

CHAPTER TWELVE

1973 – By Freighter to Brazil

Leaving Malta at the end of April 1972, there were a few days in hand in London awaiting sailing orders to Brazil. When they came, I boarded a train to Harwich and the ferry to Rotterdam with still a full day's sight-seeing there.

It was late on Sunday afternoon, 30th April, when I took a taxi from the central railway station to Verolme Wharf, Botlek, to board the German freighter *Emma Oldendorff* for Vitoria, a port on the east coast of Brazil.

There she was, a stream-lined fully automated air-conditioned bulk carrier which carried up to nine passengers on her journey to and from Bremerhaven, a round trip distance of about 10,000 miles, taking a month.

After paying the taxi driver there was time to stand and stare at the carrier's massive steel structure – four times round her main deck was a mile. Her imposing height towered above me as I attracted the attention of a passenger on deck.

Within minutes, the first officer came down the gangplank, followed by the bosun who took my luggage. The accommodation booked for me was on the boat deck and I found it to be an attractively decorated stateroom upholstered on steel blue coloured leather. In the corner near the bed was the dressing table with red and white check cloth, and an arm chair; looking out on to the deck were two large windows. Leading off the stateroom was a shower with small check stone flooring, gay nautical plastic curtains, a washbasin, toilet, mirror and cupboard.

Unpacking completed, it was time for dinner. I went down one deck to the large mess surrounded by picture windows. At table were the captain, the first officer, the chief engineer and his wife and four-year old son with golden hair and already a seafarer with his thirst for ship lore. Lastly there was Mrs Brinkman, a passenger from Germany whom I had seen on deck. I was the only Britisher.

The conversation during dinner was in German, but some English was spoken and understood. I learned that we did not carry cargo to Brazil, only water ballast; Homeward bound we were to bring back a cargo of iron ore from the mines of Rio Doco. The dimensions of the ship were interesting – tonnage 67,000 deadweight; length 252 metres; breadth 104 feet; depth loaded 41.04 feet; and height 18 metres deck to keel. The *Emma Oldendorff* averaged twenty-seven kilometres per hour.

The next evening we set sail out of Rotterdam's great harbour into the River Maas, and soon we were in the English Channel.

By Thursday we were in the Bay of Biscay in calm seas, and we settled down to the usual routine of freighter travel. I received an invitation to the captain's day room to see his aquarium, and then a tour of the engine rooms, by elevator, with the chief engineer. There was a library, a swimming pool and a sports room three decks below near the counter and rudder where we played table tennis, etc.

We passed the Canary Islands and saw a shoal of flying fish and dolphins prancing in and out of the water. Later I visited the bridge where a black pigeon was resting on the rail. The first officer caught it at dusk and it soon became tame, eating out of his hand and drinking water from the tap in his cabin. Near Cape Verde Islands he released the bird.

At breakfast time a few days later, there was excitement on board for about two hours with a number of continuous and rapid rings on the ship's bell which grew more persistent, and the engine stopped. I went to my cabin and put a few clothes together for emergency, but then heard that one of the crew had sighted a drifting lifeboat and we must help. I hurried to the bridge to find in the distance on the port side, an orange coloured lifeboat drifting on the water.

The ship's engines were started slowly again and the carrier went alongside the lifeboat which was found to be uncovered and empty. One of the crew was than slowly lowered by rope chair; he collected nine oars which he tied to ropes to be hauled up on deck. All other moveable articles were similarly brought up and included three full water containers, five dead flares which had presumably been set off to attract attention, and a couple of live ones.

The sailor was then hauled up on board and the lifeboat hoisted half way up the side of the carrier. I then went off to breakfast. On returning, the lifeboat was still in the same precarious position, but after further manoeuvring, it was gradually hauled up on deck. Cameras clicked and the captain inspected the interior for any information he could glean. Painted on the bow was *Theodor Fontaine* and *Rostock,* an East German port, on the stern. She was capable of carrying fifty-three persons, and could have been drifting for about two weeks. The cost of such a lifeboat was about £8,000. It was thought that its occupants had probably landed in the Canary Islands, taking with them all the food, the rubber dinghy and other necessary equipment.

All parts were taken away for examination and the lifeboat left on deck until Vitoria was reached when it was transferred to one of the eleven hatches and ditched into the water there. That midnight we passed the equator and next day, some twelve miles away were the islands of Fernando de Noronha, believed to be used as Brazilian prisons.

During the next day or two we had stormy weather. Vitoria, in the state of Espirito Santo, is the major outlet for iron ore and is automated for loading it on to the ships. It was then scheduled for expansion; the ore from the Rio Doco mines holds the world's record for iron content.

At noon land was sighted and by the afternoon mountains were visible, shaped like cones. We slowed, turned around, and anchored out at sea, waiting our turn. From the port side I could see stretches of mountains all along the coastline, with white buildings, some skyscrapers, in front of which stretched a bay with golden sand. To the right were more mountains, one with a large plateau, but nearby was the harbour with a ship in port.

At last it was time for our carrier to be manoeuvred into port and we tied up alongside the colossal British carrier, *Eden Bridge,* of 120,000 tons and an outsize blue funnel and red and white ensign, being loaded with iron ore.

The ore is hauled by giant trucks from the mines to the railway, when it is taken by train on a whole day's journey to the docks. It is then transferred to a conveyor belt five kilometres long, and huge Japanese machinery automatically loads the ore aboard the carrier, via a chute, into one of the empty hatches.

After an early breakfast, next morning I went ashore to Vitoria for the day that the ship was in port for loading. I walked down the long quay, past the iron ore travelling along the conveyor belt, towards the police gate where my passport was inspected and a taxi telephoned for. On the way into town there were many palm trees, oleanders in full bloom and lovely white houses. The driver drove fast through the built-up area.

My first call was to the Brazilian Bank to cash travellers' cheques into cruzeiros. There were people of all nationalities in the busy town, with hordes of school children in their neat uniforms – more than forty per cent of Brazil's population of over a hundred million were then under fifteen. The rate of population growth was then three and a half per cent per annum, one of the highest in the world.

Approximately sixty-five per cent of the population is of European stock, chiefly Portuguese; ten per cent are negroes, one per cent local Indians and the rest include various mixed races like mulattos, mestizos, caboclos, and cayusos. Several hundred thousand Japanese emigrated to Brazil at the end of the last century.

European immigrants, apart from the Portuguese, have come from Spain, Italy and Germany. The country is a melting pot of races and cultures, but Portuguese is the only language spoken apart from a few tribal tongues. However I found that English and French could be understood by some of the shopkeepers. Almost ninety per cent of the population are catholics, but there are numerous churches of other denominations and the Jewish faith is well represented.

During my day in Vitoria I came across a number of dress and material shops. Brazil is self-supporting in supplies of clothing and footwear, and is well established as an exporter of shoes and garments. Also in the shops was a large quantity of plastic ware. Brazil is a big consumer of plastic materials for a wide range of uses. I visited a large corner store, Cannes, like a supermarket, with the usual everyday requirements but when I asked for one or two items on my list the shop assistant replied in the negative by putting up a forefinger and shaking it slowly across her face from side to side – a Brazilian custom. I enquired for Brazil nuts, *noses* in Portuguese, but could not find any.

Walking up a large number of steps, past small restaurants, I came to the Rua Pedro Palacios with its cathedral and imposing marble statue of Domingos Jose Martins.

Next I took a taxi out of town to a recommended restaurant, Churrasco a Gaccha, which had the well-known Diners Club sign on the window. The interior was large and artistically designed with small tables laid up for lunch. The ceiling was adorned with wooden cart wheels. An elderly man came forward followed by a waiter who at once brought the menu and a small glass each of local dark red wine and a plate of appetisers as an aperitif. I ordered filet mignon and outsize kebabs arrived with several portions thrust through two very long steel knives.

After lunch, I took a taxi to the Santa Rita souvenir shop, though I discovered it was only a short distance away. Here I was met by a smiling Portuguese assistant in a short dress, with skin as black as jet and a pair of sparkling eyes. The local handicrafts were made of various Brazilian woods, bowls, ash trays, bangles, vases, ear-rings, etc. I selected a couple of items before returning to the ship where iron ore was still being loaded into the hatches.

The next afternoon we sailed for Bremerhaven with 63,000 tons of iron ore on board. Our place at the loading bay was immediately taken by a Brazilian carrier. Our deck was covered with red dust like a carpet; as much as fifty tons of ore dust can be swept of the decks during the voyage.

At sea again I watched the land gradually recede and settled down to the return journey. Sailors were busy washing down the decks with large hoses, while three were suspended on boards held by ropes, painting the outside of the bridge. I went for my camera to record the incident and then took my usual mile walk around the deck. The officers pedal around on bicycles.

At breakfast the next morning, after a stormy night, the first officer made a presentation to me of a pair of breast fins from a flying fish which he had found earlier washed up on deck by the spray. He fixed the fins to a sheet of white paper which the captain and chief mate signed and dated 20th May, 1973. It still hangs on my wall in my home seventeen years later.

On the Saturday before Whitsunday we had very rough seas again. At noon we crossed the equator, celebrating in the mess with a 1970 German wine Krover Nackterach. Later, the captain invited us all to his day room for drinks. The following day the engines stopped again. A shark had been sighted at the stern and the captain took a shot at it, though I don't know why. An albatross was also shot down and it fell into the sea. I was cross and did not turn up for dinner.

On Saturday, 27th May, we had more rough seas with a force seven gale; spray washed over the main mast which was lit up at night. The first officer and the bosun donned their oil skins before walking along the deck to see if all was well. An anchor was missing on the previous trip.

By now we were nearing the French coast and passed the Channel Islands and Cherbourg. This was celebrated with a drink called bowle (wild duck) in the captain's day room. The shell of an out-size Brazilian water melon had been filled with chopped melon to which had been added two bottles of white wine, a bottle of champagne, half a bottle of cognac and some soda water – a very potent German cocktail!

On 2nd June we docked at Bremerhaven, where I received permission from the captain to spend an extra day on board to coincide with my connection to Harwich. The mystery lifeboat was taken off on the starboard side and rowed away. Meanwhile I was seen off by the captain and first officer.

This article was published in the Sunday Times of Malta, Travel Supplement, *on 21st January 1973. Permission has since been granted by the editor for its publication elsewhere.*

CHAPTER THIRTEEN

1973 – Sardinia, the least-known Mediterranean Island

The Island of Sardinia is in the centre of the Western Mediterranean. Flying from Malta to Rome, I boarded the night train to the port of Civitavecchia and reached Cagliari, the regional capital of Sardinia, by ferry the next day.

My first impressions were mixed as we slowly sailed into port. The island looked drab and uninviting with old and uncared-for buildings, but ashore there were bright fuchsia-lined streets and there was an air of welcome. I managed to find a porter to take me and my luggage to the nearby Jolly Hotel where I was booked in. He said it was just around the corner; when a taxi came along, my man was bent on earning his tip and off we set on foot along the quay, over the Piazza Roma, and up some steps until we came to the hotel. He charged one thousand lire which seemed steep for so short a journey, but he had his way.

Mountainous Sardinia, from a tourist's point of view, had lain almost dormant for centuries until some fifty years ago when the scourge of malaria was overcome there.

The Italian government saw its potential and built an airport, roads, beautiful hotels and other amenities to attract visitors from all over the world. As a result, this lesser-known island with a jagged coastline, now has excellent communications by air and it can be reached easily by ferry from the Italian mainland. Corsica is just seven miles north of the island by sea. Sardinia has become very popular with the Americans.

Cagliari in the south is connected with other parts of the island such as Alghero and Porto Torres in the north, rich in pinewoods, vineyards and orchards, and Golfo Aranci in the north east. Costa Smeralda in this region was put on the map by the Aga Khan when he formed the Costa Smeralda Consortium in 1962 with a small group of landowners, with himself as president. The members in 1974 owned some thirty-five miles of coastline which includes eighty beaches. To preserve the beauty of the area the consortium set up an architectural committee with the task of upholding the highest standard of building and design throughout the Costa Smeralda. This part of the coast has now become a millionaires' paradise.

The landscape of Sardinia is picturesque with rugged mountains, but the best scenery is to be found in the valley of Ogliastra with its scattered trees, hills and villages. The island has many religious buildings and fortifications enclosed by old walls.

Sardinia is steeped in history with pre-historic Neolithic as well as Roman architecture, the museums containing bronze and sculptured statuettes. The handicraft shops are full of miniature warriors, musicians, boats, animals and other items of interest, many of which are bought as attractive presents. Ceramics, hunting horns, decorated gourds, knife handles, baskets and carved woodwork, silver and gold ware and corals are also in demand. Wall tapestries are an important industry.

Folklore predominates in the villages. The main festival was for St Efisio, celebrated since 1647 on 1st May at Cagliari, when thousands of sightseers flock to the island's capital for the parades through the streets. The custom fulfils a vow made to their patron saint of three centuries ago.

Taking a stroll near the shopping centre I wandered up hill to a large arcade crammed full of shops containing Italian leather goods, especially handbags and shoes. Sardinia is noted for its leather. Apart from handicrafts, there were jewellery and porcelain, and many book shops.

The gastronomy of Sardinia is especially inviting for its hors d'oeuvres through to its sweets, accompanied by some of the finest wines with a high alcohol content.

I came across an excellent confectionery shop called La Tarra el Oro, with a window full of Easter eggs set in pretty flowered china baskets.

Meeting a group which had just flown in from Germany, one of whom had a smattering of English, I said I was anxious to see the island. They invited me to join them for a sightseeing tour of the south-west coast. After an early breakfast in my room, I left to join the coach where I was introduced to the others as a guest from Malta.

Our itinerary was to the Phoenician/Roman excavations of Nora on the coast of St Margherita di Pula. The nearby island of Saint Antioco has a quaint little harbour called Calasseta. The island is joined to the Solicitana coast by an isthmus built by the Romans. A ferry now connects it. We were also scheduled to visit coal mining and iron ore districts, the Iglesian Grotto, and to see the Basilica of Uta, the Madonna.

After passing through the suburbs of Cagliari, we drove into open country, over a dam and the River Tirno into more open country with pine forests on one side and the open sea on the other. There were orange and lemon groves and eucalyptus trees, and in the mist beyond we could pick out the mountains.

Driving through the town of Chia, noted for its fine bay and sandy beaches, we passed an enormous oil refinery, and went through a number of poor-looking villages; cornfields and hedges were thick with prickly pears until we came to the Roman ruins of Nora which were discovered in 1952.

At low tide, part of the old city of Nora is below the sea and ancient stones could be seen through the clear waters, including many Roman ruins, piers, ports and buildings. Old temples are visible close to the tip of the promenade, under the sea,

The Roman theatre could accommodate eighty thousand spectators and is now used in the summer months for opera and drama. The ruins of a sanctuary could be seen and the Carthaginean plebeian quarter, the baths and some very interesting mosaics which were still in good condition. Entrance to the excavations was free. Wild flowers were growing in the vicinity and nearby the Spanish watch-tower was being lashed by the heavy seas.

From the promontory of Nora named after the martyr and saint, Efisio, we could see Cagliari whence we started our tour.

Leaving Nora we travelled on a Roman road and through Forte village and across rocky barren country where we looked for samples of stones which had eroded over the years forming unusual shapes. The coastal road led to beautiful views of sea and mountains, a collection of small islands and a little harbour. Eventually we reached Giba and the small mining town of Saint Antioco. There is a legend that St Anthony was thrown into the sea and waves brought him back to the Sardinian coast, landing him here at St Antioco.

We stopped at the twelfth century three-floor church of St Antioco de Bisercio, built by Benedictine monks of San Vittore from Marseilles on an old Phoenician site. Flowers adorned the church and a figure of the Lady of Monserrat of Spain stood at the right hand side of the interior of the church. In the grounds of the building was a sacred well. Two intelligent guides escorted us to the catacombs of Santa Rosa, the saint's mother, and the Gartajan tombs.

A Phoenician fortress a few miles away had grim enclosures which in the past contained the bones of children, including new born male babies, sacrificed to the gods of Tanit and Baa. On the return journey, the red-coloured surface of the iron ore mines of Iglesias were pointed out to us.

Passing through a range of mountains we came to the Grotto of St Giovanni. The road ran right through it. Our driver, new to the area, walked the length of it to the exit with a torch before driving the coach through. There are 336 grottoes in Sardinia, many of which are unexplored.

The next day I spent in Cagliari seeing the Basilica of the Virgin of Bonaria with a statue of the Madonna at the entrance. A hill led up to the Piazza Palazzo where there was the very ornate Romanesque-style cathedral, built about 1312 with a very decorative ceiling above the centre aisle. The lace-effect pulpit was of special interest, built by Maestro Gulielmo, and brought from Pisa Cathedral. On the right, in the second chapel, was a statue of the Madonna and Child in gilt painted wood. On the steps near the presbytery were models of two large lions.

The National Archaeological Museum had a wealth of pre-historic materials. It also contained a picture gallery through the ages with statuary, a jewel room and other departments too numerous to mention. The ruins of the Roman amphitheatre accommodates fifteen thousand people and is now used for drama.

On Easter Monday all shops and business houses were closed. The main roads were packed with cars making for the beaches.

Leaving for Olbia in the north-east of the island where I had booked accommodation, I taxied to the bus station. The countryside was very green and the yellow gorse and asphodel were in bloom. We passed through a residential area of attractive white painted houses with corrugated roofs, through villages, winding narrow streets and a mountain range. Olbia was an important town in the time of Carthage and in Roman and mediaeval times; it has since profited from the airport and harbour, which has daily connections with the mainland. The Golfo Aranci harbour, the terminal port for railway ferries, offers a rapid daily connection with Civitavecchia.

Leaving Olbia for Porto Cervo on the Smeralda Coast, I was given a lift to the modern Hotel Luci di la Mustagna, owned by a cousin of the Aga Khan. After my stay overnight, the manager of the hotel drove me to the terminus where I took the train to Cagliari for a hotel to await my return ferry.

CHAPTER FOURTEEN

1973 – Roaming Portugal's Algarve Coast

Have you ever had the urge to roam the Algarve in Southern Portugal under your own steam and without a car? Buses and coaches are cheap, with careful drivers, as I found along the one hundred and twenty-five mile coastline and up into the mountains. A local rail service, often unknown to visitors, operates between Lagos (pronounced Lagoosh) in the west to Vila Real de Santo Antonio for the Spanish border in the east. Second class with wooden seats is not to be frowned on to save escudos and also to escape the tourist crowds. I often hopped on this little train at the floral-decked wayside stations with the route past orchard groves of fruit of every description.

In 1973, at the height of the season, I set off for the Algarve, with hand luggage, a return open ticket for £88.30, £155 in travellers' cheques, £50 in Portuguese currency at 54 escudos to the pound sterling, £20 sterling and a Portuguese phrase book bought just before take-off.

Landing at Faro's international airport, I took a taxi for 140 escudos to the hilly coastal town of Albufeira, half way along the coast. it was a Sunday and the shops were closed, but a large open air market in a flower-decked square sold luscious fruit and vegetables. For 95 escudos I booked in for bed and breakfast with a local family for a week, and received great hospitality. During my seven weeks in the Algarve I stayed with five Portuguese families.

The town came to life next morning, with its narrow streets and pavements almost unable to cope with the heavy traffic passing through the bottleneck, causing queues and hold-ups with streams of cars, sixty-seater coaches, cement mixers, and the ever present noisy motor scooters. The duty gendarmerie somehow managed to disentangle the chaos, but the pedestrians were often squeezed against the walls as the traffic wended its way around.

The Portuguese are friendly, kindly and simple folk with a sense of humour. The women have lovely eyes, and in the villages stride along in their full-flowing skirts behind their men-folk, the heads covered with a scarf topped with a sun hat, often leading a donkey laden with produce. Old women sit at street corners, shaded by an umbrella, selling their wares. The Algarveans have large families so there is always someone in mourning. They are hard-working people, seldom idle, born fishermen and good agriculturists. Industry is one of their main sources of livelihood with the building of dams and power stations. Mining and tourism also plays a vital part in the economy.

The Algarve is famous for its fish, especially sardinhas, as the Portuguese call sardines. The industry has flourished for over a hundred years with an average of two hundred factories. Local women can the sardines by hand under perfect hygienic conditions, and most are exported. Sardines are the staple diet of the Portuguese as they are cheap, nourishing and rich in protein. I came across this little silver fish at fishing ports, caught up in fishermen's nets and sold for a few escudos to peasants who take them away in buckets or plastic bags for the next meal. I saw sardinhas being cooked over tiny braziers outside white-washed little houses. I had them served up in restaurants with salad and vino, and ate them on picnics with a papasecos (bread roll) washed down with the local brew.

Near the fish market in Albufeira I enjoyed *sardinha assada* at Ruiana's unique restaurant where my meal came straight out of the tank, was grilled over a charcoal grill, and served up at long trestle tables with a salad and a bottle of Caldeirada red wine.

One of my favourite haunts was Galeao's Bar owned by the TV and radio announcer, Peter Haigh, and his charming wife Jill Adams, who are both retired. Here I met up with other personalities of the Haigh regime who came into his social hive for an aperitif and to see Peter and Jill. At midday Jill would serve up her bangers and on Sundays her roast and Yorkshire which always attracted the regulars.

Portimao is the headquarters of the fishing fleet, and an historic town with buildings dating back to the ninth century. A must for visitors to see is the fine harbour and extensive docks. The aroma of the fish seeped into my nostrils long before I reached the docks. I stayed a while to watch the arrival of the day's catch, and the quick handling of the fishermen's haul, with baskets of fish being loaded and taken on to the quay.

Two miles from Portimao is Praia da Rocha, an ideal centre for exploring the whole coast. A great attraction are the distorted and colourful rocks and an excellent sandy beach. The views of the old fortress of St Catherine are considered some of the finest in the Algarve, and the golf courses are world renowned. A traditional horse and cart plies back and forth to Portimao for a few escudos.

Along the coast is the oldest Algarvean town, Lagos, with some excellent stretches of beaches overlooking a large bay. Partly destroyed by the 1755 earthquake, it still has some interesting old churches and monumental walls.

But the gem of the Algarve is undoubtedly the little fishing village of Sagres, twenty miles from Lagos, but subject to more earthquakes than anywhere else in the world.

Close to Cape St Vincent, Sagres has a fascinating coastline with golden beaches and wide-open spaces. It is also the historical centre of Prince Henry the Navigator, who planned his sea explorations to unknown destinations in the fifteenth century. The remains of Sagres fortress still stand with gun emplacements, battlements, cannon and the prince's School of Navigation, now a youth hostel. Many eminent sailors trained at his school of Navigation, including Sir Francis Drake. The maps and equipment were taken to London and Lisbon museums. There is a stone memorial to the prince's memory, engraved: *The U.S. Power Squadron honours the memory of Prince Henry the Navigator (1394-1460) whose School of Navigation on this site opened the way for world exploration in the Great Age of Discovery.* A museum contains an interesting nautical map with the inscription: *Portugal, the country that had contributed most to and explored nearly two-thirds of the inhabited globe.* Prince Henry paved the way for the discovery of the sea route to India by Vasco da Gama in 1498, and the route to Brazil in 1500.

Also inside the walls is the original well, close to where Prince Henry used to sit on a hillock, scanning the seas for his passing light-weight caravels, long ships worked on sails with a speedy crew. There are even the niches caused by a rope which the prince used to haul himself up and down.

Close to the fortress I visited the tiny Chapel of Nose Senhora de Guade Loupe, the only church in Sagres, where Prince Henry prayed daily for guidance and also a small house where he lived when in Sagres. His real home was in the village of Rapoise, between Lagos and Sagres.

Prince Henry, born in Oporto, was the third surviving son of King John I, founder of the Aviz dynasty of Portugal, and his queen, the English Princess Philippa, daughter of John of Gaunt. Henry, a bachelor, recluse and philosopher, was often described as the Admiral of the Ocean, preferring the seafaring way of life to the royal court circle. He was the Grand Master of the Order of Christ and his ships carried the red cross of the order on their sails. The prince was awarded the title of Infante de Sagres. He died at the age of sixty-six and was buried initially in the church of St Mary in Lagos, but a year later was moved to the monastery at Batalha, a town north of Lisbon. The Portuguese mourn him to this day.

At the road terminus, and standing precariously on the edge of the cliff at Cape St Vincent, is the Farol lighthouse, considered to be the finest in Europe. An archway leads to the interior of the lighthouse with white-washed walls, old buildings and small houses for the personnel. At the entrance to the lighthouse is a souvenir shop. I was welcomed to climb the seventy-two winding steps to the top of the lighthouse, after receiving a rum from one of the officers. The view two hundred feet below was marred by a heavy sea mist with sirens booming out to sea with a deafening sound. In the working section of the lighthouse was a huge crystal reflector, made in France in 1906, which revolved around on three hundred and fifteen kilos of mercury every fifteen seconds, with two thousand coloured wall bulbs for night use. The light is the strongest in all Europe. There is a flash every five seconds; each beam can be picked up by ships sixty miles away, and by plane twenty miles. At one time, the lighthouse operated on paraffin, but is now mechanised. Two to three hundred ships pass by the lighthouse every twenty-four hours from all parts of the world. I had another opportunity to climb the lighthouse when there was no sea mist and the view of the Atlantic below was fantastic.

The lighthouse area is a favourite haunt of fishermen; it was breath-taking to see men sitting perched on the escarpment with their fishing lines dangling to the ocean below. Frogmen, from tiny boats, harpoon fish and lobsters. Boats and tackle were on hire for the enthusiasts.

Leaving the lighthouse I took a short walk back to the village to see the old Forte Beliche with its minute white-washed church containing a gilt altar and four prayer stools.

From the village square a lane led to the Bay of Sagres, where at sundown the harbour is alive with boats coming in with the daily catch. I joined the crowd of sightseers for the landing of a large variety of fish from sharks to sardinhas. The nearby bar tempted me in for an appetiser of gambas (prawns) and bowls of cockles and squid served with a glass of vinho verde, the local wine.

Not far from Sagres and on a high promontory, stands the imposing Pousada do Infanta, tucked away from the busy coastal resorts. It is one of eighty government inns, much sought after during the summer months where one can unwind for a limited stay of five days.

Taking a taxi, I was driven up a winding road to this breath-taking retreat. Having dismissed the driver, I found that the pousada was full, but a room was found for me in the annexe. The entrance to the pousada contained a large stone plaque depicting Prince Henry with his scholars. Inside over an exquisite fireplace hung a gilt framed picture of the prince.

A bus took me down to the charming town of Silves with its thirteenth century cathedral and castle walls. in the Silves/Messina crossroads is a beautiful and ancient lace-styled cross of Portugal.

I came to the town of S. Bartomeu de Messines, arriving on one of the animal market days. Apart from a number of animals waiting in the shade for auction, there was an array of colourful horse bridles and street stalls laden with the products of local industries.

The bus took me up to the village of Monchique, the highest peak in the Algarve, 2000 feet up, noted for its Caldos Mineral Springs, and old Roman spa, and now well-known as a health centre for respiratory diseases.

Going east on the little railway is the busy market town of Loule, with unique oriental chimney pots on the top of the corrugated iron roofs of houses, and found elsewhere in the Algarve. They vary in colour from delicate blues to pinks, and are of various designs – some like iced cakes. Miniature models are sold in the shops as souvenirs.

East of Loule is another pousada set high in magnificent scenery in the delightful village of Sao Bras de Alportel. From Sao Bras there is a connection to the coastal town of Olhao, a little bit of Africa. Having spent three years in the colonies, I could quite easily have been back in Africa with the cone-shaped rondavels. There were gardens and an attractive waterfront, at the end of which the *Sea Breeze* ferry operates to the tiny island of Armona for three escudos. It was like a shot out of a film with unique summer houses.

A coach service links Olhao to the old Grecian fishing town of Tavira on the eastern end of the Algarve on the River Gilao. Tavira was at one time occupied by the Greeks, then came the Goths followed by the Moors. A large number of the older type of houses have the Greek style lace iron balconies. Tavira is well-known for sardines and tunny fish. Rich in tradition, the town has a number of old interesting churches, one or two of which are derelict. It is a town of many nationalities, where French is widely spoken. The old castle walls still stand, and the battlements command an excellent view of the surrounding country. There is little to offer in the way of hotels and restaurants but the *Tanger,* near the market place, is worth patronising if you are prepared to wait. The Portuguese there underwent four years of military training for overseas. As a result, many servicemen, immaculately turned out, were to be seen in the streets.

The last coastal town is Vila Real de Santo Antonio, an important old fishing town with an unusually designed shopping centre called the Fraco do Marques de Pompei, with a mosaic paving of the rays of the sun, for pedestrians only. For a few escudos I boarded the ferry over to the Spanish town of Ayamonte, a favourite with the Algarveans as it is cheap for shopping.

Leaving Vila Real de Santo Antonio en route for Faro is the small town of Monte Gordo with modern hotels, flats and first class silver sandy beaches. The Gacola Camp is set among pines. The trees of Portugal are well preserved and cherished, in fact almost sacred; a builder would rather build round a tree than cut it down.

Faro, the ancient fishing town, is the centre of the tourist industry, and crammed full of shops selling local ware made up into household goods, imprinted with the legendary Cock of Barcelos in bright colours, said to be lucky. According to the myth, a rich landowner in Barcelos gave a banquet and his silver was stolen. A guest was accused of the theft. After being tried by the court, he was found guilty in spite of overwhelming evidence in his favour. The magistrate granted the man a final chance to prove his innocence. 'If I am innocent, the cock will crow,' said the man. At once the cock crew, and the prisoner was set free.

Booking in at the Hotel Faro, there was time to tour the old city, the walls of which still remain. Walking through the archway is the old quarter with narrow streets, many steps, quaint shops and an ornate cathedral in the square.

The Algarve is noted for its high class food, especially fish. At one pavement restaurant, while enjoying a fishy meal, I was serenaded by a guitarist with the national song, the fado. Confectionery is another speciality of the Algarve, with almonds and caramels high favourites.

The Algarveans tend to entertain in restaurants rather than in their homes, leaving invitations on the door mats of open doors.

Bull fighting takes place in the Algarve at certain times of the year. Considered a fine spectacle for the Portuguese and some visitors, the bull is not allowed to be killed.

At the end of my fifty-eight days roaming the Algarvean coastline, all that was left of my currency was three hundred escudos, worth then about £5; thus I averaged about £5 a day for expenses.

CHAPTER FIFTEEN

1973 – Cyprus in the Spring
Birthplace of Aphrodite, Goddess of Joy

The best time to see Cyprus, I was told, is in the spring, when the island is a blaze of colour with various flowers and the citrus trees are laden with fruit. Cyprus is described as the 'Isle of Eternal Charm' and is the third largest island in the Mediterranean.

After an overnight stay in Nicosia, which has over 100,000 Turks, I joined a tour and went through the capital via the theatre, the Cyprus Archaeological Museum, the British Council, the Nicosia Race Club, where races take place every Sunday, and through villages with pine and cypress trees. The wide, barren Mesaoria Plain separates the Kyrenia and Troodos Mountains. From here we travelled in convoy to Kyrenia, where I was to stay, via the Turkish sector, seventeen miles from Nicosia. Soon, we approached more fertile land and orange, lemon and grapefruit plantations; the trees were laden with luscious fruit.

Kyrenia, on the Kimo coast, came into view, a Greek area with a small Turkish minority and a population of about five thousand. Described as the gem of the island with its picturesque horseshoe shaped harbour, crammed full of yachts and little restaurants, it is an artists' paradise, and a delightful place to relax, with a quiet way of life and attractive countryside.

At one end of Kyrenia harbour stands the massive Kyrenia Castle, once a Byzantine fortress, now a tourist attraction. Built in 1211 by the crusader Lusignans, the kings of Cyprus, the stout walls and vast towers at each of the four corners dominate the harbour. Inside the castle entrance is St George's Chapel, built into the walls, the Lusignan coat of arms and the tomb of a Turkish admiral. Only the ruins of the apartments are left, and the square tower at the top of the castle is approached by a number of winding steps, well worth the climb for the panoramic view of Kyrenia. In the lower part of the castle are the dungeons.

In one section of the castle is the wreck of the Kyrenia ship, believed to be fourth century BC, which was brought up in sections by a diver from the sea bed in 1967. It was in the process of being rebuilt by the Pennsylvania University Museum Expedition, and was expected to be completed by November 1973. Also in the castle is the Shipwreck Museum containing a large number of relics from the Kyrenia ship, including beautiful jars, some of which were in excellent condition and in which almonds were found.

Behind the harbour and stretching for about a hundred miles is the imposing Kyrenia mountain range, with its three famous castles on its peaks, St Hilarion the fairy castle, Buffavento Castle the Defence of the Winds, and Kantara Castle situated at the eastern end of the range. Also on this range is the legendary Pentadakytylos Peak, five fingers, about eighteen miles north east of Nicosia.

By the harbour is the Folk Art Museum; the building belonged to Lady Lock and was donated by her to the Antiquities Department in 1966. The museum contains eighteenth and nineteenth century exhibits. Also in Kyrenia there is a Greco/Roman tomb.

Four miles east of Kyrenia are the ruins of the fourteenth century impressive Bellapaise Gothic Abbey, the Abbey of Peace, with its beautiful cypress trees, growing on the terraced slopes of the hillside, and said to be the finest on the island. The abbey is built on the edge of a cliff with the snow-capped Taurus mountains of Turkey visible on a clear day forty miles away. The abbey was destroyed in 1570 but the Greek Orthodox Church and the interior remains intact today.

Not far from the abbey is the Tree of Idleness where every Thursday night and on festive days traditional music and folk dancing is performed, and local food snacks containing meats, cheese, fish, such as octopus and ink fish garnished with salads and yoghurt, are consumed at a nearby restaurant.

Kyrenia was an excellent base for touring the six regional districts of the island with Nicosia in the centre, where I walked leisurely around the old Venetian part of the city with its immense circular wall and eleven bastions, and the presidential palace built by the British in 1882, and the archbishop's house. Also famous is St John's Cathedral used in the fifteenth century used as a monastery, and subsequently the seat of President Makarios, the Greek Orthodox Archbishop of Cyprus. Close to the cathedral is the Folklore Museum with its fine collection of national costumes and handwoven work.

One of the priorities in Nicosia is the archaeological museum with treasures from neolithic to Roman times, including an exquisite marble statue of the goddess Aphrodite from Soli, first century BC. One of the most important exhibits is the larger than life bronze statue of the Roman Emperor Septimius Severus.

Also of great interest and said to be the finest in the world are the two thousand Cypriot clay terracotta figure pieces of warriors, arranged in their original grouping in 650 BC, from a sanctuary in the Kyrenia district.

Nicosia is a large modern city with tall buildings, including its Hilton Hotel. The bazaar quarter with bargains in silverware and copper was well worth a browse. The city connects up with the regions of Famagusta in the east, Limassol in the extreme south, and the Paphos region on the west coast.

The second largest town in Cyprus is Famagusta with St Nicholas' Cathedral, built by the Lusignans, and now called the Lala Mustapha Pasha mosque. To the right of the cathedral is Othello's tower, the scene of Shakespeare's tragedy where in the play the murder of the beautiful Desdemona took place. At the entrance to the tower is the winged lion of the Republic of Venice, together with the name of a Venetian captain who remodelled the castle in 1492.

My next visit was to the ancient city-kingdom of Salamis with its theatre, Roman baths and gymnasium.

The third district, Limassol, in the south, is well-known for its carnivals and festivals. Each spring the Great Orange Festival is held when people travel from all parts of the island for this delightful occasion. The inhabitants are known for their gaiety. Limassol has a twelfth century castle, municipal gardens and a zoo. It has historical connections with Richard Coeur de Lion during the third crusade when he married Berengaria of Navarre. It is also the town of the Knights Templar and the Knights of St John of Jerusalem who established their headquarters there.

Limassol is now a busy harbour exporting cattle, carobs, citrus fruits and wine. Limassol is the centre of the wine industry with vegetables, minerals and cereals also being prolific. Interesting side products are artificial teeth and sponges. Among its imports are woollen goods, tobacco and domestic necessities.

Seven miles to the west of Limassol is the tall eighteenth century tower of Kolossi, built by the Knights of St John of Jerusalem. The area is noted for its carob trees from which are manufactured cosmetics, medicines, alcohol, cattle food, diet chocolate and many other commodities.

I passed through citrus orchards and vineyards to visit the mediaeval castle built by the crusaders in the thirteenth century. Through Pissouri village with its tall eucalyptus trees from Australia, I went on past the largest British base in Cyprus.

My next stop was at Petra Tou Rominu, the legendary birthplace of Aphrodite (Venus), goddess of love and beauty. A group of rocks on the sandy shore depict the place where the classical Aphrodite was said to have been born from the foam of the sea. On the opposite side of the road I could see the remains of the sanctuary of Apollo.

Driving on to Paphos, I came to a very fertile part of the island with many almond trees. Nearby is the birthplace of the late President Makarios. The Museum of Antiquities, in the centre of which is a marble torso of Aphrodite Greco, is near the beach, with deserted tombs of unknown kings or saints, now in ruins. St Paul's Pillar is said to be that to which he was tied and lashed.

There are some interesting mosaic pavements of Roman villas not far from the museum, including the house of Dionysius, third century AD, which was found by a workman operating a bulldozer in 1963.

The city of Curium is reached from the main Paphos highway and contains an amphitheatre capable of seating three thousand five hundred spectators; it was uncovered in 1950 by the Pennsylvania University Museum Expedition. Classical drama and other plays are produced in the ruins of this magnificent theatre during the summer months. To the left of the theatre, on raised ground, there are some fifth century mosaics which have been badly eroded over the years.

The last district is Larnaca on the south coast, about half an hour's drive from Nicosia or Famagusta. This very peaceful and pleasant centre has the exquisite St

Lazarus Church from the ninth century. It is built on the site of one of the ancient city kingdoms and, according to hearsay, was founded by Khittun, the grandson of Noah.

A favourite drive from Kyrenia or from Nicosia is to the hill resorts of Platres, Prodhromos and the mountains of Troodos, 6,500 feet above sea level, through pine forests where the only species grown is *Pinus nigra.* The area is renowned for its orange and grapefruit plantations.

The Troodos district is a leading summer and winter resort. There people bask in sunshine on the slopes and in the early months of the year ski at Sun Valley where there are ski lifts, The highest point on the island is at Troodos, on Mount Olympus, where tents can be hired in summer.

On the return journey are the asbestos mines and several villages surrounded by orchards. The Greek Kykko monastery, twelve miles from the summer resort of Pedhoulos, is set in beautiful forestry, and is the largest and most important of the ten monasteries in Cyprus. It stands on a mountain road over three thousand feet up and was founded in about 1100 AD. The interior contains a much-prized icon of the Virgin Mary, believed to have been painted by St Luke. The monastery was destroyed by fire several times, but the icon has always been saved.

Shopping in Cyprus is absorbing. Makarios Avenue in Nicosia is the main centre with numerous boutiques where one can buy beautiful linen with lace from Lefkara, though some is made in Hong Kong now from Cypriot designs, made into tablecloths, handkerchiefs and many other types of handiwork. Crochet work, too, is popular for shawls and ponchos. Cypriot costume jewellery is in much demand; it is made from stones found on the beaches and mountains; after it has been highly polished it is made into bracelets, rings and brooches. Gourds, beeswaxed and design painted, are sold as ornaments or wine containers.

There is also a great demand for pottery and ceramics, many with designs copied from antiquities on show in the museums. Sheepskin products are everywhere in slippers, hand and shoulder bags, rugs and many other gifts. Receptacles made of goatskin or leather, and suede handbags are good buys. The local weave, cotton and wool, is made up into various forms, and Cyprus-made silverware produces some pleasing filigree work, including brooches and pendants. Some coppersmiths near Nicosia make up vases, trays, pans and pots.

Men's suits can be ordered to be made at very reasonable prices, and finished by the end of one's stay; also women's and men's shoes.

The hotels and restaurants range from five to one star categories and cater for various nationalities. The cost of living is high, but vegetables are good and cheap, although consumer goods are expensive.

There are plenty of taxis with fast service between main towns at regular intervals and seats can be booked. Bus companies operate all over the island, and a regular service links up with Nicosia.

Cyprus would not be complete without a mention of vast groves of lemons which grow in profusion on the island; most of the fruit is exported.

The writer Lawrence Durrell lived on the island for a number of years and wrote

Bitter Lemons. During my amble through Belapaix in Kyrenia, I came across his white and blue house set in trees; it appeared to be deserted and forgotten.

A Cypriot invited me into her home nearby, which had a delightful view of orange and lemon plantations and the blue Mediterranean beyond. Before leaving, she handed me a bunch of fuchsias from her garden.

In Kyrenia I also met a visitor, named Nigel, of Cornwall; he gave me a signed copy of *Bitter Lemons.* A landscape gardener also offered me a copy of the book.

This article was published in The Sunday Times of Malta, *on 21st January, 1974. Permission has since been given for it to be published elsewhere.*

CHAPTER SIXTEEN

1974 – Bide awhile in Alderney

Stepping off the yellow mini plane you will be intoxicated by the fresh clean air around you, and the peaceful atmosphere with the famous Guernsey cows in the nearby meadow. A taxi will whisk you off to your hotel or apartment but, first, cast your eyes around the sundial near the airport which reads, 'Do as the sundial does, count the bright hours.'

On this friendly little island, the third largest of the Channel Island group, only three and a half miles long and one and a half wide, there are many such bright hours as you sojourn through green countryside which is a mass of wild flowers in spring and summer, and packed with blackberries in autumn. Wander along the gorse-covered cliffs and the golden uncrowded sandy beaches, so safe for children, but the sea is cold for swimming even in summer.

During your stay there will be time to stand and stare, to turn aside your cares and the bustle of everyday life. You could even leave your watch behind as time seems to stand still; you certainly would not need your car. Radios and transistors are not welcomed, in fact they are taboo, including on the beaches! There is no importation of caravans and no coaches. The only camping site is at Say Bay and permission has to be applied for and equipment brought.

For the enthusiast, walking in Alderney is a sheer delight – yachting shoes for the job can be bought in the town or at the harbour for as little as £1.25 (that was in 1974) but for those less energetic there is the Riduna bus service in the season. Cycles could be hired for about 50p a day. and as a last resort there are taxis and hire cars. There are no juggernauts to mar the country roads; the little streets are cobbled with quaint shops – no supermarkets.

The island is steeped in history dating back to the Iron Age, evidence of which can be seen in the town's museum, formerly the school, with its numerous glass-case exhibits containing Neolithic pottery and bronzes and many other exhibits including relics from the five-year German occupation. The Hall Library in Royal Connaught Square has some very interesting books on Alderney which I borrowed for two pence each per week plus a refundable deposit.

Peter-the-Potter's shop near the German water tower, should be visited to see its large assortment of handmade stoneware and porcelain.

There are several hotels worth mentioning in some of which I have stayed. These include the Royal Connaught owned by Stan and Liz Parkin, Belle Vue Hotel, Georgian House, Chez Andre, and the ever popular comfortable and homely Town House in Main Street owned by Owen and Jane Trought. In all there are thirteen licensed houses. For the odd noggin, try a local buck-trout gin! Restaurants are in short supply but Le Courier provides luncheons and dinners, and there is the odd snack bar.

On the sports side, there are golf, squash, football, tennis, riding, yachting, sailing and fishing. In summer cricket on the green (the Butes) is nostalgic, and all can join in.

Very popular is bird watching and half-day boat trips can be booked to Burhou Island, and around the island to see the largest colony of gannets in the world – a sight not to be missed.

The Aurigny Air Service Ltd connects with Jersey, Guernsey, Southampton and Cherbourg, and in the season the *Condor* hydrofoil plies on Tuesdays and Thursdays to Jersey, Guernsey and Sark and on to St Malo with a chance to sight-see in Brittany and Normandy on a five-day tour or longer. Alas, my experience was horrific when I was caught up in a severe storm and stranded in Brittany and then in Jersey.

For indoor amusements, when the weather is unkind, there are bridge, whist drives, bingo in the Catholic hall, and on Saturday night a film in the Island Hall.

Alderney is blessed with five churches – the beautiful parish church of St Anne known as the cathedral of the Channel Islands on account of its size, the Catholic church, the Methodist church, the Society of Friends and the Salvation Army.

The Mignot Memorial Hospital takes care of minor illnesses, but for more serious cases one would have to be transferred by charter plane to Guernsey or England.

There is an animal welfare clinic affiliated to the RSPCA. The importation of dogs and cats is permissible and welcomed, provided there is no rabies.

The island has fourteen forts, two policemen and one traffic warden; there is no crime and the only industry is the states dairy.

Shopping is all done in Victoria Street, adjacent to High Street, so you will not have far to hunt around for your last-minute duty free purchases. The traditional Guernseys (handmade knitted pullovers) are a good buy and in great demand.

Accommodation in Alderney in the season is difficult with the hotels chock-a-block, especially in the first week of August, Alderney Week, when the island is full of visitors lapping up the entertainment laid on by the town, finishing with a torchlight procession of several hundred people who parade through the streets to the Butes where an outsize bonfire is blazing away. I joined in fully.

You are advised to make your reservation and flight well beforehand to avoid disappointment. London's Waterloo Station is only two hours away. The States Office, New Street, Alderney will supply you with all you want to know.

It was in August during my stay in Alderney that I crossed over to Brittany by hydrofoil, With four hours at sea on the outward journey we called at Guernsey, Sark and Jersey. Arriving in St Malo, I booked for two nights at Le Louvre Hotel at forty-five francs a night for bed and breakfast.

One of the highlights of St Malo is a climb up the enormous rock of the Shrine of St Michael the Archangel (St Michael's Mount) connected to the mainland by a long causeway. At certain times the Mount is cut off by the sea which is said to go in and out faster than a horse can gallop. St Michael's Mount is a great pile of granite, some one hundred and seventy metres high covering sixty two acres. Many of the buildings have been turned into hotels, restaurants and shops.

It was while I was on the Mount that a strong wind blew up with threatening gales. I was due to return to Alderney next morning. In the evening I went down to the harbour to see if the hydrofoil would be leaving. I was told it was unlikely. However, being full of optimism, I booked out of my hotel and arrived at the jetty with my case only to be told that the hydrofoil was cancelled, though there might be a possibility at four o'clock that afternoon. Meanwhile the weather was fast deteriorating. I was later told that the crossing was cancelled indefinitely so I rebooked in my hotel.

After two days of marking time in St Malo, I was told that we would be leaving that afternoon at four o'clock. Six other passengers bound for Alderney and I were all prepared to risk the return passage, though a gendarme on duty said we were mad to attempt it.

We all boarded the hydrofoil. Six miles out at sea the wind speed reached fifty-one knots, a force 10 gale, with sixteen-foot waves pounding over the hydrofoil, and long over-hanging crests lashing the deck. Dense white patches of foam blew along the sea with the wind, and the surface of the sea assumed a white appearance. The heavy rolling of the waves became almost shock-like, while visibility was down to nil.

With approaching nightfall, conditions looked grim until the captain sent word by his bosun that he was turning back. The conditions were worsening every minute, described as horrific and the worst for fifty years. After a stormy run back to St Malo, we arrived shaken, drenched but thankfully safe.

Booking in at the Commerce Hotel, I paid regular visits to the harbour for news of the return journey to Alderney and two days later I was told that we would be departing that afternoon, but only to Jersey.

It was another rough crossing to Jersey. On arrival I requested a taxi to a hotel, but they were all full with several hundred stranded day trippers from Weymouth. It was the same at the tourist office; everywhere was full. The receptionist tried a dozen hotels with the same plea, 'We have a lady stranded, can you help her?' Eventually, a private house could take me, where I was to stay for a week with several other passengers until weather conditions improved. Each time I went out, I met strong winds and very poor visibility.

At last the storm abated, and the captain was prepared to take us back to Alderney, where I arrived ten days late.

It was a hair-raising experience, but I am ever grateful for the captain's decision to turn back when six miles out of St Malo; we would never have reached Alderney that night.

CHAPTER SEVENTEEN

1975 – Around South Africa in eighty days

It was a tight schedule to cover three thousand miles in eighty days. In Cape Town, Table Mountain showed up clearly; it takes just five minutes to reach the top by elevator. The best way to see the city is on foot; joining a walkabout, organised by Betty Hughes, we walked our way through history, including Old Cape Town and the Malay Quarter.

On the outskirts of the city lies Stellenbosch, the oldest settlement and a place for vines and wines. I saw the workings of this vast production in old homesteads and farms.

I made a tour with a difference with my friend Ena, a resident of Cape Town, to the High Noon complex, covering thousands of acres in a unique valley. To reach it we travelled over four of the most spectacular mountain passes – a safari in a real world animal kingdom enclosed in a nature reserve.

One of the highlights of my South African tour was the enchanting Garden Route, extending from Mossel Bay to Port Elizabeth. The whole area is a perfect blend of magnificent forests, deep gorges, salt-water lakes and fantastic seascapes.

Travelling in January 1975 with *Springbok Tropicana* on safari, our party had six overnight stops. For the first part of our journey we completed three hundred miles to Oudtshoorn, set in the unique Little Karroo landscape, famous for ostriches. On the farm we learned all about these flightless birds. There 2,500 ostriches roamed the farm. One was tethered and blindfolded; I volunteered to mount it, holding on to its great neck while cameras clicked. Mr Logie, the manager, took us by jeep to see the fantastic industry which has developed including forty-eight breeding camps and an Ostrich Palace, a relic of those famous and romantic years when women adorned themselves in prime ostrich plumes.

Along the Garden Route is the stretch of coastline known as the Wilderness on which is built the Wilderness Hotel, where we stayed. It lies in an historic and romantic setting dating back a hundred and fifty years to when a young farmer attended a sale at Uniondale. On impulse, he bought a large tract of land for £317 which included this stretch of coast. He fell in love with a young maiden and she promised to marry him provided they lived in the Wilderness, away from civilisation.

He built a house on his new land and called it *The Wilderness.* The house still stands; enlarged it is now the Wilderness Hotel, a favourite with honeymooners.

It was a good two hundred miles to Port Elizabeth, the centre of the timber industry and noted for furniture. Driving through a government forest reserve, there was danger of elephants though we did not see any. Prancing monkeys eating wild bananas were on one stretch of road. We entered the dense Tatakama Forest with trees up to two thousand years old, and crossed over the Great Storms River to Port Elizabeth and the end of the Garden Route.

Port Elizabeth is notorious for shipwrecks. The shores were uninhabited until the early nineteenth century when a British garrison guarded passing ships. It remained a struggling settlement until 1820 when four thousand settlers came ashore at Algoa Bay to start a new life, historically called the 1820 settlers.

Sir Rufus Donkin, acting governor, named Port Elizabeth after his wife, who had died in India of a rare disease the previous year at the age of twenty-one. He built an impressive Donkin memorial to her memory at Fort Frederick. Port Elizabeth, with a population of over four hundred thousand, is very English. Queen Victoria's statue stands in Market Street on a stone dais and a monument commemorates the landing of the settlers.

On the journey to Durban I went through Grahamstown; steeped in history, the city still retains old-world charm and well-preserved buildings as capital of the province. We passed some boys of the Abarwata tribe with snow-white faces and bodies having been coloured by their witch doctor for their initiation into manhood.

Our safari continued through vast bush country, once held by the Xhosas. Crossing Settlers' Bridge Province through scrub country, we reached Great Fish Canyon which was impassable in 1947. Over Buffalo River we arrived at East London, which was established as a supply base in the Kaffir Wars of 1846/7. It is now the fourth largest port of South Africa

In 1857 there was great excitement in East London when the teak ship *Lady Kennedy* sailed into harbour with an unusual cargo of a hundred and fifty Irish colleens. They landed safely amid great jubilation. Later a storm caused the ship to sink. The sailors on board reached the shore; some settled in East London with a happy ending to shipboard romances.

Durban's history dates back to 1842 when the fort was besieged. A local boy, Dick King, volunteered to ride over treacherous country for help. He rode at night to avoid robbers and wild animals. After nine days he reached his destination giving news of the situation. Help came by ship to Durban. The Dutch republic of Natalia collapsed and became the British colony of Natal.

In pioneer days mail came by ship. Durban's first post office was a front room in Mrs Schonoberg's house where mail was sorted and letters collected. Mail for Pietermaritzburg went by native runners by night carrying mail bags shoulder high. Postage was paid in cash until stamps were issued in 1857. Letters for England were sixpence each in old money, irrespective of weight.

Durban is one of South Africa's largest cities, a bustling industrial centre with a busy harbour, a pulsating way of life with a cosmopolitan community, but keeping up old traditions. The rickshaw boys still trot up and down the four-mile promenade.

Vernice, my hostess, drove me to the headquarters of Tangaat Sugar Company where we toured the modern mill. Sugar became recognised as a crop in South Africa in 1852 when a sample of locally-grown processed sugar was exhibited.

The Marianhill Monastery was worth visiting. It was founded in 1882 by Abbot Francis Planner and his band of Trappist monks.

A fun and wildlife tour started at the Blue Waters Hotel in Durban. I joined a seven-day Springbok Atlas Safari party to Lourenco Marques via the Kruger National Park, Swaziland, Zululand and Hluhluwe. We travelled through lush green countryside, via Pietermaritzburg and Ladysmith, both landmarks in South African history. Through the mighty Drakensburg mountains we reached Johannesburg. We passed such places as Stanger and Gingindlovu, meaning 'Swallow of the Elephant', and the former kraal of a chieftain who won a battle against his brother and became king of the Zulus. Zululand seemed to be all rolling sugar plantations and forests of Australian gum trees.

We arrived at Hluhluwe Game Reserve, home of the white rhino, set in a twenty-three hectare sanctuary, spotting many species of wild life surrounding our hutted camp. We dined at the intriguing Zululand Safari Lodge Ranch, and spent the night at the Holiday Inn.

Leaving Hluhluwe, we set off northwards, skirting the imposing Lebombo escarpment running along the eastern length of the low veld with lush vegetation and tall wind-breaker pines.

Swaziland and the Kruger National Park

We entered the colourful, tiny kingdom of Swaziland which is three parts surrounded by South Africa and the eastern frontier with Mozambique. The middle veld is densely populated with fertile rolling grasslands. the low veld lies in typical African open country, once inhabited by a handful of people and wild animals.

Lemombo, the site of the kraal of the Queen Mother, who is known as the 'Great She Elephant', is the spiritual capital of Swaziland. Two great annual festivals are held in the town: the Newala heralds the Swazi new year and is the most sacred of the Swazi ceremonies; and the colourful Umblanga or Reed Dance is composed of Swazi maidens paying tribute to the Queen Mother's kraal.

The Swazis are a cheerful and hospitable race, rich in custom and tradition. Their handicraft market was eye-catching with women dressed in brilliant costumes. They were encouraged to wear their tribal dress by their king, Sobhuza II, who was then was world's longest reigning monarch.

Left to ourselves, three of our party, with interpreter, sought Swazi witchcraft. At the kraal, shoeless children scampered among chicken. We removed our shoes at the entrance to the kraal, and the witch-doctor appeared wearing a khare tanna headdress made of porcupine quills. Around her wrists and ankles were small skin bags filled with stones, and her face was covered with white powder. In the 'Holy of Spirits' the witch-doctor performed a ritual dance and went into a trance uttering strange noises while pounding the floor with her stick. Our fortunes were told and the session ended with the ancient custom of the witch-doctor 'throwing the bones' on to a mat. This entertainment cost us one rand each.

We left Swaziland and entered the Transvaal before reaching the Kruger National Park. This vast stretch of nature reserve, larger in size than Wales, lies in the north-east corner of the Transvaal between the Crocodile River in the south and the Limpopo River in the north, with Mozambique on the east.

After booking in at Lower Sabie Camp, we entered the Crocodile border gate, and drove northwards along the Lower Sabie Road which is where lion looking for game could often be seen. At night I could hear the roar of lions which seemed to be close to the fence of the camp where we stayed.

We were up at dawn the next morning for more game spotting. We had heard there had been a kill near a sausage tree and our luck was in; there was the beast devouring its kill while white-tailed vultures, awaiting the carcase, hovered overhead or sat impatiently in barren trees.

Leaving the Kruger National Park, we reached the little town of Sabie nestling in the forest-covered hills of the escarpment. We travelled some eighty miles over the Long Tom Pass, the highest road in South Africa, to the peaceful Bambi Motel, ideally situated in the Drakensburg range at a height of 5,000 feet.

Our next hop was to Pretoria, South Africa's administrative capital, many of whose streets are lined with jacaranda trees whose blossom drop on the pavements to make a lilac-coloured carpet. After a short stop in Pretoria we went on through miles and miles of maize fields to Ladysmith and Pietermaritzburg before we returned to our starting point in Durban.

A Visit to a Surface Gold Mine

In Johannesburg the chance came to join a party to tour a surface gold mine, through the courtesy of the Chamber of Commerce in Holland Street.

I was collected from my hotel by Mrs Diana Griffin, our guide, for the thirty-five mile drive to the Eisburg Gold Mining Company Ltd in one of seven gold mining areas, producing two-thirds of the world's new gold production.

Our conducted tour included the production works where the massive machinery was almost deafening. Our visit to the mine coincided with smelting day where we actually witnessed glistening molten liquid gold trickling from the blast furnace into house-brick size moulds. The bullion bars were then refined at a central refinery, producing almost pure gold and silver bars. Each bar was stamped by a hammering process, weighed and recorded, the odd bits of gold being put into a bag and padlocked.

Then came the great moment! I was invited to lift one of the gold bars. It would not budge an inch from the table. After an hour's tour we were allowed to search the mine grounds for pieces of gold. Of course, we never found any. Four and a half thousand men are employed in the underground mine, many from far away places. They all have to learn a common language, Fanakale. No females are employed.

The Kingdom of Lesotho

From Johannesburg, I travelled in stages back to Cape Town; first to the Kingdom of Lesotho. Taking the overnight train I arrived at Marselia in the early morning. To reach Maseru, the capital, meaning red sandstone, I had to board a bus to passport control as there were no taxis. I was offered a lift to Maseru and driven to the town's oldest inn where I booked in.

The independent Kingdom of Lesotho is a delightful tiny mountain paradise. This massive amphitheatre rises in steps from west to east, where the mighty Drakensburg Alps join a natural boundary with Natal. A gigantic history book, Lesotho stretches back millions of years to the time when dinosaurs once trod the muddy swamps. Footprints of theses strange creatures can still be seen in stream rockbeds near Leribe.

For many years, only the yellow-skinned tiny bushmen inhabited this land; examples of their rock art and stone crafts are found in many parts of the country. The bushmen were finally driven out by the southward migration of the African tribes.

As a nation, Lesotho did not come into prominence until 1818 when Moshoeshoe I, then a minor chief, gathered together remnants of the various clans that had been scattered by the raids of the Zulus. He established his stronghold at Thaba Bostu, meaning Mountain of the Night, near Maseru, and successfully resisted the attacks of his enemies. In 1868, he placed himself and his people under the protection of the British government. In 1965, after almost a hundred years as a British Protectorate, the nation requested independence. On 4th October, 1966, Basutoland became the independent Kingdom of Lesotho, and King Moshoeshoe II became head of state.

The people of Lesotho call themselves Basotho (singular, Mosotho) and their language is Sesotho. English is the second language. The population is about one million of whom two thousand are whites. Most of the people live in the western lowlands, including about 29,000 in Maseru. Their religion is predominantly Christian.

Lesotho offers mountain scenery and healthy climate. The distant Drakensburg mountains are capped with snow in winter, turning the Alps into a fairy-like scene.

To get about there are no taxis, only hire cars. A novelty is an old buggy drawn by two horses which trotted around the town for fifty cents when I was there. I sought out the British High Commissioner's office in the Square, where I met Mr C. W. Reid who sketched a plan of the town and, armed with a visitor's guide, I set off to see Maseru.

A walkabout was the best way for an insight into the ways of the people. Their tribal greeting is 'khotso', meaning 'peace to you', and well meant.

Near the cathedral was an open air market where colourful traders were selling fruit, vegetable and local handicrafts.

I walked along Kingsway, so named in 1947 when our King George VI and his family visited Basutoland. In Moshoeshoe Park I climbed a hundred and fifty steps to see the old king's statue which commanded an excellent view of Maseru and the mountains beyond.

The Maseru Handicraft Industrial Centre, one of the largest in South Africa, contained a great variety of bead work, fertility dolls and fossils. The symbol of the nation is the tall Basutho hat worn by the coolies. At the Basutho shop, itself shaped like a Basutho hat, I bought one of these open-work straw hats.

Kimberley, City of Diamonds and the Big Hole

In South Africa's vast territory lies the home of the world's diamond industry, its main attractions being the Big Hole Diamond Mine, well-known the world over, though now worked out.

At midnight, I reached Kimberley railway station, and booked in at the Grand Hotel nearby, close to the Big Hole, the largest in the world.

It was in this mine that the great orange-yellow diamond, the Tiffany, was found; when cut it weighed 125 carats. The Star of South Africa, 83 carats rough and 46 carats cut, was found near the Orange River in 1869, only a couple of years after the first diamonds were found in South Africa; it was purchased by the Earl of Dudley for £25,000.

Alongside the Big Hole is the historic museum where the original Kimberley has been faithfully reproduced; it was fascinating to wander around the old timers depicting the way of life of the pioneers.

On Kimberley's outskirts is the Duggan-Cronin Bantu Gallery showing tribal dresses and costumes, also a unique collection of photographs and natural objects of black African people, and other non-white races of Southern Africa. The best collection of South African art is in the Humphrey Art Gallery. Duggan-Cronin originated in Cork in Southern Ireland; he put in about fifty years studying almost every tribe in South Africa. He died in 1954 at the age of eighty.

Kimberley is called the City of the Firsts; it had the first street electric lighting, was first to have a stock exchange, and started the first school of mines in South Africa. It is also very English, a large number of people having emigrated from Britain and settled in Kimberley. A remarkably clean and peaceful city, it has wide streets and a market square with old-fashioned shops.

The Drakensburg Express

Boarding the coal-driven Drakensburg train at Kimberley, I settled down for my 647 miles overnight journey to Cape Town.

After leaving the suburbs, we trekked through open country and alongside the fascinating highway of the Diamond route, which runs for 658 kms from Victoria West in the south into the vast Karroo, passing South Africa's two mightiest rivers, the Vaal and the Orange.

As evening drew near, I donned my full-length skirt for dinner, as was the custom, and took my seat in the spacious dining car decorated with real flowers; it was a gourmet meal with wine. Coffee and liqueurs were served in an adjoining coach with large picture windows from which I had a clear view of the sunset settling over the Little Karroo.

We stopped at De Aar, the second largest railway junction in South Africa, with time to stretch my legs along the platform before the remaining three hundred and fifty miles to Cape Town, the end of my three thousand mile tour of South Africa in eighty days.

CHAPTER EIGHTEEN

1975 – By Banana Boat to the Caribbean

'Those banana boats book up twelve months ahead. You'll never get on,' said my friends. Undaunted, I took up the challenge and, as a seasoned ocean sailor, I went to London in search of a passage. Walking into a shipping company I enquired for a booking. To my surprise, a cancellation fell into my lap. I was to sail in two weeks' time. As I set off on a shopping spree on a bleak November day in 1975, I felt I was already on my way for my first voyage to the Caribbean.

At Cardiff I was met by the company driver of the Geest Line and driven ten miles to Barry. There she was, the *Geest Crest,* her white paint glistening in the autumn sunlight, one of four passenger cargo liners of the Geest Atlantic Fleet, with weekly sailings. Her gross tonnage was 8,000 tons and she was all set to sail eight thousand miles on a regular schedule for a round voyage to the West Indies. We were to bring back thousands of tons of Geest bananas in her refrigerated holds. Our destination was the Windward Islands and we would be travelling in waters first sailed by Christopher Columbus on his great voyages of discovery.

Each ship carried twelve passengers, with single and double state rooms and the owner's suite. My room for the next twenty-three days was luxurious, with temperatures adjustable to my personal requirements. In the well-equipped nearby lounge there was a welcoming bar (with rum at twopence a tot) with a spacious dining saloon and willing and helpful stewards awaiting our bidding. The captain, his officers and crew, with first-class organisation, did all they could to make our voyage comfortable and happy. Good food was served, especially Barbadian fare.

Our cruising hours were spent lounging on deck, watching flying fish leap from the waters around the propellors or trying our luck on the tote on the ship's daily run. The seamen's library passed away many an hour. After dinner, horse racing was popular. At night, myriad stars in a velvet sky would beckon us on deck to see the familiar North star (Polaris) located by the pointers of the Big Dipper and the Plough or Great Bear.

The ports of call were Barbados, Dominica, Grenada, St Lucia and St Vincent, each island with its individual charm and character. The calypso island of Barbados, where we docked for a day, is a tourist paradise with a bustling English-style city; the bond between Great Britain and Barbados goes back to the 1620s. Wandering around Bridgetown I felt at home in this melting pot of nationalities, one of the world's most densely populated areas, with its universal way of life. Everyone speaks English, yet mingles happily regardless of race, creed or colour. The Barbadians call themselves Bajans; mostly of negro descent, they have soft pleasing voices. It proved to be an hospitable and friendly community with a high standard of education and a deeply religious background.

Around the city stood ancient buildings, formerly residences of wealthy planters. As I came to The Green, as it was known until 1903, history almost tapped me on the shoulder; standing supreme in the centre was a bronze statue of Lord Nelson. Barbados is a fantastic place for shopping. It was while I was browsing around a jewellery counter in a store that I met a Barbadian resident; we introduced ourselves (her name was Frances). She offered to drive me around the island in her car seeing many places I would have missed on a conducted tour.

Docking at Roseau, capital of Dominica, known as Sunday Island, there was time to take a jungle safari into the interior. Full of lush vegetation, this never-to-be-forgotten nature island is heavily forested and rich in banana and coconut plantations.

At Vieux Fort in Lucia, I watched women loading bananas by hand. About thirty girls, in Bermuda shorts and mini dresses, placed fibre rings (coltas) on their heads ready to load a box of twenty-eight pounds of bananas. By law, only females were employed on this and they were paid four cents a box.

Shopping in the Caribbean is exciting. Local handicrafts were out of this world, and the spices irresistible. At St Lucia it was Women's Day in Bagshaw's Boutique. We all flocked in for their divine beach-wear, tropical but not too touristy.

Enjoying one of the best climates in the West Indies, the beaches of the Windward Islands are chalky white, clean, uncrowded and unfenced. They stretch for miles in an unbroken line leading into one another. St Lucia has some of the finest beaches and most attractive hotel complexes out of the whole Caribbean.

The spice island of Grenada, where life is easy going, is attractive and photogenic. Most of the film *Island in the Sun* was shot here. The capital, St Georges, has a most picturesque harbour with little white houses dotted here and there.

There was peace and tranquility on the friendly and cultivated island of St Vincent, considered one of the prettiest of the Windwards. It is said to resemble Tahiti more than any other Caribbean island. Forested mountain peaks, rivers, streams, waterfalls and spectacular land and seascapes left me spellbound. It was on St Vincent that Captain William Bligh (who lost HMS *Bounty* by mutiny on a previous voyage) finally planted a number of Tahitian bread-fruit seedlings. One of these fully grown trees is in the Botanical Gardens.

Some days later we disembarked at Barry, each carrying a box of Geest bananas from the company, and all longing to sail again by banana boat to the Caribbean and relive the freighter voyage of a lifetime.

This chapter was published in The Lady, *25th November, 1982. Permission has since been given for it to be published elsewhere.*

CHAPTER NINETEEN

1976 – Tunisia Bound

In 1976 on a cold winter's day, I set off from London in search of the sun, Tunisia being my goal, a land of contrasts. After crossing the English Channel and catching the train for Sicily, I arrived at Palermo at midnight. It was not a good time to search for an hotel, but with the help of a Sicilian also stranded, I found the Grand Albergo Sol and had a single room for six thousand lire.

Next day was Sunday when only a night ferry service operates to Tunis. It meant a day in Palermo, but there was so much history and art to see in this rich Italian city.

As the ferry came into port, the quay was already swarming with people, with Arabic traders unloading their carts, while women sat around wrapped in their white hooded gowns, one end clutched between their teeth. Reporting at the Tyrrhenia Line I was told I would be allocated a berth at sea.

Docking next morning at La Goulette, a taxi took me to the Tunisia Palace Hotel via a causeway. With no Tunisian currency, I relied on the hotel to advance the fare. My luck was in and I booked in.

Tunis is the gateway to Tunisia, crossroads of Africa, a great metropolis, and Tunisia's first city. Mostly of Arabic origin, it is rich in agriculture and the largest world exporter of olive oil.

Dating from the Carthaginean period, Tunis became the administrative centre in the late ninth century, when it grew in splendour. By the fifteenth century its magnificence compared with that of Baghdad. Built on the west bank of a shallow lake it comprises two adjacent districts widely different in character – the old town specifically oriental in character, and the modern one. The Medina, the original city enclosed by high walls, is one of the most beautiful in the Islamic world.

The souks are shopping with a difference. Craftsmen were at work, but ready to bargain with the passer-by. There were silver and coppersmiths, cobblers, makers of chenhia (traditional red skull caps), mint sellers and stalls with embroidered garments, to name just a few. As I ambled along rubbing shoulders with Arabs, Berbers, Turks and such like, I came to the Souk of Attarine where fragrant essences were displayed in large oriental jars and the perfume seeped into my nose; jasmine was prescribed for me!

There was everything for local weddings. I was fascinated with daintily made-up baskets with padded silk and fine lacework, which the bridegroom buys a few days before the wedding; in the basket, the bride-to-be lays candles in the shape of a hand, scented soap, perfume, imitation fish for fertility, and dark red powdered henna to dye her hands and feet three days before the day. From a mixture of plants she will dye her hair. On the wedding day, she wears a gold and silver embroidered waistcoat to adorn her wedding dress.

As a contrast, the modern town has fine broad avenues, parks, good-class hotels and shops; I found the shop keepers were always ready to chat to the English visitor. Efficient policewomen, dressed in well-cut black suits, direct the traffic. A good taxi service operates with the small Bebe type to Minis. Two-seater Hippomobiles cater for tourists. The flower market on Bourguiba Avenue is a colourful scene. I was there at Easter time, and white arum lilies stood like sentinels in painted petrol cans, among other coloured blooms.

But Tunisia is a man's world. The Cafe de Paris, at the corner of the Avenue de Carthage, is a favourite meeting place. Men sit for hours at the pavement tables sipping black coffee, passing the time of day.

Three miles from the city centre is the Bardo Museum, once the Bardo Palace, residence of the Beys of Tunis, with the world's finest mosaics from Roman villas, Carthaginean remains, Greek and Roman statuary and Islamic art.

I made my way to the little railway station to take the train to the ancient Moorish village of Sidi Bou Said and to Rome's powerful rival, Carthage. The station was built by an English firm at the request of a British official stationed in Carthage. The 'prima' coach appeared to have lost its status as the seats were wooden!

Sidi Bou Said is legendary. Until the present day, it has borne the name of the man whose baraka (spirit) still haunts the place, his mystic retreat; he still lives in repose in the shelter of his mosque of Zaouia, one of the most venerated in Tunis.

Perched on a headland overlooking the Bay of Tunis, Sidi Bou Said is a world of serenity where time hangs motionless, a meeting place for musicians, artists, poets and writers. Sweet-smelling orange trees line the winding cobbled streets leading to the square, with its skinny cats. Local handicrafts, especially wrought-iron bird cages, adorn the tiny shops.

In the square is the Cafe de Natts, said to resemble the Cafe Flora in Paris. Up a number of steps, on a wooden bench, I sipped mint tea while watching the unique world below. The Berbers' mosque of the holy man of Sidi Bou Said is open to the sky.

On the way to the beach the trees were laden with oranges and tangerines and gardens were full of sweet-smelling mimosa. An old man at his gate picked a red rose for me.

Reboarding the train I reached the city of Carthage with its well-maintained archaeological ruins. Among them is the Tophet of Carthage, in ancient times reserved for child sacrifices. So worth seeing were the Punic havens, the Baths of Autinius and the Amphitheatre. The museum housed a collection of Punic, Greek and Roman objects. A guide showed me round the grounds, pointing out the tomb of St

Louis of France facing Mecca. A path led to where Sir Winston Churchill addressed the victorious allied troops in 1943.

On Easter Monday I joined a French party for a two-centre tour of Tunisia. We picked up more passengers at the fashionable seaside resort of Hammamet and went on to Nabeur, a paradise for birds and an important pottery centre where the skilful hands of craftsmen were imitating the style of their ancestors.

We came to Kairouan, the centre of Tunisia, and the old Moorish capital, founded in 671. By the ninth century, it had become a flourishing capital housing stately monuments. The town is enclosed in a buttressed wall and has developed around the Medina with souks and compact stalls. The great mosque of Kairouan is the oldest mosque built by the Moslems.

From the highway leading to Libya and Cairo we saw camels working in the fields. We came to what appeared to be water but was, in fact, a mirage formed by air, heated by the burning salt flats, distorting the landscape. Islands and palm groves appear where there is nothing but desert waste. We reached the area of the Tunisian campaign with British, French and German cemeteries.

Through more flat country, the only sign of life was farming families tending their flocks. Mist descended and we ran into a sandstorm. Two women on horseback, with colourful flowing capes, raced past us; it was an eerie moment, until we were back in the sunshine.

We reached Kaserine, stopping at the Gilliam Roman Baths of this ancient and historical town with its forum, amphitheatre and mausoleums.

We entered the legendary south at Gafsa, known to the ancients as Gappa and the most important southerly town with nine thousand palm trees growing around an oasis. The tiny pink-washed hamlets, with teams of camels trekking down to the oasis for water, with their heavy tread and dreary countenance, gave a picture-postcard effect. In the town centre, we entered a Byzantine citadel to see the only remaining Roman pools of that period. Boys were diving for coins.

In the desert the Bedouin people lived in primitive conditions of simple black tents. They depend for their livelihood on their herds of camels, sheep and goats, with a constant search for new pastures and water for their animals. They had no objection to our cameras and were grateful for coins. Weaving is the only developed craft.

Tozeur is the date-palm country and a most important town in the Djerid, earning a reputation for the lush beauty of its oasis in which thrive two hundred thousand date palms in a number of orchards irrigated by two hundred cool springs. The houses in some districts date back to the fourteenth century and are remarkable for the style of the facades of solid rock laid in curious patterns.

A few miles on we stopped at the desert zoo set in a garden called Paradise, with an animal and bird sanctuary. In a building I witnessed a hair-raising demonstration by a reputed snake charmer. He produced from various pens many kinds of snakes, including a horned viper. To amuse or scare us, he twined a reptile around his head. Before returning a non-poisonous snake to its box, he tried to entice me to be wrapped around with the venomous-looking reptile.

Chott el Djerid was known to the ancients as the Lake of Tritons. it extends from

Gabes to the Algerian frontier over a stretch of two hundred miles. Filled with brackish water during the rainy season, it is reduced in summer to a flat expanse of sparkling salt, indented here and there by camel tracks. In the desert peasants were selling rose-stones.

Through more date plantations and olive groves, backed by the mountains, was the unique village of Matmata, renowned for troglodyte dwellings hollowed out of disused wells. Our lunch was served in a circular wall cave dwelling built around a courtyard with a separate section for the animals. The women turned away when we brought out our cameras.

Medenine is conspicuous for its ghorfas, a sort of stone or mud pigeonholes once used as storehouses by the nomad tribes in the region. Spikes in the walls enabled dwellers to climb up.

Crossing a narrow causeway we came to the lush island of Djerba. From Homer onwards poets have celebrated Djerba, the isle of the lotus eaters, opposite the desert town of Gabes. A great abundance of palm, olive and fruit groves makes it a perfect island oasis; its sandy beaches are unequalled for relaxation in a temperate climate. The people are unmixed Berbers, stocky, with long hair and sallow skins, an intelligent race whose ancestors were scattered over the Maghreb. Our two overnight stops were at the Der Jerba complex with four hotels along a stretch of beach. Fishing is the chief industry in Djerba, followed by rugs, blanket weaving, pottery and Berber and Jewish jewellery.

The island is a mass of domed mosques. We took an excursion to Houmt Souk to see the mosque at Manbhoubine, the fortified mosque of El May, the Strangers' Mosque and the Turkish Museum. At the curious and dilapidated village of Gueilala, potters were at work on replicas of Roman oil lamps, their only industry. About a thousand families live in dried mud huts. One village was renowned for the yearly pilgrimage to Mecca in Saudi Arabia. It is one of the tenets of Islam that believers should make at least one pilgrimage to the holy city of Mecca.

Along the blue Mediterranean coast the islanders engage in diving to fifty feet for sponges.

Retracing our route at Gabes, our last overnight stop was at Raspina with a stretch of white sandy beach. Raspina, from the Greek Rasupouna, was the name the Romans gave to what is now the city of Monastir, the birthplace of President Bourguiba. Typically Arab-looking, the great mosque dates from the tenth century.

Sousse is the third largest city in Tunisia. It is now a go-ahead town, but it suffered bombardment by the Germans during the Tunisian campaign. Back on the highway, I neared the end of my two thousand kilometres tour of Tunisia.

CHAPTER TWENTY

1977 – Overland hopping from the Mediterranean

In 1977, while living in Malta, I had the urge to travel to England by sea and rail. There were regular three times weekly sailings to and from Malta to Syracuse and Catania in Sicily and Reggio di Calabria and Naples on the mainland.

Sicily is volcanic. From the enormous circumference of the summit of the 10,900 foot Mount Etna, (meaning burning mountain), the whole of Sicily is visible. In the north lay the Pelorita, Caronie and Modonie mountains, the most important chain on the island with heights rising to 6,500 feet, while the southern part is much flatter.

Sicily is blessed with a mild climate with an average of six hours sunshine a day, never too hot in summer as there is always a breeze.

The island is full of history with Phoenician, Greek and Roman periods and relics of invasion by Goths, Byzantines and Arabs. It is also rich in architecture and sculpture. In recent years, many digs have unearthed archaeological remains, resulting in unique museum, gallery and library exhibits from various sites.

Along the coast are several resorts where sea bathing is possible all the year; in the mountains there is peace and quiet.

Sicilian food is rich, colourful and highly flavoured on account of the variety of herbs on the island. in the open markets were a mixed display of these culinary preparations, together with an excellent show of fruit and vegetables. The Sicilian wines are first class; grapes grow in profusion and the vino complements the food. A favourite wine of mine was Marsala.

My first port of call was Syracuse, an important city in ancient times, with many monuments, but now modernised with cultural, sporting and folklore events taking place, attracting overseas visitors.

There are over a dozen hotels of varied standards, from the highest to the modest pension catering for local in habitants. I found the little Grand Hotel adequate; it is near Porte Grande, the harbour, and within walking distance of the ferry. Near the harbour and in the town are several trattorias (restaurants), rosticeries (grill rooms) and posticeries (snack bars).

Syracuse is one of the most interesting towns in Sicily, dating from the eight century BC and surrounded by beautiful scenery. There is much to see including many famous archaeological ruins; the Greek theatre of 467 BC and the impressive Doric cathedral are two of the highlights. I found the Oratory of Via degli Orti, the Sanctuary of the Madonna of Tears, somewhat ostentatious – a showplace ill-fitting the island's ancient background, though entrance was free. More in keeping was the little chapel dedicated to the Madonna which I discovered in the old quarter of the city.

The ferry sailed on to Catania, with a lengthy breakwater and an unusual coastline. The chief attractions are the cathedral with interesting works of art, sculptures and picture galleries. The Greek theatre close by towers up to a hundred feet; in bygone days it held 16,000 spectators. Mount Etna stands out on the horizon overlooking the city, and elegant and gracious eighteenth century buildings open up into wide streets. Catania is a town of character dating back to the Greek period.

Among the hotels is the *Jolly,* one of a chain in the Mediterranean, expensive, but convenient. The bus service links up with Syracuse and Catania.

At Acireale, near Catania, are the Santa Venera Spa mineral baths, open all the year – a curative establishment for such maladies as rheumatism and arthritis.

Lying close to Catania, and on the bus route, is Sicily's enchanting gem, Taormina, one of the most beautiful resorts in Italy, and known for its scenery; terraced high up, it overlooks the sea and the white slopes of Mount Etna. Originally Greek, and later a Roman colony, Taormina was destroyed and rebuilt by the Arabs. The ancient ruins of the Greek and Roman theatre are worth seeing; also the medieval castle, a sixteenth century church and other classical monuments.

Reggio di Calabria on the mainland, a city as well as a port, was founded in 750 BC. It was completely destroyed in 1908 by an earthquake, and rebuilt. In 1943 it again suffered during the war when the cathedral was extensively damaged.

Most of the northern coast is in the province of Palermo and the busy port is one of the richest Italian cities in history and art, originally Phoenician; it has left its mark in Roman mosaics, churches adapted from Arabic mosques, French monuments, the cathedral and German tombs, while the streets and piazzas have a Spanish flavour.

Palermo has some ancient thermal springs which are known to be very effective for numerous health disorders. The province is also a land of contrasts and unique with its tiny 'sugar-cube' houses. Every Sunday evening the mv *Leopardi* ferry crosses over to Tunis, the gateway to Tunisia which was a French protectorate for seventy-five years.

The province of Messina has three important spas at Castroreale, Ali and Linard. Castroreale is the number one spa in Sicily with excellent sulphurous and carbonated waters effective for a number of disorders.

Messina connects with the toe of Italy and is a hopping off spot for the Aeolian Islands with their rocky coastlines. Seven in all, they are Lipari, Vulcano, Salina, Filicudi, Alcudi, Panarea and Stromboli which is the best known because of its volcano. Together they are shaped like a flower. These islands are ideal for a summer vacation that is different and fascinating.

Some two hundred miles north of the Strait of Messina, the ferry docked at its final port, Naples. The Grand Albergo Hotel was within minutes of the harbour.

Founded by the Greeks and later becoming a Roman colony, Naples lies in one of the most splendid natural settings in the world. Tours are organised to such places as Pompeii with its Roman ruins, the ancient town of Salerno and breath-taking Amalfi and Positano, paradises for artists.

The two sister islands of Capri and Ischia lie close to Naples and can be reached by frequent ferries and hydrofoils from the harbour. Capri is always popular with English visitors; I visited later the lesser-known isle of Ischia, called the Green Isle, which has a bunch of health-giving mineral springs.

Always a must is a stop-over at Rome. Apart from its innumerable monuments scattered over a wide area, there is a circle of surrounding hills with abbeys, monasteries and temples to see. It is a marvellous shopping centre, and you are guaranteed to return if a coin is dropped into the Trevi Fountain.

The next stop on the train was Florence, famous for its art and culture. Without pre-booking I was able to stay at the charming Hotel Balestri in Piazza Mentana Ponte Vecchio and Ponte Alle-Grazie. I needed at least a week for a walking tour of Florence's important buildings and works of art, armed with a guide book and map. An informative and illustrated one I came upon was *You in Florence.*

Coach tours and excursions should be booked. CIT organise regular trips to Pisa and its Leaning Tower. Siena is delightful and, away from the city, it has an interesting picture gallery of Sienese painters. The town's pizzas were very tasty. San Gemignano is famous for its numerous towers.

A bus from Florence took me to Fiesole, one of the most loved and celebrated places in Italy, renowned for its natural beauty and for its history and art, its olive trees and cypresses. The town is exquisitely situated among the hills which surround Florence, and has often been described as a haven of tranquility. There are many good buildings to see.

England can be reached from Naples in two days. A taxi from the port to the central railway station cost me 3,000 lire. There I caught the Rome Express and changed at Rome for the train to Calais/Boulogne. The ferry took me to Folkestone and the boat train to London's Victoria station. As an alternative I could have boarded a train to Rome at Syracuse in Sicily.

My journey was made easier by booking my sea, rail, cabin and couchette tickets well in advance. I also took refreshments for the rail journey from Syracuse as there was to be no dining car on the train and the station trolleys were somewhat sparse. Armed with a timetable on central and southern Italy from Sealink Travel Ltd, I was able to travel care free.

Published by The Times of Malta Travel Supplement *on 15th January, 1978, and permission has been given to print it again.*

CHAPTER TWENTY-ONE

1978 – The Bridge over the River Kwai

In 1978, our party on a Far East expedition travelled by bus on highways six and seven to the little town of Kanchanaburi on the Mae Klong River, about eighty miles west of Bangkok, the capital of Thailand.

In the province of Kanchanaburi, considered the most beautiful in Thailand, are the impressive site of the Bridge over the River Kwai, the Burma-Siam Railway and the great Donray Kanchanaburi Cemetery. Visiting these sites was the most memorable part of my Far East tour.

In the war, the Japanese forced English, American and Malay prisoners-of-war to build the bridge, where much drama and suffering were enacted. Two bridges were constructed by the prisoners. The original wooden bridge was dismantled after the steel bridge had been completed about a hundred metres downstream from the wooden one which was used to transfer supplies and materials to the camps before the main bridge was completed.

The present steel bridge was bombed before the end of the war by the air force, and the three centre spans were destroyed. These sections were replaced by the Royal Thai State Railway, the two square spans of which can now be seen.

Thousands of servicemen labouring on the railway died as a result of disease, starvation and lack of drugs. On show close to the 'Death Railway' is an old World War II locomotive.

Pierre Boulle's well-known book and film on the story of the bridge is no doubt familiar to readers and film-goers. Regrettably the site is now very commercialised, and has become a tourist attraction with a general store doing lucrative business, especially in souvenirs of this historical setting.

At the entrance to the building is a bronze memorial tablet recording the names of eleven soldiers of the Indian Army buried in Moslem civil cemeteries in Thailand whose graves are unidentifiable.

The great Kanchanaburi Donray Cemetery lies in a the forest about two hundred yards from the railway station on the north-western outskirts of the town, and is surrounded by country of light jungle and hills. It is one of three war cemeteries (one in Thailand and two in Burma) on the notorious railway. The War Graves

Commission records 6324 identified burials in Thailand, including three hundred men who died during an epidemic at Nieke Camp and were cremated; their ashes now rest in two graves in the cemetery. Their names are commemorated on Portland stone panels in the shelter pavilion which stands at the end of one of the two main avenues, facing the Cross of Sacrifice at the intersection at the opposite end. Over the two graves are bronze plaques bearing the inscription, 'Here are buried the ashes of the three hundred soldiers whose names are inscribed in the Memorial Building in this Cemetery.'

The burial ground is in a field given by the Thai people as a perpetual resting place, and is surrounded by a neat hedge where many soldiers, sailors and airmen are honoured. Row upon row of immaculately-kept graves, each with an inscribed headstone and some adorned with flowers, are lovingly tended by the Thai people. The graves stand as memorials to those thousands who died for their country laying the lines of the Death Railway.

I recorded the names on two graves in Row 2F: '1874307 Sapper A. C. E. Potter, 21st September, 1943, aged 35, *Faithful unto Death,*' and '3855161 Pte A. Naylor, the Loyal Regiment, 13th September, 1943, *Whatever else we fail to do we never fail to think of you.*' I also photographed the two graves.

Relatives may rest assured that their loved ones are well remembered, and are at peace in this beautiful sanctuary.

CHAPTER TWENTY-TWO

1978 – Ischia, Island of Health and Beauty

It's just a stone's throw from Naples to the enchanting green island of Ischia by hydrofoil, steamer or car-ferry. The ferry is a restful way of reaching the island. On the horizon I could see Mount Vesuvius, and in the distance there were more islands.

Soon the vine-covered hills of Ischia appeared, and in the foreground the quaint circular harbour. Of volcanic origin, Ischia is famous for its abundance of natural resources – thermal mineral baths, mud baths and ovens, which are to be found in many parts of its thirty square miles, five times the size of Capri. Several hotels have their own thermal establishments offering beneficial treatment for physical disabilities; in the luxury class is the Regina Isabella Hotel at Lacco Ameno in the north-east. The Apollon Hotel in Sant Angelo in the south offers various forms of thermal treatment in their Garden of Aphrodite. The island's hotels cater for all pockets and a booklet listing them is obtainable from the information office at the harbour where mini taxis are lined up to take you to the hotel of your choice.

There are also the Giardini thermal baths at Poseidon on the west coast, seven miles from Ischia Porto in a garden complex under Swiss/German management, and popular with visitors all the year round for the wonderful food. There is a cafe, and ancient wine grotto, a medical wing with private cabins, a sun terrace, rose garden and boutiques. There are nine heated pools, eight open air and one indoor, with varying temperatures and sizes set in the magnificent Bay of Citara, which is truly a paradise in a tranquil setting.

These specially equipped curative pools conform to all the latest technical and medical knowledge, and are very beneficial for arthritis, chronic bronchitis, rheumatism, circulatory diseases, gout, slipped discs, gynaecological disorders and accident injuries. During the summer hot sand-packs are in demand for certain maladies on a private beach facing the garden.

Ischia, with one of the best climates in the Mediterranean, is always teeming with people, especially around the harbour. Apart from the cheerful Ischians and the influx of tourists, Germans predominate, many with their own villas.

Shopping is excellent. In Via Roma, beautiful Italian leather, linen, jewellery, ceramics, basketware, even skin gloves are to be found. I came across shops selling exclusive Capri models for the connoisseur. The food stores are first class with luscious fruit and vegetables.

If you prefer one of the main centres, there are regular steamers to get you there; in Sant Angelo on the south coast (a favourite seaside resort and a spa noted for its healing waters) your suitcase will be carried from the boat to your hotel strapped on the back of a donkey, the only means of transport on this last bit of paradise where cars are taboo.

Restaurants in Ischia are plentiful; it is pleasant to take an evening stroll along the harbour jetty with its numerous trattorias – modest eating places noted for their tasty home cooking. You will probably be tempted by a displayed menu to step inside a trattoria and sample succulent locally-caught fish, or choose from the live assortment in the outside tank. If it's lobster you fancy, two squirming clawless monsters may be held up for your selection, one of which is doomed for the pot. To round off your meal sample one of the island's excellent wines.

For a general view of Ischia, take a morning bus from the harbour; it travels through the main centres. Go north first to Casamicciola Terme, a small coastal town of great archaeological interest and with thermal springs which are said to be the most radioactive in the world.

The next main stop is at Lacco Ameno with its luxurious and elegant hotels which make it exclusive, attracting the jet set. Around the coast is the natural and unspoilt Forio, the chief area of grape-growing; in September, the locals gather, with visitors giving a hand, for the vintage and customary wine-tasting fiestas. Forio is also the home of artists and writers.

Following on is the promontory of Sant Angelo, a charming fishing village, and one of the most beautiful parts of the island; it is especially suitable for people who have difficulty in breathing. Connected by a narrow isthmus of sand is the tiny island of Punta Sant Angelo where the charming Hotel Conte hugs the rock face, with the Ristorante Peppino nestling close by.

From Sant Angelo, you will pass the well-known Marconti Beach, near Barano, the largest beach in Ischia. A walk along the sands at low tide will bring you to the unique centre of Acqua Cavascura where a huge spring gushes from the rock at boiling point. Here you can indulge in one of the Baths of Tiberius in a cubicled trough carved out of rock into which is piped warm volcanic water, where you relax and gaze at the sky over a tarpaulin-covered door. This inland centre can also be reached from Sant Angelo headland.

A visit to Ischia would be incomplete without a trip up to the island centre of Serrara Fontana (again from Sant Angelo) with its individual rural charm and impressive panorama. At Fontana there are mountain mules for hire to trek to the breath-taking summit of the extinct volcano, Mount Epomeo, which is 2,500 feet above sea level. But walking is very rewarding, first up a side-walk, then on to the mountain road terraced by vineyards and fruit orchards, followed by a climb up a narrow stony path. On a clear day from the top of Epomeo the whole of the Sorrento Peninsula is visible, including the islands of Capri and Procida, Pozzuoli on the mainland and Naples beyond.

Mount Epomeo, the highest point on the island, is topped by the hermitage of St Nicola, formerly a monastery and now an inn offering an overnight stay. But first, having arrived there by mule or shanks's pony, you will welcome a deck-chair and a glass of Epomeo wine followed by lunch on the patio, prepared by the innkeeper and his family. Later you will be invited to visit the first church built on Ischia, adjoining the inn. The downward trek to the base on foot is delightful, giving one the chance to scan the incredible landscape.

When you have explored Ischia, there are always steamer excursions to the nearby small islands of Procida in the Bay of Naples, which has not yet been discovered by tourists though three hotels are listed. From there, another steamer will take you on to Pozzuoli on the mainland, the mountainous city of the Phlegraean Fields. A visit should be made to the territory with the impressive Solfatara volcano; it is fascinating to walk around this ancient crater with its hot bubbling magma. From the ground around you columns of vapour pop up from a number of cracks causing tiny eruptions. A guide, surrounded by tourists, caused a flame to be lit near the Bocca Grande and, in seconds, thick clouds of smoke drifted from seams around the bowl of the crater, enveloping the encircling hills. Leaving this area, a stop is recommended at the Sibilla Acropoli, destroyed by the eruption of Mount Vesuvius in 70 AD. Also on the outskirts of the town is an amphitheatre, a complete circular theatre dating from the first century, with underground tunnelling.

This chapter was published in The Lady, *6th April, 1978. Permission has been received for it to be printed here.*

CHAPTER TWENTY-THREE

1979 – Orient Hopping

Our Singapore jet flight from London started a sixteen-day tour of the Far East in luxury. The batik-dressed hostesses pampered us with tasty meals, and drinks were on the house. After flying over Germany, Austria, Greece and Saudi Arabia, we touched down at Bahrain in a glorious sunrise on its stretches of golden sand. Singapore is a thriving freeport with masses of shipping in the harbour but from the aircraft it looked like children's toys on a pond. As we came in to land swaying palms and high-rise flats could be seen. At Paya Leber International Airport the temperature was in the nineties.

The Singapore Forum Hotel in Orchard Road was our stopover for two nights. Singapore takes its name from the ancient Sanskrit words *singa* and *pura,* meaning Lion City. Singapore, the Garden City, is one of the smallest nations in the world, the size of the Isle of Man but with some forty times the population which in 1979 was over two million. The official languages are Malay, Mandarin Chinese, Tamil and English. Over half of the people are under twenty-one. There is compulsory army service for two and a half years. Men retire at fifty-five. There is no immigration. Family planning operates and abortions are available.

Half of the government revenue is spent on education and Singapore required good English schoolteachers. The main religions are Islam. Buddhism, Christianity and Hinduism.

The Gateway to the East, Singapore is a healthy nation with first-class medical facilities, but cancer is the main killer having taken over from heart disease. Some twelve per cent of government revenue is spent on health services and there are seventeen government hospitals.

In this green and modern city with its wide tree-lined avenues, all Asia mingles together in a melting pot of Chinese, Malay, Tamil, Indonesian, Sinhalese, Eurasian, European. American and the native Singaporeans. Each seems to have its own religion, rituals, customs and mode of dress. Yellow-robed monks walk around the streets popping into shops for gifts of food.

Singapore is an independent, democratic republic, a member of the United Nations and the British Commonwealth of Nations. The city is economically sound, backed by the Singapore dollar, one of the world's strongest currencies. It is a mecca for visitors from all over the world. One of its great attractions is its continual sunshine with a maximum temperature of 87 degrees Fahrenheit, and a minimum of 75. Nights are cool. This lush, fertile, tropical land has an average rainfall of ninety inches a year with no specific monsoon or rainy season. Most rain falls in quick showers.

It is a city that has everything. I was impressed by the people. Singaporeans are courteous and friendly, attaching importance to visitors' welfare. The Malay phrase of greeting is *selamat datang,* meaning 'we welcome you and wish you a pleasant stay.' The city is noted for its cleanliness, with stringent laws and littering fines. Long hair for men is taboo; one in our party, with hair past his collar, was frowned on and told to have it cut! Drug peddling is a crime punishable by heavy fines, imprisonment or even death. On 24th April, 1978, a drug-trafficker was hanged in the Changi Prison which was notorious in World War II days.

For a feel of the city we went on a tour, driving to the waterfront, the Esplanade, City Hall, Queen Elizabeth Walk, the president's house, Victoria Memorial Hall, the cricket ground, Parliament House, Supreme Court, and St Andrew's Cathedral built by slaves from India. We also went by the Singapore River, the landing point of Sir Stamford Raffles over 150 years ago, a picturesque scene of sampans, junks and bumboats, bustling with activity as labourers heaved cargo on to their bare shoulders.

We visited Chinatown and were told that it may cease to exist in a few years. For example, high-rise flats have been built in Sago Lane in place of the old death houses. The Chinese keep their dead for two or three days before burial or cremation.

Mouet Faber Park at 582 feet is the highest point on the island and gives views over one of the largest and busiest harbours in the world located at major crossroads of Asia with some two hundred shipping lines represented. On average one ship enters the port every fifteen minutes.

An outdoor Instant Asia cultural show was a pageant of Chinese, Indian and Malay culture and we were invited to join in a coconut shell dance. The nearby Tiger Balm Gardens were a fantasy land of grottoes and caves depicting famous Chinese legends carved into the rocks.

The Hwa Yan Chinese Gardens were a show of beauty with ancient pavilions, palatial courtyards, weeping willows, lotus lakes and a seven-storey golden pagoda. The Mandal Orchid Pavilion contained thirty thousand orchid blooms grown in charcoal and brick. It takes five to seven years to produce the first bloom. Singapore exports more orchids than almost any other country. The Japanese Garden in Jurong was orderly and tranquil; it is the largest such garden outside Japan with greenery, streams and summerhouses.

The Botanical Gardens cover an area of eighty-eight acres of natural beauty with a fine collection of tropical flora. Monkeys wandered freely and black swans drifted across the lake. In a cage in the park was a huge gorilla mothering a kitten at its feet.

Queenstown was one of the government's new high-rise public housing estates with flats costing fifty Singapore dollars a month to rent, or twelve thousand dollars to buy on instalments. There were no washing machines in 1979 – Chinese laundrymen were very cheap.

A drive to the east coast included the Meredeka (Independence) Bridge, and along the waterfront by a string of boatyards there are wooden stilted kelongs (houses) jutting out into the water forming fishing traps; visitors are welcome and overnight stays can be arranged.

On Mountbatten Road we saw one of the residential quarters. We were told that Singapore's public housing project constructs one low cost living unit every twenty-six minutes. On then through a middle class farming area, we passed Changi Prison and Shanga village. There were coconut, rubber and tapioca plantations. We passed the president's house and the Temple of a Thousand Lights with a statue of Lord Buddha made from three hundred tons of concrete. The House of Jade contained a valuable collection of jade dating back to the Sung dynasty.

At Crocodile Farm were live reptiles and handicrafts such as batik and jade carvings. Down Shenton Way and along the seven-mile stretch of docks we reached the free Jurong Chinese Bird Farm with seven thousand various singing birds showing off their splendid plumage against a tropical green background and a magnificent waterfall. Jurong was once a swamp but has been reclaimed and now accommodates five hundred factories.

From Singapore's Clifford Pier we cruised on the ancient but sturdy Chinese junk, *Fairwind.* Crossing the eastern anchorages were modern liners, steamers and small craft which make Singapore one of the most important ports in the world. Our course swung towards the picturesque southern islands and by Malay fishing villages. On either side, coconut palms leaned over sandy beaches.

Singapore is a shoppers' duty-free paradise, with the cream of merchandise, often cheaper than in the country of origin. The handicraft centre complex has twenty-six shops offering crafts from sixteen countries – reptile skin bags, batik, straw and shell craft, ivory, jade, jewellery, rosewood, cane furniture, Thai silk, Persian carpets, pewter ware, Chinese clogs, paper sunshades, etc.

To save time, shopping was best done in the hotel shopping complex. I was intrigued with intricately-designed and hand-painted historical batik and Kelaton silk, native to the area. For men, there were suit materials with a twenty-four hour tailoring service. The Thieves Market in the town had an off-beat collection of secondhand goods and genuine antiques.

There are masses of licensed yellow and light blue topped taxis for hire. For a run around town, I hopped on a three-wheel trishaw, pedalled from behind by a Chinese youth with sinewy legs and baggy breeches.

Eating out in Singapore was a sheer delight, feasting my eyes on the local dishes with lavish floor shows. There was also food from China, India, Indonesia, Japan, Korea and the west. In the Peking restaurant in Orchard Road, our party pooled a variety of dishes aided with cold, wet napkins. For local colour there were dozens of hygienic open-air street stalls, including the renowned 'Car Park' where we munched oriental titbits on sticks. Small boys act as waiters, and the night is illuminated with kerosene lamps. Satay, a succulent Malayan special, was meat on skewers grilled over a charcoal brazier and dipped in chilli sauce.

It was a night with a difference at the gaily-coloured Banana Apollo restaurant with home-style fare served on a banana leaf, representing the traditional aspect of the restaurant. There were juicy dishes from Madrid and India; it was the custom to eat with the fingers, hence the wet napkins.

A visit to Singapore would not be complete without patronising the stately Raffles Hotel, established in 1886 and named after Sir Stamford Raffles, the founder of modern Singapore. In the heat of the day, we relished a Singapore gin fling cocktail, created by a barman in 1915.

We boarded the overnight *Southern Cross* State Railway Express train for three days in Kuala Lumpur.

Kuala Lumpur

The Moorish-style railway station of Kuala Lumpur, with administration buildings, is considered to be the oldest and finest landmark in the capital city of Malaysia; constructed in 1917, it is even portrayed on picture postcards. Other symbols of KL are the picturesque post office, the secretariat and the clock tower.

We were taken to our luxurious hotel in the heart of the cosmopolitan city, and from my large bedroom window I had an excellent view. Kuoni, our tour operators, had placed a welcome basket of fruit on a table in my room.

Kuala Lumpur is a city of brilliant and fascinating contrasts, an independent federal territory, rapidly expanding with all the colour and glamour of life. I was charmed by the warmth of the people and their friendliness and traditions.

On a coach tour of the city we drove by Parliament House (which cost seventeen million Singapore dollars to build in 1961), the National Museum and the mosque, where we had to remove our shoes and don black capes and white head-dresses before entering. We had a sight of the National and Meredeka (Freedom) Stadium, the king's palace and the University of Malaya where every year seven thousand students from all over the world attend for education. The football stadium holds fifty thousand spectators. The new satellite town had been built for industry. The Hilton Hotel has seven hundred rooms.

A countryside tour included Government House, the Indian Embassy, the British section, the British High Commissioner's house and ambassadors' row. Outside the town we witnessed rice-ploughing by buffaloes, for Malaya used to be a tropical jungle and has been partly cleared to grow rice. We saw tin mines and tin dredging – a most practical and economic method of mining tin from the country's rich soil. Malaysia's prosperity is based on two great industries, rubber plantations and processing factories.

We went by a Chinese cemetery where paper money is burnt for the next life. Around Pampong village there were masses of banana and coconut plantations and six-year old rubber trees.

At a batik factory I watched the various stages of fabric printing. At a pewter demonstration centre I saw the skilled workmanship that goes into the fashioning of the famous Sesanger pewterware, the history of which dates back two thousand years.

At the silver factory, men were at work making exquisitely-designed Taba products from Malaysian tin.

As a contrast an excursion was made to the most northern part of KL to the limestone Batu Caves where there are vast illuminated caverns rising with imposing grandeur.

I strolled through Kampong Bahru's Sunday night market off Hale Road for a sight of local life. On stalls every conceivable product was to be found, including a large variety of Malaysian food and delicacies. A weekly Sunday arts and craft centre, Pasa Seni, displays rattan work, wood carving, embroidery, copper, tools and ceramics. Paser Mingu weekend market, the Malay counterpart, has traditional wares and exotic food stalls.

A giant ebony Buddha lined one side of a temple. Dice throwing was in progress by the altar, being a kind of fortune telling. If two dice came up even the answer was yes; if odds, the answer was no. Joss sticks were burning in a nearby bowl and offerings were made of tins of milk, fruit and sacred wine.

Templar Park was noted for its flowers, also being a reserve for animals. It was a cool haven, profusely green with tumbling cascades and rushing waters.

Eating out in KL was a gourmet's delight with a wide range of Asian food, from spicy Malaysian meat and vegetable curries to a score of Chinese dishes. Shark's fin soup and bird's nest soup are worth trying.

At sunset we wandered around Chinatown in the old city, with its thousands of cars, noise and bustle. We were expected to bargain at the stalls. The evening wound up at the Yasmin restaurant complex, with Malay traditional dancing, including a wedding dance. We were invited to go on stage and bless the bride with flowers and perfume before a candle and national dance were performed.

At the end of our KL tour we boarded the overnight express train, *Northern Star,* for Butterworth and Penang Island which is twinned with Sicily.

Penang, Pearl of the Orient

Of all the far-away places I have visited, I fell most in love with Penang, a tropical island with fabulous palm-fringed bays, clear blue skies and seas – a second Hawaii I am told, Pearl of the Orient.

Originally named Prince of Wales Island, Penang takes its name from the betel-nut palm (or Penang tree) which is found in profusion on this lush island of exotic adventure, full of animation, scenic beauty and tranquillity.

A multi-racial society contributes to a fascinating variety of customs and cultures. Malaya has a predominantly Malay government, and in the country as a whole the Malays are in the majority, though in Penang state the Chinese are more numerous.

The national language is Malay, though I was understood in English. Hokkien, a Chinese dialect is spoken by the Chinese residents. The state religion is Islam, but with freedom of worship.

George Town, the capital and warehouse of the east, is one of Asia's oldest and best-known trading centres, where I found low-priced shopping. Almost anything could be bought, from junk jewellery to bric-a-brac.

Although Penang has a moderate climate, some of the days were hot, around 80 degrees Fahrenheit. Rainfall comes regularly from April to May and August to September in short sharp showers.

Getting about the island during our four days stay was easy with air-conditioned coaches, metered taxis, hire cars and an adequate bus service. For a touch of class, limousines, with driver, were to be had. But for novelty I hopped on a trishaw as in Singapore, a three-wheeled vehicle for two, bargained for beforehand, and headed for Chinatown in Campbell Street. Again, a Chinese wallah with the usual spidery legs and baggy breeches pedalled away behind. As we chugged along in and out of the busy traffic, through streets lined with old-fashioned shop-houses and bazaars, I thought every minute was my last! Suddenly and without warning, my Chinaman stopped. We were outside the Goddess of Mercy Temple (Kuan Ying Teng), the oldest temple in Penang, built in 1880 by the first Chinese settlers. I went inside to find the place was crowded with worshippers. Joss sticks were being burnt and prayers offered. I did not stay.

Penang is a sightseers' paradise. The best way to see the whole island at one stretch was on a conducted tour. The half day spent touring the forty-mile perimeter stays vividly in my memory.

Heading east, we reached the historical Fort Cornwallis, the oldest structure on the island and a reminder of Penang's colonial past which started under the East India Company in 1785. The residential area included the general hospital, the governor's house, the polo ground and the sports club. Along Northan Road I marvelled at the old British-style architecture.

The natural harbour had a fantastic conglomeration of craft, from Chinese junks and coastal steamers to tiny Malay and Chinese fishing boats. Along the throbbing waterfront was a string of unique stilted houses. Not many liners call in Penang nowadays and P&O ships no longer dock.

At Sungel Kluang, we entered the awe-inspiring Snake Temple; it held me spellbound. Uncaged, languid-looking snakes, in a variety known as Wagler's pit viper, had a highly toxic venom and are said to be divine disciples of a Chinese deity. They were coiled around the altar and other parts of the temple as if intoxicated by the incense-filled interior. The local picture-snapper tried unsuccessfully to persuade me to be photographed with one of them. In olden days, the temple was inhabited by huge pythons, Chang Loon, meaning green dragons. The monks fed them on poultry and eggs brought in by the devout.

Further north, an aquarium contained forty tanks housing fresh and sea water life. We visited the spice, fruit and rubber plantations. At the latter we witnessed the tapping of rubber. Between forty and forty-five trees are required to be tapped to produce one sheet of rubber.

We came upon miles of terraced paddy fields which seemed to drop down into the grey-green water of the Malacca Strait, the longest strait in the world, over four hundred miles long, separating Malaya from Java.

At a Malaysian roadside fruit stall, vendors were selling dried banana chips, spices and the famous Tiger Balm ointment, Pahking Palm from Singapore, effective for numerous muscular maladies.

We toured a batik factory and saw traditional block printing. It was fascinating to see how sarong batik was designed and produced and then fashioned into exquisite dresses. I could not resist buying a yard or two.

We passed through quaint fishing villages and a new settlement for fishermen. Fishing extends as far as the Indian Ocean and the catch is more than enough for Penang's market.

A mini-jungle half-hour climb to the top of Penang Hill on board the quaint funicular railway was a novel experience; it is the only train of its kind in Malaysia. The panoramic view form the peak of George Town and the mainland was well worth seeing. On the summit there was an hotel, a school, a mosque, a police station and bungalows – in fact a little hamlet in itself.

Back at base, we entered the magnificent Buddhist Temple called Kek Lok Si, used as a monastery; it was built in 1890 with granite steps leading up to the temple. On higher ground there was the 'Million Dollar Precious Pagoda', built in 1930 and donated by Aw Boon Haw, the Tiger Balm king.

In Murman Lane was the Siamese temple housing a reclining Buddha, Wat Chayanmangjakaran, measuring 108 feet in length and covered with gold leaf. Devotees continue donating gold leaf for this gigantic statue.

We came to Tanjong Tokong after passing countless white sandy beaches and caves for which Penang is famous.

The Botanical Gardens were laid out by the British and cover seventy-five acres of natural beauty where monkeys wander freely. They are sometimes known as the Waterfall Gardens because of small cascades of water down one of the hills leading into the gardens. All around are evergreen jungle-clad hills, tropical plants and trees growing in profusion.

There are some delightful hotels in Penang. We stayed at the Rasa Sayang on the north coast at Batu Ferringhi. It stands in a superb position ideal for relaxation in casuarina and palm-filled grounds adjacent to a gentle rippling shoreline. The words Rasa Sayang mean a love for life and its pleasures and is the title of one of Malaysia's best-loved folk songs. The hotel has been described as one of the most romantic and satisfying in the world. It is also one of Asia's leading beach complexes, designed architecturally on Malaysian traditions. It offers first-class facilities with international cuisine served in an unusual setting and background. I could dine under the stars or enjoy the unique facility of grilling my own steak on a charcoal grill in one of the restaurants.

Eating out in Penang is a novelty. In the top hotels, where dress is formal, the gourmet man can eat his way around the world with a different dish every day of his stay – Malaysian, Indian, Muslim, Japanese, Thai, and even European food. Alternatively there are the simple, moderately priced small restaurants. For local colour, roadside open-air stalls are popular and numerous. The food is cooked on the spot hygienically. In the seafood restaurants live crabs and lobsters crawl around in tanks before landing up in the pot. The national dish is Satay, those skewered chunky morsels of meat strung up on stems of coconut fronds, roasted on charcoal burners and dipped in spices and groundnuts. These succulent sticks, or kebabs, of satay are usually served with kutupat, a local rice cake. An ideal refresher is iced coconut water, or perhaps a toddy, a fermented alcoholic drink from the sap of certain palm trees. Something more pungent is See Koe Thing, a finely ground rice, nuts and various types of jelly. For those with a sweet tooth, Chendol is cool and pleasant for a dessert; it is available on town stalls.

In the fruit line, apart from the cheap and perpetual papaya and pineapple, seasonal fruits with a tangy flavour include water melon, star fruit, rambusten, mangosteen, riku and the king of fruits, the durian, the most intriguing of all fruits. Because of the smell it has been called carrion in custard! It is reputed to be a great aphrodisiac and tigers relish it. The fruit goes best with a glass of port wine. It tastes like a mixture of honey, cream cheese, strawberries and cream, and petrol or tar! Watch out for this fruit; it has a peculiar odour, but is a delicacy among the locals for its luscious flesh.

Penang is a treasure house for merchandise, some of it duty free. In the air-conditioned emporia and department stores prices were fixed. Penang's 'cheapside' is along Penang Road where bartering was expected and enjoyed by all. Good buys were Malaysian pewterware and Kelantan silver. Women of fashion welcome the chance to buy batik and Kain Songet fabrics with gold and silver embroidered borders, woven on cottage handlooms in the east coast state of Malaya. This material is ideal for glamorous western style evening gowns. Meungkuang leaf products are of special appeal; the leaves are woven by villages and made up into mats, fans, hats, bags and purses; I chose a leaf-designed long white skirt. There are textiles from Japan and the west, silk from China and India, perfume from the orient, together with curios, handicrafts, works of art, watches, cameras, glassware and intricately-woven rattan furniture. Men are especially catered for, tailoring being a chief feature; a suit can be made up in two days.

A night tour included a seafood dinner and a visit to Chinatown, an area almost exclusively Chinese. The Malays live mainly in the Kamongs. The night floating market, the Pamar Malan, was a great attraction.

Penang has a bustling night life with night clubs, international floor shows, a theatre hall and, for the young at heart, swinging to hot music at discotheques. A thirsty visitor welcomes the many licensed houses, each with its own decor and service.

Later we left for Bangkok by air.

Bangkok, the Hub of the East

Reluctantly, we left the tranquil world of the Rasa Sayang Hotel and became airborne to Bangkok, Thailand's capital. For the remainder of our stay in the Far East we were based at the unpretentious Thai family hotel, the New Imperial.

Bangkok is not a city which can be seen easily under one's own steam. First of all, there is the language barrier, then the bartering for taxis, and problems with entrance fees to the temples. It is much better to go around in an organised group.

It is a cosmopolitan city with an air of continual bustle and life around the clock. In the day the streets are clogged with lines of large cars and military vehicles driving at a snail's pace, bringing traffic almost to a standstill. Our driver read his newspaper while waiting to move up in the traffic queue. Buses of gleaming teak with chrome ornamentation and gaudy hoods wait their turn with the cries of the street vendors selling ice cream and steaming noodles. There is high air pollution; dirt and dust prevail everywhere.

At night the streets are illuminated with a blaze of flashing neon signs advertising the city's varied potentials, bordering on vulgarities of east and west.

Bangkok is called the Venice of the East because of the many klongs (canals) in the city which were once the transportation system. Today many of the downtown klongs have been filled in and transformed into main roads, but in the area around the city the klongs are still the best mode of transport. Many city workers commute by boat or water-taxi. Road taxis are fairly numerous, but one has to barter. Air-conditioned limousines with English-speaking drivers stand outside the smart hotels.

The city is steeped in Buddhism and gold, with a blend of religious traditions and twentieth century sophistication. In the West our curiosity about Siam, or Thailand as it is now known, by the musical and film, *The King and I.*

Lying in southern Asia, Thailand, which translates as 'Land of the Free', is roughly the size of France. It borders Burma in the north and west, Laos in the north-east, Cambodia in the south-east and the Gulf of Thailand and Malaya in the south.

It is a mass of ornate palaces, temples and pagodas. The most important building in Bangkok is the Grand Palace and the Emerald Buddha Temple which took a hundred years to build by slave labour; it was subsequently transferred in 1784 from Wat Arun on the Thonburi side of the river to its present home in Wat Phra Keo. A colossal demon with up-turned toes guards the entrance to this most sacred temple in Thailand. Made of jade or jasper, it is used for ceremonial occasions, such as royal weddings. Photography inside the temple was forbidden. Everyone, on entering the temple was expected to be respectably dressed, and we had to remove our shoes. In the magnificent throne room we were asked to sit in a group in the centre of the floor, but not cross-legged as this was considered an insult to royalty. We were permitted to saunter around the outer courtyard and palace grounds to take photos of the mirror-encrusted towers, gilded spires and famous statues of mythological gods and goddesses, one of the settings used for *The King and I.*

Although the royal family do not live in the palace, two hundred relatives occupied nearby buildings. One of these buildings was used by our Queen of England on her state visit.

There were some interesting ceremonial sheds containing the royal barges, each uniquely designed and decorated in great detail. They were once used on royal and ceremonial occasions, as well as functioning as war vessels. The most beautiful barge is the Suphaahong, used by the king when he made his royal river procession for the Kathin ceremony, a Buddhist function of offering robes to monks during the months of October and November.

After a session of temples, a contrast was a barge cruise in a long-tailed speedboat, through winding klongs to a typical Thai farmer's house with rural life at its best; we drifted back in a converted rice barge.

We were up at dawn the next day for an unusual and varied all day launch trip to Damnersaddan along the busy Chao Phya river and klongs among Thailand's most fascinating and quaint floating markets. The locals do their shopping from these hand-powered boats laden with tropical fruits and vegetables as well as household equipment. Gaily-dressed peasants were topped with their traditional Thai mushroom-styled straw hats. Some of the women were cooking on board. We stopped at one of the stilt-markets on the river for us to browse among the local handicrafts.

Thirty kilometres from the heart of Bangkok is the delightful Rose Garden Country Resort where Thai culture is on display in fifty acres of landscaped gardens, with parks, orchards and traditional Thai architecture. It is a beautifully-presented setting of breath-taking fascination. Among the attractions was Thai musical instrument playing, a wedding ceremony, sword fighting, and Thai boxing in which feet, elbows, knees and shoulders are included in the use of weapons allowed. There were dancing displays and Seladen pottery making. Pretty girls were painting coloured paper umbrellas for export. In another section elephants were at work.

Opposite Bangkok's stadium is the house of Thailand's late silk king, Jim Thompson, an American who came to the country at the end of the second world war and started the silk industry. His disappearance in the Malay jungle remains a mystery to this day. His house has been skilfully made from six very old Thai houses joined together. It contains an outstanding museum displaying Jim Thompson's collection of Asian objets d'art, such as his blue and white chinaware, Cambodian wooden Burmese statues and other fabulous antiques. Close by, girls were processing and weaving Thai silk by hand.

It was a thrilling experience to visit the world's largest and most uncanny crocodile farm in Samut Prakarn Province some thirty kilometres from Bangkok. Two thousand fresh and salt-water crocodiles are kept as well as a large number of other creatures including elephants, lions and snakes. Three times daily the crocodile handler enters their pond to wrestle with the crocodiles which are all destined to end up as leather goods.

The hill tribe people of northern Thailand have a unique and fascinating culture of their own. There are nine main ethnic minority groups with more than twenty sub-divisions. At the Hill Craft Foundation, under the patronage of our Queen Mother, we came face to face with some of these lovely people with their very ornamental and colourful head-dresses.

At this Foundation the handmade products were skilfully made and exclusive. On sale were shoulder bags interwoven with wool patterns and wool pom-poms, wall hangings, table runners, children's caps and many more souvenirs from the hill tribes. The Foundation uses its profits to encourage other hill people to produce items for sale. There were musical instruments like a mouth harp made with bamboo and a gourd organ played by the Lahu tribes, made of dried gourd with bamboo pipes and reeds. There were silver-stemmed pipes and tobacco boxes, plus the inevitable chains, bracelets and pendants as worn by the hill tribes.

We walked on our own through one of the main street markets of Bangkok among the gentle, friendly Thai people. With my nose as my guide, I wandered through the narrow streets where vendors were ready for us, calling out their wares and eager to barter. I was intoxicated with strongly-smelling jasmine perfumes and odours of nutmegs and chillies. It was easy to be lost in the hustle and bustle. One square mile of stalls displayed every conceivable item, even stuffed turtles!

Bangkok is the city of dressmakers and it is possible and inexpensive to have dresses made within a day or two, either at the premises of the shop or at one of the hundreds of little dressmaking establishments throughout the city. For men, fine suits and shirts can be made by skilful tailors during one visit, provided enough time is allowed for the garment to be completed. Fabrics can be chosen on the premises.

One of Thailand's major exports is pictorial art, highly valued all over the world. Many young painters demonstrate their skill with a pronounced local flavour, depicting Thai scenes of distinction and colour.

Handmade shoes are cheap in Thailand. One must allow three to four days for them to be made. Leather and suede clothes were all reasonably priced. Skin goods, such as crocodile, snake and lizard, are often copied in plastic; it is wise to make sure which it is before buying.

Bangkok is the home of antiques; in fact, it's an antique collectors' paradise. A knowledge of Asian antiques is needed and to know how to bargain. Thai antiques included Buddhist sculpture to be bought for pride-of-place in the home.

The two thieves markets are havens of secondhand goods of every description, even from pawn shops! But if in doubt as to the value, it is wise to take along a Thai friend to haggle over prices. Among the collection were musical instruments, electrical goods, uniforms and camping equipment. For lovers of antiques and objets d'art, both Chinese and Thai, there was porcelain, brass and copper ware and inlaid mother-of-pearl furniture.

To wind up our far eastern tour, we had an evening with a difference at Piman's palatial Thai theatre restaurant. On entering, we were asked to remove our shoes. We dined on delicious authentic Thai food, in an atmosphere of six hundred years ago, off very low and long tables under which we somehow managed to fit our legs. We were waited on by Thai ladies-in-waiting in attractive costumes reminiscent of an historic age of days long gone by. There was a tasty soup, prawns, sweet corn and curry, accompanied by rice-wine and various sweetmeats. A French master of ceremonies described the stage show in English and French.

Before our plane took off, Kuoni handed out boxes of orchids to members of our party.

CHAPTER TWENTY-FOUR

1979 – Robbed in Tangier

In 1979 I was wintering in Gibraltar and decided to visit Marrakesh in Morocco, but disaster befell me en route!

It happened in a flash. After ferrying over to Tangier, I made my way on foot to the already packed railway station for the three o'clock train to Marrakesh. As I boarded the train with my suitcase in one hand and my handbag slung across my shoulder, a voice behind me said, 'More room further down'. Walking the length of the second class coach I came to the first class. Retracing my steps I found an empty seat and was about to sit down when a voice behind me said, 'Can I put your suitcase up?' I looked up and there was a Moroccan youth standing beside me. Glad of some help, I let him put my case on the rack, and I sat down. To my horror, my handbag had been zipped open and my wallet and purse, together with my documents, had gone! I was penniless and the youth had flown.

Quickly collecting my case from the rack, I left the train as it was still standing in the station. On the platform stood the youth. Going up to him I said, 'My money; you have my money!'

'No money, no money,' he said. Passengers peered curiously from the windows of the train. By this time, two Moroccan policemen had appeared from nowhere. I tried to explain my predicament, but the men did not appear to speak any English; they talked to the boy in Arabic. Then a police officer made signs for me to follow him. With the youth carrying my case, we set off to the police station.

I sat on a hard bench; on my left was the youth, and on my right a crying child; her papa, standing by, had been caught stealing, or was he an accomplice? I would never know.

Again I tried to make the police understand, when suddenly one of them asked me in English, 'Do you accuse this boy?'

I said, 'I did not see him take the money, but he put my suitcase on the rack.' Local youths are trained to thieve in twos; it was apparent his pal had taken the money and they hoped to share the spoils at the extreme end of the platform.

A senior police officer arrived and sat at a table opposite me to investigate the case. Meanwhile I had signed several Moroccan forms which he went through.

By seven o'clock in the evening my patience was exhausted. I requested Moroccan money (dirhams) for an overnight stay at an hotel, but these were not forthcoming. I also indicated that I wished the police to contact the British Consulate. I did not appear to be getting anywhere with either request. By this time the youth had gone, when in came a man in civvies. 'Come,' said the man, and ushered me outside to a police van. I was asked to go in the back of the open van and had to climb up. The child sat in the front with the driver and police officer.

It was now dusk, and where were we going? We drove through the town and eventually stopped outside a large building. The police officer knocked on a small trap door, and outside stepped a Moroccan in uniform, a red fez on his head. I was signalled to go inside. I had arrived at the Consulat anglais!

With the Moroccan servant only speaking French, in my 'petit francais', I explained what had happened. A telephone call was put through to the English accountant. I listed all the money, travellers' cheques and other items I had lost. The porter offered me tea from his flask, but I had a small tot of brandy which I very much needed.

After discussing my case, the accountant drove me to the Astoria Hotel, owned by a Dutchman, where he booked me in for the night and paid the bill as I had no dirhams. He recommended a restaurant to me for dinner and advanced sufficient money for expenses. I was requested to report by taxi the next morning, with my suitcase, at the British Consulate.

The accountant asked me to take a taxi at nine o'clock next morning to return to the consulate. I said I was due to report to the police station, but he said to ignore that! So after an early breakfast, I took a taxi and arrived at the British Consulate which is set in beautiful grounds. Meeting the staff, I was asked to sign forms. I said I had no alternative but to return to Gibraltar, and was assured that arrangements would be made for that evening. My passport number was obtained from my hotel in Gibraltar.

I needed more dirhams for the taxi, etc. With no identification, I was taken at face value and received the necessary expenses to return to Gibraltar. I was then escorted into the town by the man in the red fez for a temporary passport and photos.

On my return to the consulate I was asked if I would like to see the library. I browsed among the books for a while until a secretary came in and invited me to join her for lunch at her home. I was whisked off by taxi to her flat and, soon, I was sitting down to a tasty meal prepared by her servant, accompanied by a bottle of wine. Walking back, I called at the little nearby English church; it was closed but a Moroccan opened it for me and I went inside.

Back at the consulate, I received my air ticket, made my farewells and left by taxi for the airport with the intention of catching the evening plane back to Gibraltar.

At the terminal there was chaos, with crowds of passengers waiting for delayed aircraft. Owing to poor visibility on the Rock, the plane to Gibraltar had not yet arrived. There would be no flight back that night. I wondered what to do as I had only ten dirhams left.

Near the airport desk stood an attractive young passenger. I told her of my problem. 'Not to worry,' she said. 'I have some money and am also going to Gibraltar.' After introducing ourselves (her name was Frances), we parked our luggage and set off by taxi with light cases. After trying a couple of hotels we were offered a double room at Hotel Paris. We said we would take it, but it did not live up to the hotel's name. We decided to eat out.

Next morning we arrived at the airport for the ten o'clock flight, but there was no plane. After a light meal, we hung about while passengers and staff tried to date my good Samaritan! At four o'clock the plane arrived and we were soon bound for Gibraltar.

But the hotels were chock-a-block and Frances could not find anywhere to stay. I managed to find her a room in my hotel, where she stayed for a few days awaiting a plane to the UK. I paid her hotel expenses to repay her mine in Tangier.

Six weeks later she was back again en route for Tangier and Casablanca where she was living. I met her at the airport and she stayed again at my hotel, until she set off for her final destination.

I paid my dues to the consulate and my travellers' cheques were refunded, but the contents of my wallet were never seen again.

My trauma in Tangier had a sequel. Two or three years later, I was invited to stay with my good Samaritan and her husband in Casablanca. From there I made my another attempt to see Marrakesh, this time without incident.

CHAPTER TWENTY-FIVE

1979 – Minorca, the Radiant Island

At the peak of the season, with only a return flight ticket, I took off from Luton for Minorca in the Balearic Islands. In two hours we reached Mahon Airport.

Set in the Mediterranean, 140 miles south-west of Barcelona and seventy-five miles north-east of Majorca, Minorca (spelt Menorca by the Spaniards) is thirty-five by nineteen miles; its population then was about 52,000 with half the inhabitants settled in Mahon, the capital. In 1723, Mahon replaced the town of Ciudadela on the extreme west coast, on account of the gigantic port facilities in Mahon. the three-mile long has one of the finest and deepest anchorages in the world, big enough to take the largest ships. It is of great historical interest through connections with Lord Nelson. There are regular sea connections with Barcelona, Palma and Alcudia.

It is a compact and easy-to-explore island with infinite charm and restfulness, and a refreshing break from the whirl of busy tourist centres, yet accessible to the more sophisticated island of Majorca, a quarter of an hour away by plane.

Shortly after my arrival on the island, an ex-Malta artist friend boarded my bus. Sylvia invited me to the flat she owned and drove me round the island by car, when I met some of the locals. The Minorcans are friendly, honest and hard-working people. Their language, Minorquin, is intermingled with many English words, reminiscent of the British connections in the past. I had no difficulty in making myself understood.

Minorca is noted for its brilliant summer sunshine, especially appealing to the camera enthusiast and artists who cannot fail to capture the sun's reflection from the little snow-white houses dotted around. Property built before 1723 must by law be painted red to show its antiquity.

There are miles of golden beaches, some only accessible on foot, but rewarding for their quaint coves and inlets. The seaside resort of Caldana, on the south coast, has as its main feature a magnificent bay set in a semicircle of clear blue sea, surrounded by masses of pines – a paradise for children. It was several days before I could leave the place, lazing and bathing from the Cala Caldana Hotel. I eventually made my way back to Mahon, the centre of business and popular with visitors; its narrow and steep streets lead off the main Hanover Street and the unique shopping centre, Calle General Goded, decked out with potted plants. The houses were without balconies and the windows were the old fashioned English style with sash cords.

The shops were crammed with Minorcan manufactured goods – shoes of every description, pretty costume jewellery and some furniture. Cake shops were packed with luscious fancies filled with cream of various tempting flavours, even whisky! A traditional buy was the round flaky sugar-coated bun, ensainmados, of a light texture, often served in hotels with continental breakfast. Macaroons (amarcas) were another customary speciality and much sought after in the village of Mercadel, for their freshness. Great care was put into the wrapping of my purchases.

The big covered market in Plaza del Carmen did a brisk trade in fruit, vegetables and meat, beef being one of the island's biggest exports. Minorca also processes cheese in large quantities for export, particularly the creamy farmhouse brand and the older and sharper cheeses. Other products are lobsters and oysters which were expensive. An outdoor Saturday market sold shoes and clothing.

One of Minorca's main manufactured products is gin, said to be made from an old English recipe acquired when the British occupied the island, but it has a different taste as it contains a lot of juniper and various herbs. The locals drink it for breakfast; it is said to be good for the kidneys. Made up in stone bottles, the gin makes an ideal and inexpensive gift. The gin distilleries are open to visitors where I also sampled the local wines and export liqueurs.

The restaurants were international – continental, Indonesian, Chinese, French and Spanish. One English-run restaurant where I enjoyed good food was the Buen Guato Bar, down a few steps, near the market. Worth trying were the Spanish tapas – tiny pieces of fried fish and meat served hot, though these appetisers are now no longer on the house. The Cafe Europe, just off the main square, was my favourite for tapas.

I did some of my sightseeing the lazy way, by organised coach, though a hired car would have been care-free. Cars were often delivered to the door full of petrol and picked up again at the end of the hire.

It was very pleasant travelling by public transport. The main coach station, Imes, was at the corner of the Esplanade Square with a connecting service to the various villages, and through the island's centre to Ciudadela, Minorca's second town.

I wandered through this ancient historic town, still the ecclesiastical capital, built in Moorish style with attractive arcaded streets, one of which lead to the unique Plaza Espana, and through a number of Moorish-style archways. I came to the fourteenth century Gothic Cathedral, the interior of which was well worth seeing. Just behind the cathedral is the bishop's tiny renaissance garden. In the same street a delightful bakery provided luscious elevenses.

The main part of the town, called Borne Square, in Plaza del Generalis, continued on from the cathedral, a peaceful traffic-free area, except for the tourist packed coaches. The town hall (Ayuntamiento) is on the square; originally a Moorish palace, it is open to visitors. Sauntering around, I noted the Arabic influence in the mayoral chamber, and the ceiling with the local coat of arms. The first floor contained a varied assortment of museum pieces.

Leading off the Borne is Ciudadela's fine harbour. Down the steps and along the quayside were many restaurants, some set into caves. The Casa Mano lo Nostrum served excellent food. At the Aurora restaurant, near the Cafe Mollo and the bus terminus, I was served with a cool refreshing Sangria made up of fresh fruit juices, local red wine, mineral water (or brandy) in an outsize glass jug overflowing with sliced fruit. With it I relished tasty gambas (prawns).

Back in Mahon, a half-hourly bus service operated from Plaza San Roque to the old garrison town of Villa Carlos, formerly Georgetown, built by the British during the two occupations of the island from 1708 to 1756 and 1762 to 1782. The old Barrack Square is now the esplanade. The straight streets still have English names – Victoria, Stuart, etc., and are based on the old tent lines.

There are many hotels in Minorca but, owing to the temperamental winter climate, most of them close down at the end of October until May when the tourist world sleeps and many of the residents seek warmer climes. The Minorcans revert to indoor activities, such as art and music.

I booked in at the three star Agamemnon Hotel. From my balcony I had a superb view of the picturesque bay. In the summer months the hotel organises two-hour trips around the bay from the jetty. Taking one of these tours we called in at all the little creeks and past the imposing Villa San Antonio, set high on a hill and better known as the Golden Farm; it was occupied and so closed to visitors. Lord Nelson is said to have stayed there with Lady Hamilton.

On the little boat I was invited to try my skill drinking wine from a two-funnelled bottle, without my lips touching the rim. it was quite a feat, but I mastered it.

The two little harbours in Villa Carlos had a fishermen's atmosphere. At night I joined in the merry-making with visitors and locals in this unique setting.

Not far from Villa Carlos is the French town of San Luis, founded by the French in the eighteenth century, during their short occupation of the island.

Having covered the main areas of Minorca, I still had to see the hundred or so beaches on the south-east coast. The well known ones were Cala Alcafar, S'Algar and Plaija de Punta Prima, all with their different characteristics.

Around the bay lay the most photogenic place in Minorca, the breathtaking fishing village of Minibeca, tightly packed with minute and decorative white cottages in streets so narrow that neighbours could almost shake hands with each other across the streets, and could certainly hold a conversation. It was an Alice in Wonderland atmosphere. A tiny church was in course of erection among the houses. Nearby, the Mini Inn had a varied menu to tempt my palate.

Along the south coast I came to Cala'n Porter, a new town in the making, which was attracting settlers. On the north coast was Fornelis, a typical fishing village in pine groves, with a fine harbour. A popular summer resort for the unsophisticated and famous for its lobsters and stray cats!

North of Mahon and a little off the beaten track, was Sa. Mesquida where I enjoyed a dip from the pine edged sandy beach.

Minorca's history dates back to early civilisation in the Bronze Age, when the inhabitants lived in caves. Remains of this period arestill being found. Particularly outstanding were the three types of ancient monuments – the Taula, the Talayat and Navesos, scattered around the island, and marked on the map.

I was impressed by the large variety of bird life on Minorca. About two hundred species are said to live on the island or come at certain times of the year.

Flamenco and folk dancing is a highlight at certain times of the year. The traditional Spanish fiestas also are celebrated. In September, the Mahon fiesta, with firework displays, goes on for three days with about forty horses performing in the streets. In the winter months, there are films in English at the Victoria cinema to while away the time.

Minorca is an island that captures the peace-seeking traveller with time to stand and stare.

CHAPTER TWENTY-SIX

1979/80 – Christmas in Australia

The first human beings known to arrive in Australia were the Aborigines. Experts believe they came from south-east Asia about 12,000 years ago. There are now about 130,000 of them living in Australia, of whom 45,000 are full-bloods. Many live in protected reserves. Those areas classified as aboriginal reserves are not open to tourists, unless they hold entry permits. Many live in government settlements, or on mission stations. As they increase in numbers, they gradually drift to the towns.

The first white settlers arrived from England at the end of the eighteenth century. They came by ship via the Cape of Good Hope, journeying 15,000 miles in six months. Most of them were convicts condemned to exile for the rest of their lives. In 1850, when gold was discovered, others came of their own accord and joined them. Some of the settlers from England were from Portsmouth with their fresh complexions and rosy cheeks, like pomegranates. Hence the name Pommy for English-born Australians.

The Australians today are noted for their great hospitality and generosity towards visitors. The women are much more refined than the men, cultured and well-bred. The men, used to a hard life, often in the bush, are hearty, but rough diamonds.

My first glimpse of Australia was on my arrival at Melbourne airport. After passing through health security, my porter whisked me away to a waiting taxi and would not take a tip. The cheerful driver drove through the fast-moving traffic along the side thoroughfares to the Graham Hotel in Swanston Street where I was to stay. The temperature was in the sixties, and people were doing their Christmas shopping dressed in summer wear. The Australians boast of four season in one day.

At the hotel I was welcomed by reception. From my bedroom window I could see opposite an illuminated Christmas tree, while surrounding buildings were floodlit with the spirit of Christmas.

The next morning, on a walk-about, I was impressed with the Christmas window-dressing. In Burke Street, Myers had tastefully depicted reminiscent scenes of various countries, England, Italy, Spain and Germany.

Streets were lined with entertainers playing musical instruments, clowns and Scottish dancers. A notice outside a cinema said 'topless usherettes'!

The next day was Sunday and all the shops were closed. Walking along Duke Street I came to Pancake Parlour where I relished one of their outsize and tasty traditional pancakes, topped with a blob of ice cream and maple syrup from the table dispenser. Opposite to me sat a resident. I chatted with her and told her how much I was enjoying my first time in Australia. Suddenly she produced a large box of chocolates. 'You have them,' she said. 'I don't eat chocolates.' Her name was Miss Veronica Barry of Syndal.

The beautiful cathedral of St Paul was close to my hotel. I was able to attend a midnight carol service.

On Christmas Eve, two days after my arrival in Australia, I found myself singing carols lustily with hundreds of Australians. This Festival of Carols, in aid of the Royal Institute for the Blind, is held annually at the Sidney Myer Music Bowl in Victoria Gardens in Melbourne; it takes place under an awning in the form of a steel shell. The auditorium accommodates 20,000 spectators.

As I took my seat in this vast arena, which overflowed into the gardens, everyone around me held a lighted candle. I was given one by a good neighbour. The orchestra struck up and the Australian Boys' Choir, a hundred and fifty strong, opened the evening with the first carol in which we all joined. Other choirs followed and a blind boy sang solos. Television personalities gave a few sketches and the evening wound up with everyone linking arms to the tune of *Auld Lang Syne.*

Christmas Day was fairly quiet in Melbourne. As my hotel did not cater for lunches, it was arranged that I should lunch at their sister hotel nearby. En route, I met an Australian family who invited me to join them for a Christmas lunch. Unable to accept, I arranged to take a taxi that evening to their home. It was a 'take a plate' meal, an old Australian custom, when each guest takes a plate of a speciality food. My hosts were Mr and Mrs Michael Clausing of Clifton Hill.

On Safari to the Red Heart of Australia

On Boxing Day, I joined an eleven-day coach tour with AAT to the incredible red centre of Australia. We were a mixed bag of nationalities – Canadians, Dutch, New Zealanders, South Africans, Americans, a couple from Zambia (the Richards), one or two Australians, and myself, English.

Our safari coach for this down under tour was well-equipped for the strenuous journey which lay ahead to the red heart of Australia. Our driver and captain, Max, kept us posted with his travelogue over his relay system, giving us history, facts, figures and bush-lore as we went along. On desert safari picnics he produced tasty eats and his notorious bushman's billy tea. We all helped to set out the tables and prepare the meal, including the pet of the coach, a five-year old boy named Scott. Sometimes we could see in the distance, coming towards us, a cloud of red dust; we knew that a truck was approaching, enveloping us in its trail as it drove by.

Our tour hostess, Linda, attended to our daily wants, plying us with ice cold drinks through the parched desert areas of the Australian bush, keeping us amused and interested on lonely stretches of the road for miles, often on unmade tracks, and planning the next day's programme.

Travelling through this deserted country was an unforgettable experience. Only a small minority of Australians have the urge to see this untamed outback.

We passed through many varied types of country, from arid expanses of astonishingly red sandy desert with its vast and startling emptiness, isolation and heat, traditional enemies of the outback people, to prolific pastures. Yet it is not only the vast emptiness that startles, it is the colours – yellow browns of the desert plains, the vivid whites of the salt lakes, and above all the incredible reds of the desert and the rich Namatjira ochres.

The desert is not always empty; sometimes we caught sight of herds of wild camels; 16,000 are known to roam the outback. There are galloping brambies (wild ponies) and stately pacing emus. Campers often hear the weirdest of all cries, that of the dingo, or wild dog, howling at the dawn.

On the first day we drove westwards along Calder Highway, past Digger's Rest, site of the gold fields, to Ballarat, one of Victoria's largest cities, renowned for its gardens and marble statues of past Australian ministers. South of Ballarat is Sovereign Hill, once an old mining village. Mining technicians have re-created a pub, a bank, a theatre, shops and houses. A museum displays mining relics. One hundred years ago, Ballarat was a booming gold town packed with lusty miners, each hoping to strike it rich.

Lining the road were dozens of burst tyres and empty beer cans from thirsty travellers. There were warning signs – *Don't burn Victoria; One spark can destroy a park; High fire risk;* etc. Australia is very fire conscious on account of the seasonal dryness causing great bush fires. Another notice read, *Never underestimate the power of M.A.N.* M.A.N. is a diesel truck, but women's lib objected to the advertisement.

We drove on to Princess Highway; many years ago it was farmland. Through old volcanic country we came to a ten-mile Avenue of Honour of English elms to mark the war dead of country towns. Then on to Western Highway and over Australia's largest and most important river, the Murray, which flows through three states.

We reached South Australia and the fine cathedral city of Adelaide, the gateway to west and central Australia. We were booked in at the Travel Lodge where I met the Australian cricket umpire, Colin Edgar. On hearing I was going to Alice Springs, he gave me an introduction to his cousin, Senator Bernie Kilgariff, whom I had the pleasure of meeting later. I also had an introduction to the senator from Derek Nimmo, the actor, before leving home.

We toured the city on foot; it is well known for its gardens, parks and the gracious colonial home of seven-times State Premier Sir Henry Ayers. Adelaide was also the home of the explorer Charles Sturt, 1799-1869, who opened up much of inland Australia.

Driving north we reached Port Augusta, a small modernised railway town, and our overnight stop at the Acacia Ridge Motor Inn. Next morning we left on the Stuart Highway, known as the 'Bitumen' or the 'Track'; it runs from south to north, from Adelaide to Darwin and was named after James McDouall Stuart, the first white man to traverse the Macdonnell Ranges.

Leaving the last of the sealed highway, we headed for the outback via Woomera, a wheat-growing district and forward base of the rocket testing range, extending into Western Australia.

We crossed two hundred miles of mostly salt-bush (sheep and cattle food). At one point we caught sight of a goamer lying in the scrub, a kind of lizard, nine inches long. There was just time to snap it before it scuttled away.

Also in the bush was a striking flower, Sturt's Desert Pea, which grows in the desert of the Flinders Range and was named after Captain Charles Sturt. This rare and tiny bush plant is the state floral emblem of South Australia and has red and black petals and bright green leaves. At the roadside were wild green melons, whose seeds and flesh are enjoyed by cockatoos. We passed wild cows and dead kangaroos which had been blinded by truck headlights and run down.

We came to Lake Hart, a vast shining lake, and drove on to the town of Kingoonya, on the Trans-Continental railway. Another hundred and fifty miles brought us to the impressive open mining centre of Coober Pedy, known as the Great Australian Loneliness, the opal capital of the world. We spent the night at the fascinating Opal Inn.

In Coober Pedy we experienced a way of life very different from any other country. This lonely opal mining field is situated in the Stuart Range and is where some of the finest white of milk opals are mined, set and exported.

Opals were first found in 1915 but it was not until 1925 that the mining camp was given the name of Coober Pedy, Aborigine for 'man in hole'. The miners work in holes, one of the most remarkable bodies of white men in the world, totally independent and employing themselves, working in small partnerships.

About twenty-six nationalities help to make up a floating population of some five thousand inhabitants; a large percentage of them are of Chinese extraction. Eighty per cent of the miners and townspeople prefer to live in underground homes or dug-outs, eight feet below ground. This gives them protection from the searing summer heat. The day we were there the temperature was 113 degrees Fahrenheit. Only about three inches of rain fall each year. Summer is from October through to April with high temperatures and the nights remain warm. Winter is May to September when day temperatures are in the sixties, but freezing at night.

In summer the coolest place is underground. We were shown over a dug-out belonging to the Umcona Opal Mine Company; it was very cool down there and well equipped with all home comforts. There was even a lounge with a fire-place, not forgetting the wine cellar! What surprised me was the indoor swimming pool. Water is imported by tankers and electric power is laid on in Coober Pedy. The natural stone-coloured walls and floors of the dug-out are kept at a low temperature during the summer by lime and by spraying. The Aborigines are given rent-free furnished homes, but prefer to live in the open.

Near the dug-out was one of the world's most unusual catacomb churches, over a hundred years old. This tiny house of prayer was built by three women. The stone interior contains a pulpit and altar draped in red and gold cloth, with matching chairs. A crucifix on the outside wall is the work of miners.

Main Street comprises a post-office, tourist shop, a branch of New South Wales Bank, a Greek butcher's shop, a boutique where I bought a pair of navy shorts for coolness, and three inns.

In the Umcona Coal Mine Cave an experienced cutter gave a demonstration. Then he showed us the boss's exquisite private collection of gem stones. We could buy opals.

The opal fields yield up most of the world's supply of this brilliant gem stone. Nine mining companies work the mines away from the camp. We saw the solar distillation water plant, early diggings and an open cut mine. Miners often sleep down the mines. They earn good money for mining, but there is little use for it at Coober Pedy. Robberies are almost unknown on account of the distance the thieves would have to flee, but fights occur between the nationalities. We were told we could fossick for opals, but were warned that we could easily be lost in a hole and the mine squad would have to be called up to rescue us.

Schooling for the camp children reaches a high standard, with ten teachers and sixty pupils. on Hospital Hill there is a hospital and nurses' home. Entertainment for the community consists of forty radio programmes but no TV. Sport includes baseball, tennis, swimming, nine-hole golf course, cricket and a racecourse with three- day October meetings.

We crossed the border into Northern Territory. After another long drive during which we saw glimpses of Mount Connen, we stopped at Curtin Springs and then drove through desert oak country, one of the oldest type of trees. We reached the great red sandstone Ayer's Rock, lying in the centre of Australia. It rises 1143 feet above open desert plains and is about 250 miles from Alice Springs. The rock is five and a half miles in circumference. Geologists say that nine tenths of the rock may be underground. The base of Ayer's Rock supports relatively lush vegetation.

We stopped for the night at Elura Motel close to the rock. Elura is aboriginal for 'the rock'.

From dawn to dusk, the rock is fascinating in its spectacular colour changes; pale yellows to vivid purples, fiery reds to orange. Every evening there is a mystic miracle when the sub's rays turn the rock from a brown, whale-like shape into a blood-red ruby colour. As I gazed at Ayer's Rock, it gave me an eerie sense of primeval nature, of how it all began.

The evening we arrived we joined sightseers and camera enthusiasts to witness this phenominal sight and to take pictures.

After a rainstorm the cliffs are veiled in superb waterfalls which trickle down the foothills and then fade away.

We toured the caves at the base of the rock to see aboriginal designs carved over the centuries into the rock surface. Ayer's Rock was a home of the Aborigines with their dream-time mythology. Now only a section of the rock base is reserved for them.

On the eastern side of this great monolith is a climb to the summit for rewarding views of the vast plains and distant mountain ranges. But the climb is only for the sure-footed and extremely fit climber. People have been known to fall to their death and evidence of this was to be seen on the warning plaques inserted on the rock. Going up the rock face is said to be hazardous, and coming down a nightmare. A young man in our party had to be escorted down from the chicken run, the first stage of the climb. Another climber managed to reach the summit and return safely. He said he would not do it again for £100, it was too unnerving.

Driving twenty miles from Ayer's Rock we came to Mount Olga, the highest peak of a group of thirty cone-shaped reddish-brown monolith rocks, famed for their unusual formations and colours. They are known to the Aborigines as katajuta, meaning nine heads, which have been rounded by the wind, or by the sea when the continent was submerged thousands of years ago. Manganese is present as streaks through the rocks.

We returned to Ayer's Rock to see and photograph the interchange of colour by day. We passed again through Curtin Springs and into sandy hilly country, crossing the dried-up Finke River which comes down from the Macdonnell Range at Glen Helen Gorge.

At last we reached Alice Springs and stayed at the lush haven, Oasis Motel, owned by Senator Bernie Kilgariff and his family. The motel stands in beautiful grounds with gardens, individual unit accommodation for guests and a small swimming pool.

The senator invited me to his home where I met his wife and members of his family. He gave me a copy of *The Alice* booklet, signed by him, and wished me a pleasant stay in Alice Springs.

Alice Springs had been the senator's home for over fifty years. Since 1975, as a member of the Conservative Country Liberal Party, he was one of the Northern Territory's two senators in Canberra.

The town lies in the Macdonnell Range, a thousand miles from any sizable habitation. The settlers called it Alice Springs, now affectionately called The Alice, after Lady Alice Todd, wife of the builder of the overland telegraph line from Adelaide to Darwin. The Aborigines used to call the town Turiera, meaning large water hole. Readers will recall Nevil Shute's book and film *A Town like Alice,* which brought the town into greater prominence. Since then Alice has been visited by the Prince and Princess of Wales.

Alice Springs was founded in 1872 as a station for the overland telegraph. It is now the centre for the outback cattle industry. Touring the town of Alice, first we ascended Anzac Hill, on which stood a war memorial, for a scenic view of Alice from the summit. In Hartley Street we were taken to the art gallery to see a collection of paintings by the Dutch artist, Henk Guth, including those of the ghost gums, trees of particular interest to visitors.

In Art Studio Guth is the largest painting in the world, painted by Henk Guth and his assistant. This panorama is a three hundred and sixty degree landscape of Alice, stretched across thirty three pieces of linen; it took the artist and his assistant two years to complete.

In Head Street is the School of the Air, a unique education system for children in certain outback areas. Teachers conduct lessons by two-way radio to pupils they have never seen. Family classes are scattered over hundreds of miles.

The old telegraph station used to be one of the links of the overland telegraph service between Alice Springs and Darwin; it has now been restored.

Alice has over forty sporting clubs, including some of the most unusual events staged in Australia. one event is the annual Henley-on-Todd regatta organised by the Rotary club to raise funds for an outback children's holiday to the seaside. Young and old make merry in the sand of the River Todd, carrying papier-mache bottomless boats, attracting a large crowd of spectators.

On the eighth day of our tour we left the Oasis Motel, skirted the Eastern Macdonnell ranges and drove through some of Australia's most rugged country. Going south through Heavitree Gap to Pitchi Richi Bird Sanctuary, we passed Emily and Jessie Gap. At a camel farm we had a ride on one of the beasts and finished up at a date farm.

Then we came to Ross River Homestead, set in an outlandish stretch of farmland, but to be our overnight stop. After meeting our hosts, Gill Green, we were invited to an ample home-cooked lunch. To accompany it was the traditional bushman's bread, the damper, and the renowned billy tea.

There was a lot to see at the homestead. First we were shown how to throw a Hawes boomerang and to make it come back. we could ride a tame horse, trek through the working station with 11,000 cattle, or walk to the nearby N'Dahla Gorge to see Aboriginal rock paintings dating back to pre-historical times; or visit Triphina Gorge, a large creek well-known for its ghost gums and pastel colourings.

For our evening entertainment, there were yarns by our host, and the history of Old Love's Creek, as the homestead used to be called, before retiring to our air-conditioned log cabins.

The following day we toured the Western Macdonnell Range, renowned for its beautiful scenery.

At Tennant Creek we drove to the foot of Mount Gillen to see the burial place of the Reverend John Flynn (1894-1951) a Presbyterian minister who founded the Australian Royal Flying Doctor Service which today covers over five million square kilometres of outback Australia from Fort Augusta in the south to Darwin in the north with a base at Alice.

West of Alice Springs is Standley Chasm, a strikingly colourful cleft in the Macdonnell Range, only five metres wide but seventy metres high. As we walked through the narrow gap the sun, at noon, was overhead illuminating the great walls above us. In the national park we saw the cutest rock and black-fanged wallabies in their native habitat. We were asked not to feed them.

We came to Corroborree Rock Native Reserve and also an Aboriginal initiation point, a great ridge which spurs from the plains. in the Valley of the Eagles there were many native birds and plants. Nestling in the George Gill Range is the magnificent King's Canyon with walls up to 214 metres, enclosing hidden mysteries, pools of crystal clear water and giant ghost gums. Returning to Alice for our flight back to Melbourne, we took off from the air-strip in a small plane.

Before leaving England for Australia, I received an introduction from Lady Peel to the Hospitality Committee of the Melbourne Branch of the Victoria League. After returning from Alice, I contacted Mrs Dorothy Lansell-Smith and introduced myself. She arranged a get together through Mrs Frank Hobill-Cole, both of South Yarra, Melbourne. Taking the tram, I spent a very pleasant day with the members of the Hospitality Committee, followed by snapshots in the attractive garden.

A Fairy Penguin Tour

I booked a tour to see a unique parade of fairy penguins which regularly emerged at sunset from the Tasman Sea during the breeding season.

I joined hundreds of spectators to see this amazing spectacle. Apart from coach loads, people came in cars and on foot. Many had brought rugs, prepared for a chilly evening. A microphone had been set up overlooking the beach, and the whole area was floodlit. Two wardens patrolled the beach. No-one was permitted to take flashlight photos of the penguins who were under the protection of the Wild Life Trust.

Soon, word went round that hundreds of these little creatures could be seen coming out of the sea on the incoming tide, strutting along the sands in little groups. They looked almost unreal with their stout and tiny bodies, short necks, small heads and strange webbed feet which they use for steering, their white fronts adding to the scene. Up Summerland beach they waddled, and through the tiny pathway which they had imprinted over a period of time. Only the tops of the heads of these friendly and care-free nine-inch creatures could be seen above the reeded sand dunes, as they trudged along, their wings flapping like swimming paddles. On and on they toddled until they reached the top of the dunes, almost exhausted, pieces of fish visible in their mouths. They had no fear of human beings who were often obliged to step aside to avoid treading on some of them.

Eventually they found their way to their individual burrows where their young were patiently awaiting their parents' arrival with food, their minute heads popping in and out of their nests for any fish that could be transferred from their parents' beaks to their own.

Adult birds remained at sea for extended periods and could travel for long distances under water. During the breeding season each parent took it in turn to collect fish at sea during the day.

Often eggs were laid beneath grassed dunes, or under overhanging rocks. Since my visit to Summerland in 1979, I have been told that many of the fairy penguins at Summerland Beach have sadly died.

The Old Melbourne Gaol

The Old Melbourne Gaol was a complete contrast to other buildings in the city. It was built in 1841 and is on Franklin Street with elegant entrance gates, the courtyard and the chapel, while the three storey cell block fronts Russell Street.

My hotel had already telephoned the warden to say that I was on the way. On entering the cell block, I was given a welcome!

Wandering through this somewhat gloomy edifice, I was surprised to see such orderliness. The existing interior had been retained, the walls were clean and sealed in such a way as not to offend the eye. The first cell (16) had been painted white to provide a comparison. At the end of the cell were records of prisoners' documents and torture exhibits. There were four suits of armour made and worn by members of the Kelly Gang, the notorious Irish family of outlaws.

I climbed the gruesome stairway to the second tier and was confronted in one cell with the standing model of Harry Power, the bush ranger. In another cell was a model in solitary confinement. The eerie execution area was intact and in working order, with the exception of the beam. The original one had been removed to Pentridge at Coburg, a northern part of Melbourne; the one on display was a mock-up installed when the film *Ned Kelly,* starring Mick Jagger, was shot in 1970.

On leaving the gaol, I signed the visitors' book, carrying away thoughts of prison life of long ago when the old Melbourne Gaol was used for penal life sentences.

The Barque Polly Woodside

They mark our passage in the race of men,
Earth will not see such ships as those again.

John Masefield

As I walked from my hotel in Swanston Street, from the mouth of the Yarra River I could just see the tip of a moored vessel, with its tall masts, her outline framed by modern skyscrapers. As I neared the moorings at the Old Duke's and Orr's Dock, her bright new paint glistened in the sunlight and her hull and graceful lines were a delight to behold. I decided to go over her.

Polly Woodside was 192 feet in length and 30 feet in the beam with a registered gross tonnage of 648 tons, and a maximum speed of fourteen knots. She was now a wreck being restored but when at sea she had been manned by a master and usually two officers, whose quarters were in the poop, and by twelve to eighteen seamen accommodated in the deck-house aft of the foremast. Her main deck comprised accommodation for stewards, pantry, master, stores and slop chest, wash space and W.C. Her fittings included bunks, settees, wooden swivel chairs and camp stools. The whole of the area below decks was available for general cargo. Later it contained 230 tons of concrete for ballast.

Polly Woodside in 1979 was nearing the end of her restoration, although research had been going on for a considerable time. The idea to take up this challenge came from Dr Karl Kortum, the director of the San Francisco Maritime Museum, who had restored the sailing ship *Balclutma.* As a result, the late Dr E. Graeme Robertson, first chairman (1963-76) of *Polly Woodside,* impressed by this accomplishment, utilised his courage and tenacity to make the restoration of *Polly Woodside* a reality.

A proposal to save the ship was accepted by the National Trust of Australia (Victoria) in 1962. A photograph was displayed in the Maritime Museum of Dr Robertson's daughter, Joan, who named *Robertson's Wharf* in memory of her father.

This was the last resting place of *Polly Woodside* which is now a memorial to a breed of ships and men the world will not see again.

From the beginning of the community project, all Melbourne was agog with enthusiasm for this labour-of-love, with the larger part of the work being carried out on a voluntary basis. Hundreds of people from all works of life worked tens of thousands of hours repairing the ship. Volunteer seamen daily assisted the rigging and many companies donated their skills or their services.

The restoration of this sailing ship was expected to be completed in the year after I was there, an achievement of which all Melbourne citizens can well be proud.

Repairs to the deep-water commercial square-rigged sailing ship began in 1972 when, as a coal hulk, she was dry-docked at Williamstown in Melbourne, for repairs to her underwater hull.

Polly Woodside was built of riveted wrought iron and designed for maximum cargo capacity with lines which gave her excellent sea-faring qualities for sailing in the American trade – out with coal, home with nitrates or grain. She was launched from the Belfast, Northern Ireland, slipway of Workman Clark & Co. In December of 1885, she was described as 'the prettiest vessel ever launched in Belfast'. Many years ago she was one of a vast fleet, but now almost a loner, one of a dozen survivors of her class in the world.

As a seafarer and lover of freighter travel, I climbed the forward gangplank to tread the decks of this historic vessel and had no difficulty in visualising the precarious and turbulent life of *Polly Woodside.* Built for W. J. Woodside, a well-known ship owner of Belfast, and named after his wife Marion Polly Woodside, the ship is a typical small merchant sailing ship of her era. By 1897, she had rounded Cape Horn no less than sixteen times, each voyage taking a year to complete. Her estimated sailing distance between 1885 and 1922 was 415,000 nautical miles.

Photographs and a model of the ship were on view in the Maritime Museum near where *Polly Woodside* was berthed until she was completely re-built. One photograph depicted ninety-two year-old seaman Charlie Rouse talking to a reporter about his time on the *Polly Woodside* in 1906. Another, by the *Herald Weekly Times,* showed *Polly Woodside* on tow to her restoration berth at No. 9 South Wharf, Melbourne, 12th May, 1973. Her history is long and eventful, and worthy of commendation during her ninety years afloat.

In 1903 *Polly Woodside* was acquired by a New Zealand firm, A. H. Turnbull & Co., and renamed *Rona,* trading first across the Tasman Sea to Australia, and later through the Pacific to the United States of America.

The post-war slump hit the sailing ships hard and they were laid up or hulked in large numbers. *Rona* was no exception and was grounded in Wellington Harbour, New Zealand. In 1923 she was sold to the Adelaide Steamship Company, brought to Australia and converted to a coal hulk.

In 1930 there were over a hundred and twenty old sailing ships serving as coal hulks in Australia. By 1962, only *Rona* remained, docked and covered with coal dust. She was the last sailing ship in Australia. In 1968 her owners, Howard Smith Industries Pty Ltd., donated the ship to the National Trust of Australia (Victoria).

Since my visit to *Polly Woodside,* I received from Melbourne a coloured postcard of the historic barque, taken at dusk, and with pride of place in the Harbour Museum, under the National Trust of Australia (Victoria). The ship is now returned to her former glory and is open to the public for inspection.

In comparison, I also received a black-and-white postcard of *Polly Woodside* in commission under New Zealand ownership, as *Rona* in the early 1900s.

Sydney, the Magnetic City

On my arrival in Sydney, I came up against somewhere to stay. Hotels in the city were pricey and the ones in the lower bracket difficult to find. All I was offered was the Hampton Court on the Bayswater Road in King's Cross which was known as the red light district of Sydney. I was given a suite, complete with kitchen. The nearby Italian restaurant, *The Little Hut,* served my purpose for meals. Meanwhile 'the girls' were on the prowl!

Sydney in New South Wales is built on sandstone and is one of the most populous and sophisticated cities in the Commonwealth, strongly reflecting American influence, the hub of the South Pacific around Port Jackson.

The harbour has been claimed as the world's most beautiful deep-water anchorage; it is known to be full of sharks! A walk-about city, Sydney is bustling with life, supporting varied and colourful high spots with up-to-the-minute entertainment. But Sydney's smog was fast becoming the world's worst; it could even have the heaviest air pollution in the world according to the New South Wales Pollution Commission.

The opera house, known as the glittering giant, dominates the harbour. It takes up the whole of the tip of Bennelong Point, the flat promontory next to Sydney Cove and Circular Quay. The opera house has water on three of its four sides. On the fourth, landward, side lies the greenery of the Royal Botanic Gardens and Government House grounds. Many architects consider that the opera house has been given the finest site of any public building constructed in the country. It was originally a tram depot site.

The shore of Bennelong Point has been extended to allow a pathway for pedestrians and vehicles to be constructed around the opera house building, known as Broadwalk, where I met people of all nations.

The opera house itself consists of a huge concrete base, upon which have been placed three sets of roof systems. One set of roofs coves the concert hall, another the opera theatre, and the third and much smaller set the Bennelong restaurant.

Above both the concert hall and the opera theatre there are four shells placed in a row, forming both the roof and walls of a larger covered area. The shells of the concert area are larger than those of the opera theatre, and its auditorium is therefore bigger. The Bennelong Restaurant consists only of two main shells.

This great white pointed edifice took fourteen years to complete and was opened in October 1971 by H.M. Queen Elizabeth. Distinguished artistes from many countries consider it to be a great honour to perform in the opera house, and welcome invitations for symphony concerts through to jazz sessions.

It is a haul up the main steps to the buildings, said to be the largest exterior staircase in the world.

I was fortunate in being shown around Old Sydney by Mrs Frank Hobill-Cole of the Hospitality Committee of the Victoria League, whom I had met in Melbourne. Old Sydney was well worth seeing; it is a great family town and an old colony. It was interesting to wander down the old streets and by the market place, quenching our thirst in one of the old taverns.

From No. 6 Wharf, I took a two and a half hour harbour cruise showing the opera house and the harbour bridge in all their glory.

The people of Sydney are happy-go-lucky, friendly and exhilarating. They have an exuberance which they express in sport, politics and the arts.

While staying at Hampton Court, I spent a very pleasant evening in the suburbs with the brother of Frances, my good Samaritan from my trauma in Tangier in 1979.

My stay in Australia was all too short.

CHAPTER TWENTY-SEVEN

1980 – The Friendly Isles in the South Pacific

The Kingdom of Tonga consists of about 160 islands, many of them small and uninhabited, lying between eighteen and twenty-two degrees south of the equator, and about four hundred miles south-east of Fiji. The kingdom has a total land area of only 269 square miles, but it is divided into three main groups – Vava'u in the north, Ha'apai in the centre, and Tongatapu, meaning Sacred Tonga, in the south.

In January 1980 I boarded the P&O liner *Oriana* at Sydney Cove Passenger Terminal. We were bound for the tiny ancient Polynesian islands of Tonga, which lie just to the west of the International Date Line, and south of Samoa. On our arrival we were welcomed by the Tongan Police Band.

Tongatapu is a flat coral island about eighteen miles long and nine miles across at its widest extent. The capital, Nuku'alofa, is on the northern shore of Tongatapu. The town is small but charming, with public buildings and private houses set among flowers and shrubs, open green spaces and great cedar-like ovava trees, characteristic of Tonga. In fact, at Captain Cook's landing place stand the very same trees under which the famous explorer is alleged to have rested after anchoring the *Endeavour.* A monument was erected in 1970 to commemorate the landing two hundred years before.

Archaeologists claim that Tonga has been inhabited since the fifth century B.C. The present monarchy can trace its origin from the Yu'l Tonga who inhabited the kingdom more than a thousand years ago. It was first discovered in 1616, when the Dutch navigator Jacob Le Maire, arrived. They were followed by Tasman, Mallis, Cook, Bligh (the Mutiny on the *Bounty* occurred in Tongan waters) and in the 1820s by the first of the missionaries. The late and beloved Queen Salote and the present King Taufa'ahau Tupou IV are descendants of Tupou I who died in 1893 and was of the lineage of sacred kings who ruled from at least the tenth century.

The Tongans are a delightful race of people, frank, happy and self-reliant. The women are graceful and both men and women wear skirts called valas. Uniformly, they have a fine physique. Their health standards are better than other Pacific islanders, with modern medical hospital facilities. There is free medical attention from the island's own well-trained doctors. As a result of this health education and increasing adjustment to modern conditions, their housing has improved; the thatched roof, reed walled and earthen-floor houses are being replaced by small up-to-date cottages with glass windows and metal roofs.

A mixture of Fijian and Tongan blood, Tongans are the most progressive of Polynesian people. I saw no real poverty. Every Tongan has a farm of his own given by the kingdom, which prevents poverty and promotes equality, independence and is an effective system of social security in keeping with the dignity of free men. Tongans at sixteen can take up an allotment of seven and a half acres of country land, plus two fifths of an acre in a nearby village for his living quarters. No more than two hundred acres of land are ever leased to a European.

Education in Tonga is free. Every boy and girl is entered for elementary and advanced education in any of Tonga's government-supported schools. In native colleges boys grow all their own food on plantations.

The Tongan economy is mainly agricultural; the principal export crops are copra and bananas and, to a lesser degree, pineapples and water melons. There is only one factory, which produces dessicated coconut. The Tonga Construction Company employs a large number of local residents. The sea abounds in fish so the locals are great fishermen, one of their strangest methods being that of catching sharks by noosing them. There are plenty of turtles.

One of the chief industries is tuna fishing. Tongans grow bananas, yams, corn and tapu trees on the best land. Taro and tapioca do well on poor soil. Citrus fruits, melons and pineapple are excellent. Pandanus is grown for mats, sugar cane for thatched roofs and shrubs for scents and dyes.

After docking at Queen Salote Wharf, about two miles from the township, we took a bus ride to Onolei Beach to see various groups of ancient Polynesian dancing performed by men and women. The men wore banana thongs, their neck and waist garlanded. For a drum they used an old tin can. The women were dressed in pretty pink sun-dresses with black tapu trimming, and were also garlanded. Red feathers and shell combs adorned their hair. Sitting in a circle beside a Mina cave, we entered into the spirit of the occasion.

It was a Saturday and a holy day in Seventh Day Adventist Tonga and the Tongan people especially enjoy a feast.

A barbecue followed the dancing, with Tongan and European dishes. There was curry and rice, pork, paella, paw-paw, to name a few, and delicious tropical fruit juices. There were more dances with girls attired in straw skirts and men with long poles. Then the clouds burst and down came the rain! But the dancers happily carried on.

We were driven through coconut and banana plantations, past the royal palace and tombs. The Victorian white-framed palace and chapel were surrounded by massive Norfolk pines and sprawling lawns, which dominated the sea front. Construction of the palace was completed in 1867 and it has remained unchanged since 1882 when a second storey verandah was added and the royal chapel was built. The coronation of the kings and queens have since taken place there. We were not permitted to enter the palace grounds and a sentry was on duty. But we were allowed to take photographs of the Tongan royal residence from the walls that surrounded the grounds, which contained a giant scarred turtle which Captain Cook presented to a Tongan noble in 1775.

Near the centre of the town we came to the royal tomb, the burial place of Tongan royalty since 1895. The late Queen Salote is buried there.

Before returning to the ship we stopped at the Mala'e or park. Although there was no mass production of handicrafts in Tonga, we were able to see exhibitions of the manufacture of tapu, cloth made from bark that has been softened, pounded to paper thinness and pointed, basket weaving and kava making.

As we sailed away from this friendly island the Town Police Band was there again, fading us out with *Now is the hour for us to say goodbye!*

We were bound for the next island island group, Fiji.

A Day in Fiji

Fiji is a group of three hundred islands ranging from coral outcrops to lush atolls surrounded by golden sandy beaches. Among these are some larger islands with tranquil-flowing rivers running from island mountains to the sea.

We docked for twelve hours at Suva, the capital, on Viti Levu, the largest island. Recommended was a three-hour coach tour, seven miles from the port. We drove to the Fijian Orchid Cultural Centre, a place where we could best receive an introduction to the many attractions which Fiji has to offer – history, tradition, customs and wild life. The Orchid Island entertainers actually reside in the village of authentic thatched bures (houses). We were shown a replica of the chief's bure laid out and furnished as it was before Fiji became a British Colony in 1874. The scene, however, was dominated by an impressive heathen temple over fifty feet high, the first temple built for over a hundred years. In the interior we were told of Fiji's past with wars and cannibalistic practices of the last century, which sent shivers down my spine.

Fiji has the largest handicraft shop/boutique in the South Pacific with hand-painted dress materials made up on the spot. Fijian women were busy making baskets and pottery. On show in the grounds were sections dealing with Fiji's natural resources of timber, agriculture and rocks. The vegetation was lush with a most extensive collection of tropical plants and flowers, including exotic orchids; also plots of agricultural crops of coffee, tea, vanilla, etc. There were pet turtles, tame mongooses and snakes, the rare banded iguana, monkeys and colourful parrots. Fiji's newest mini aquarium had a picturesque display of marine life.

Fiji's greatest assets are her people; their happy nature captured us all. The entertainment group of women performed native folk-dancing while men in the background sang to the music of hollowed bamboo sticks.

The sacred ceremony, the Yaqona (pronounced Yangonal), is said to be as old as Fiji, and is taken very seriously by the Fijians. We were invited to attend this very special occasion, but photographs were only allowed prior to the ceremony.

Several men sat around a large bowl, called a tanoa. A rush mat was spread out in front of the men. At the opposite end of the floor two guests were invited to take part in the ceremony, sitting on a wooden seat. The ceremony began with the root of a variety of the pepper plant being ground in a mortar to which water was added; the gritty pieces of root were strained by passing the liquid through a bundle of vegetable fibre. The male guest was asked to clap his hands once, and the yaqona, on a small shell, was passed to him; he then had to clap his hands twice. The woman guest went through the same ritual, and the ceremony ended. Also known as kava, yaqona is non-alcoholic, but if drunk in any large quantity it can have a numbing effect. It is said to work wonders on one's love life!

We attended a gala night at the Hotel Isa Lei, built in the shape of a turtle. Dancing was to the Isa Lei Band; isa lei means welcome. A buffet supper consisted of Fijian, Indian and European dishes.

Two floor shows followed – Fijian meke, songs and group singing, together with a skilful blend of Polynesian dances with some artistes attired in brightly-coloured straw skirts and head-dresses. We drank bula talei, a mixture of gin, orange and lemon, topped up with sliced cucumber and a red cherry, decorated with a Fijian flower. Hot salted coconut made an appetising accompaniment. We ended up joining in a frolicking meke!

For island night on board ship, there was a rush at the dockside for the cheap straw skirts and garlands which were 'going for a song'.

Oriana sailed on to New Caledonian and our last port of call in the South Pacific Islands.

New Caledonia, the France of the South Pacific

New Caledonia is a little bit of France in the South Pacific and little English is spoken. The island was discovered by Captain Cook in 1774 and was annexed by the French in 1853; it has remained French overseas territory ever since.

This exotic and very French, large cigar-shaped island, with its elegant and well-dressed women, enticing night clubs, superb French food, chic French boutiques stocking the latest Paris creations, is a complete contrast to the islands of Tonga and Fiji which we had just visited.

The capital, Noumea, meaning 'island of light', is the second largest town in the South Pacific islands, and is on the south-west coast. The classic French cathedral of St Joseph, built in 1892, has some fine woodwork. Immediately behind is the Grotto of Our Lady of Lourdes built in 1935.

The streets of Noumea are laid out in neat squares. The centre of Noumea's life is traditionally the Place des Cocotiers, an open space with a small garden at one end.

The principal shopping area was around the central square between Rue de l'Alma and Rue de Verdue. French goods predominated, such as perfumes, scarves and pearl-shaped jewellery. All the best French wines were on sale. Caledonian products included carved beads. Prices were higher than I expected; this is on account of the cost of living there. The only cheap things were to be had at the licensed duty-free shops.

The people of Noumea are somewhat complex. The French women are chic. The

Melanesians are chocolate brown woolly-haired people, always smiling, who walk around bare-foot in floral frilly Mother Hubbard dresses.

I rubbed shoulders with a variety of nationalities – Polynesian, Malaysian, European, Vietnamese and Indonesian, to name a few. Colourful Javanese and Chinese costumes added to the spectrum.

New Caledonia's economy is based on its numerous mineral resources. The island is the second largest nickel producer in the world, and vast quantities of chrome, iron, manganese, cobalt, mercury, silver, lead and gold are believed to exist in the craggy valleys and turtle-backed ridges of the interior.

From the quay we took a drive into the countryside. Joining the highway we passed the nickel smelting works before heading towards the southern part of the island to see the pilgrim chapel at La Conception. Continuing through nickel-mining areas we went over the Col de Plus which had a decidedly lunar landscape.

The south coast was a contrasting setting with tropical vegetation and seaside surroundings where we enjoyed French pastries. A demonstration was given of the wearing of the manou, a piece of clothing worn by the natives.

After dinner on board, a tour was arranged to the Chateau Casino Royale, which took us through the city of Noumea, up Colline aux Gireaux for a view of Noumea township by night, and where our illuminated *Oriana* was berthed.

At the casino we were given five hundred francs in chips with which to play the tables. All the croupiers spoke English. The pace of the gambling was not such as to make first-timers feel out of it.

At midnight *Oriana* left her moorings and proceeded out of the harbour via Dumber Pasea, disembarking the pilot. We then set sail on a south-westerly course for Sydney.

CHAPTER TWENTY-EIGHT

1980 – New Zealand, the Land of the Long White Cloud

From Melbourne I booked a twelve-day 'Tiki' tour of New Zealand on the last lap of my journey back home to the UK. I landed at Christchurch, the largest city on South Island and known as the Garden City. Almost every house has its own garden and each year competitions are held for the best-kept garden.

Christchurch, the principal town of the Canterbury District, is considered to be the most English of all New Zealand's cities, centred on the elegant cathedral with its sixty-three metre spire and thirteen bells weighing just over six tons. From the balcony at the top of the tower there is a panoramic view of the city and mountains beyond for those prepared to climb the 133 steps to get there.

We were a mixed bag as regards ages, but our breezy driver/courier soon had us all in a get-together mood. After a night in Christchurch, we made our way southwards through the Canterbury Plain, a highly-productive mixed farming area. Over the twenty mile width of the plain with its millions of sheep, the scenery changed from the blue Pacific on one side to the snow-capped Alps on the west.

After an overnight stop, we set off inland via Gore and Lumsden, past the mountain range of Takitimu and across a dried-up river bed to the township of Te Anau sited on the eastern shore of the lake of the same name, the south's largest lake, the centre of the Fiordland National Park and the hub of many tourist attractions like the Te Anau caves, trout observatory and scenic flights over the mountains and glaciers.

The Southern Alps are home to the takahe and kakapo, two of the world's rarest birds. The national bird of New Zealand is the shy kiwi.

There was a delightful day's excursion from Te Anau to Milford Sound on the coast, via Cascades Creek and the Homer Tunnel which runs for a mile through the mountains; it has a single track and the direction of traffic flow alters each half hour. Milford Sound is one of a series of scenic fiords, which penetrate deeply into the western coast and is the only fiord catering for the overnight visitor with an excellent hotel.

We cruised from the sound's freshwater basin on to the deep, dark, still waters, out past Mitre Peak, rising 5,000 feet sheer out of the water, along the fiord towards the

Tasman Sea. Milford Sound is one of the most amazing waterways in the world and has to be seen to be believed; it is the grandest of the inlets of Fiordland National Park and an ancient glacier bed. The Bowen Falls, the Stirling Falls and many lesser cascades plunge down into the fiord sometimes bringing with them the dense growth of threes and undergrowth which cling to the sides of the sheer walls of the fiord. In season, red is superimposed on the green foliage when the scarlet rata and other flowering shrubs come into bloom. In wonder at all we had seen we returned the seventy-five miles to Te Anau.

Next morning we left the sparkling waters of Lake Te Anau to retrace our steps to Lumsden in order to reach Queenstown on Lake Wakatipu on a road that skirts part of Lake Wakatipu on the left and the Remarkables mountain range, which change colour three times a day, on our right. Queenstown is surely one of the most beautifully situated of towns, on a corner of this 'Z' shaped lake and looking down two arms of the lake.

A half-day excursion started with a nine mile launch cruise on the *Rau Maori steamer* across the lake to Walter Peak Sheep Station. The old homestead was sheltered by Walter Peak and set among lovely old trees and green willows. With several changes of ownership, the property was taken over in 1880 by the McKenzie family who farmed it for the next seventy-two years. Now the original homestead, the old colonel's house which was being restored when we were there, and the wool shed are all that remain of the old farm buildings.

We were welcomed by the present owners, John Reed and his family who, after tasty eats, gave a very informative talk on the history of the station and present-day farming methods. He took us round the farm where we saw sheep dogs working to whistles. Other sheep were grazing lazily on the slopes of the peak and a few reach the top. Rabbits roam the station in their thousands and are caught for their skins. We were shown two mating possums in their breeding pen; the dark pelts fetched as much as twenty-two New Zealand dollars each.

The station is actively farmed and has sixty-four thousand acres of land. Most of the mountainous country is impassable for motor vehicles. Despite this, the station has some six thousand Merino sheep and three thousand five hundred Hereford cattle.

Back on the Queenstown side of the lake we saw a live show of the best bred cattle displayed on a stage at the Cattledrome in Skippers Park, featuring tame rams, sheep shearing, wool spinning and working sheep dogs. There were jet boat and raft excursions on the lake and up the tributary streams. There is a chairlift to the summit of Coronet Peak, a popular ski resort. We could also take a gondola to the Skyline Chalet for a marvellous view over the lake and mountains.

Leaving Queenstown, we skirted the Frankton Arm which sticks out into the lake, and drove north through the old mining town of Arrowtown, with its avenue of English sycamore trees. On to Lindis Pass and McKenzie country, famous for its sheep lands and a shepherd of that name in the last century. We reached the highest of New Zealand's mountains, Mount Cook, where many climbers have lost their lives. We stayed at the Mount Cook Hotel; my big disappointment was the bad weather which cancelled a scenic flight by a little red ski plane which would have landed on the Tasman Glacier. Leaving mountainous country, we travelled back across the Canterbury Plains to Christchurch for an overnight stop.

Early next morning we set off for the two hundred mile journey to Picton and embarked on the steamer *Aratika* for the three hour crossing of the Cook Strait, one of the roughest in the world. The first part was on the calm waters of Queen Charlotte Sound, with memories of Captain Cook. Reaching the open sea of Cook Strait, we sailed on to Wellington.

There was time to have a glimpse of the city, passing the Houses of Parliament, and up Mount Victoria before journeying northward through farm land to Wanganui, rich in Maori history and known as the River City. On the way we called by arrangement at Duralyn Sheep Farm, owned for the past hundred years by the Gloyn family. An appetising barbecue awaited us, followed by a display of farming activities, with a performance by Maurice's sheep dogs rounding up the sheep to his command. We entered the sheep pens and I was photographed sitting on the back of a sheep!

The day after we were able to see an active volcano in the Tongariro National Park, beautiful Lake Taupo, the roaring Huka Falls and the Wairakei Geothermal Power Scheme.

We reached Rotorua, the commercial centre of the rapidly developing Central Bay of Plenty region, and noted for the Whakarewarewa Thermal Reserve, called Whaka by the locals. It has thermal open-air pools and splendid public and private bathing facilities. Most inviting were the old-fashioned Priest and Radium pools, divided into four separate pools, varying in temperature and built on the rumbling pumice bed. They were very invigorating.

Whaka is New Zealand's wonderland, seething with boiling mud pools and twenty metre high geysers. We were invited to see a nearby replica Maori village and a home of the nocturnal kiwi. Whaka is the Maori Arts Centre and Carving School, where men were engaged on wood carving. The Maori art of tattooing is virtually extinct.

An evening show at Tudor Towers, Government Gardens, was given by the Maoris. The concert was staged with ancient and modern songs, followed by dances performed by Maori poi dancers costumed in the traditional poi skirts and cloaks made from specially-treated native flax, spun by the Maoris. Of the Maori dances, the Haka, or war dance was the most impressive, but very gruesome for children, with the Maoris extending tongues and bulging eyes, gestures which Maori warriors used in bygone days to frighten their enemies.

Leaving Rotorua we visited Fairy Springs and Rainbow Springs to see the enormous trout and then crossed the Mamaku Plateau, saw a hydroelectric scheme and reached Waitomo to enter the glow-worm grotto.

Our last city was Auckland, New Zealand's largest, and our final overnight stop. With a morning in hand I boarded a bus to the quaint village of Parnell with shopping precincts and interesting shops to browse around. With the party break-up, I boarded the jetliner for my flight back to England.

New Zealand's Kiwi

On the flight home I thought of the kiwi, a bird which belongs to the order Apterygiformes, and is only found in New Zealand; it stands about twelve inches high and has a long tapering flexible bill with nostrils at its tip, longer on the female than in the male. The plumage of the male and female is alike; there is no tail, the bird is flightless and it feeds at night.

The kiwi is renowned for laying the largest egg for its size of any known bird, being about five by three inches and weighing a pound. Incubation of the one or two eggs takes eleven weeks and is mainly done by the male.

The kiwi's well-developed sense of smell is assumed to be an important factor in its search for food such as worms, grubs and berries.

There are three species of kiwi – the common kiwi in the North, South and Stewart Islands; the little spotted kiwi now found along the western side of the South Island; and the great spotted kiwi which occurs from Western Nelson to about mid-Westland.

The kiwi is a commonly used symbol for New Zealand, and New Zealanders are often referred to as Kiwis.

The kiwi population appears to be falling because of land development and so many of the birds are being killed and maimed by amateur possum trappers.

New Zealand's Tiki Jewel

This is a replica of a 'hei-tiki' or tiki, a neck pendant belonging essentially to the Maori people of New Zealand. A stylised human figure known as a tiki is found in most parts of Polynesia, but probably reached its finest form in New Zealand where the Maori people used the local jade, or nephrite, an extremely hard material. The making of a tiki developed over many years before reaching its ultimate highly-polished and semi-translucent form.

Nowadays the tiki is worn mainly by women and this led to suggestions that it is a fertility charm in the form of an embryo. There is a Maori authority for this supposition but, in fact, at the time when Captain Cook visited New Zealand the tiki was principally worn by men.

Tikis were handed down from one generation to another and became associated with the reverence for ancestors. They acquired great 'mana', or prestige, to such an extent that tribal wars were sometimes fought over their possession. Each tiki had a name and served as a symbol and reminder of the ancestors through whose hands it had passed.

CHAPTER TWENTY-NINE

1980 – The Charm of China

With the 1989 uprising of the Chinese students for democracy and the atrocities inflicted on the people, it is hard to visualise the country as I saw it in 1980.

I travelled from Beijing to Dalian (now called Shahe), Shanghai, Canton and Hong Kong and found China then a land of charm and beauty. Its gentle people welcomed the westerner in a shy but delightful way. They are a tall, lean, high cheek-boned race with small piercing eyes and an olive coloured skin, full of curiosity as we were with them. Our local guide in Beijing, charming Miss Chow Lee, won our hearts as she read our itinerary in broken English from her tiny notebook. At the end of the tour she gave to each member of our party a small gift. During our journey from Beijing to Canton, Mr Hun attended to our wants and looked after our welfare. At our final banquet in Canton he was overcome with the hospitality he received, but eventually rallied.

The Chinese are family-loving people, often to be seen in family groups on their day off, sauntering along the bund and in parks and gardens. The traditional baggy trousers of the men and women were in keeping with their way of life. In winter they don extra clothes under them to keep out the cold. Some women wore slacks and coloured tops with gloves in cold weather. The toddlers took my fancy, the girls in brightly coloured dresses, their hair often topped with big bows of coloured ribbon; the boys, with their chubby smiling faces and bright baggy trousers and tops, the tiny ones with a slit up the back of their trousers for when they are taken short. Wherever we went there was general clapping of hands, the Chinese form of greeting. At a primary school we watched children at their lessons and were permitted to walk around the classroom and see their work; an English lesson was in progress. Then the small girls entertained us with dainty dances, while the boys gave a sword dance. One six-year old child graciously announced each item.

Great Tiananmen Square, the scene of so much bloodshed in 1989, was swarming with cyclists pedalling their way to work; it was not easy to cross from one side to the other in and out of the bicycle wheels. At the sides of the square, grandmas were quietly wheeling their young charges in home-made bamboo baskets, while the mothers were at work.

A charming sight in the cities, especially in Shanghai where the population is so dense, was the traditional and graceful form of slow-moving exercises, Tai Si Qua. As we set out very early each morning on our tours, young and old were going through their rhythmical motions on street pavements, in parks and gardens, in fact anywhere where there was space. The exercises were treated very seriously and were performed oblivious to passers-by. The Chinese have carried out this ancient ritual for over a thousand years. There are about a hundred different postures with names such as 'crane spreads wings' and 'wave hands like a cloud'.

More evidence of the grace and charm of Chinese culture was to be found in the opera house with a myriad of brilliant coloured movement and sound. This ancient and refined art form brought together singers and dancers in perfect harmony to provide a spectacular demonstration of Chinese theatrical skills. The women's high-pitched voices mingled with the glorious costumes and exotic screen scenery, the traditional Chinese brass instruments were manned by six players, and the acrobats were amazing and daring.

There was a property man who took charge of the props and costumes on stage and who served mugs of tea and towels to the performing and perspiring artistes; he was supposed to be invisible. The plot of the drama was taken from the old Silk Road era, the origin of which dates back to the Han dynasty. Most of the audience were Chinese families with some of the men in blue caps. We appeared to be the only English.

Arts and crafts have always played a large part in the life of the Chinese. They are rich in variety and texture and renowned the world over for their delicate figurative workmanship and style. In the factories men and women were producing intricate ivory figures, fine lacquer and metal wares, exquisite woollen tapestries, unique water-colour scenes, dainty flower motifs, gold and silver ornaments, mahogany furniture, transfers designed on silk and the traditional Chinese lanterns.

In the Universal Friendship Stores there was some good class merchandise to buy and the delightful assistants carefully wrapped up our purchases. The payment of yuans travelled along overhead rails to the cash desk, similar to our department store systems of long ago. In the local stores we tried on the blue caps like the men were wearing, much to their amusement. The monetary unit is the yuan which may not be taken out of China; in 1980 it was worth about thirty pence.

Beijing's Imperial Palace has always been China's most imposing building, with graceful monolithic contours and the only existing example of an imperial palace in China. Known as the Forbidden City, it was the home of emperors in feudal times. It became the residency of government officials. The construction of the palace went through various stages. It was finally restored to its former glory by Emperor Quan Lung who lived in the palace with his empress, children, imperial concubines and servants of the household. No-one was allowed to enter the palace or grounds, or even touch the gates. The grounds have since been turned into a park for the general public.

The Summer Palace in Beijing stands in six hundred acres and is open to visitors. For four yuans, our party was invited to be photographed in imperial regalia. As a volunteer, I was dressed up by a Chinaman as the Dowager Empress Tzu Hsi, known as the Dragon Empress, or the Old Buddha, who, through her husband, then as regent and mother of emperors, ruled the people of China with a rod of iron. Enthroned on a regal chair, I was attired in a gorgeous creation of red, blue and gold satin, the sleeves of which almost reached the floor. On my head was placed a very heavy, but exquisite, blue and gold coronet studded with stones. The original is in Beijing's historical museum. As I balanced the head-dress precariously on my head, cameras clicked.

China's beauty is also depicted in the colourful gardens, especially the Mandarin Gardens in Suzhou, a short ride by train from Shanghai and situated on the Yangtze River. Mandarin means 'beautiful water'. The gardens are the foundation of the original willow pattern seen on our Chinese plates today. Glistening water with floating lilies encircled the gardens which were enhanced by dwarf rockeries and minute bridges. It was fascinating to stroll over them and meander along classical corridors with pretty picture windows, also to see the exotic flora backed by a tall pagoda. Some of the gardens had fascinating names, such as the Lingering Garden and the Humble Administrator's Garden. Built about 600 B.C. Suzhou, noted for its beautiful women, is one of the oldest of all cities between Beijing and Shanghai. It has become a thriving industrial town, but the old part still retains much of the flavour and charm of old China. The little cobbled streets and alleyways with white-washed houses grouped together add to Suzhou's elegance and magnetic attractiveness.

We were fortunate in having as our travel escort from London during the whole tour, Sarah Allan, a lecturer in Chinese at London University. Sarah is also co-editor of the 1980 informative illustrated book *China* published by Cassell, a signed copy of which she sent to me.

I shall long remember the charm of China and its people who have contributed so much of its past glories to the traveller from other lands.

CHAPTER THIRTY

1981 – The Whistling Island of Gomera

On a visit to Tenerife in the Canary Islands in 1981, I set off for the day to the Whistling Island of Gomera.

The islanders are renowned for their whistling language, the silbo, across the headlands, the only language of its kind in the world. Handed down from father to son, whistling has been the islanders' main form of communication, except at close range when Spanish is spoken. Since the arrival of the telephone, this unique tele-whistling is slowly dying out and becoming folklore. It is no longer taught in schools and has chiefly become a tourist attraction. A restaurant waiter will often give a demonstration.

Boarding the *Benchijigua* ferry, already packed with passengers and cargo, I found the upper deck was a vantage point from which to see the receding shoreline of Tenerife.

As we neared the island of Gomera, resembling a large pebble in the ocean, the port of San Sebastian came into view. The town has some seven thousand inhabitants and lies in a rich and leafy valley on the east of the island. It was here that Christopher Columbus made ready his ships and took on provisions and water for his voyages of discovery.

The Gothic Church of Our Lady of the Assumption, where the explorer prayed for guidance, is now a museum. The old red-bricked fortress, Torre del Conde, guarded the treasures shipped back from the Indies.

Gomera is swept by the winds of Africa. It is rich in vegetation in the valleys with a profusion of banana plantations and fields of tomatoes which are marketed overseas. Three potato crops grow yearly and sub-tropical fruits such as avocados, mangoes, pears, paw paw, grapes and oranges grow on the island. Tree heathers reach a hundred and fifty feet and there are fifty different kinds of Australian eucalyptus.

Because of the mountainous terrain, Gomera, a mushroom shaped island covering 146 square miles, is the only island in the archipelago without an airport; neighbouring islands are reached by an excellent ferry service. My crossing from South Tenerife to San Sebastian took forty minutes, at a cost of 1,850 pesetas for the return journey.

I boarded a bus for a drive up to the north of Gomera, and this turned out to be a hair-raising experience! Dozens of snake-like bends overlooked rugged cliffs, volcanic formations and a sharp coastline. The central highland of Garajonay rose to 4,500 feet above sea level. Dotted around the terraced and cultivated slopes were tiny snow-white settlements. Our drive was through some of the most characteristic zones of Gomera, including El Cedra, famous for its cedar groves. In the fishing village of Playa de Santiago, a delicious lunch was put on for us, with wine on the house.

Gomera is noted for its continual sunshine; rain falls for roughly forty-five days a year and then for only about two hours at a time. Parts of the island are therefore completely barren and, with agriculture the chief industry, problems arise because of the hard, dry, stony soil, causing terraced land to be cultivated by hand, machinery being useless.

The people of Gomera are a happy-go-lucky race and very industrious. Most of the workers are aged 16 to 18; the older ones tend to emigrate to other islands or to South America. In a handicraft shop there was a collection of ceramics, pottery, fine worked linen, colourful table mats, ponchos and pictures made of dried banana leaves.

The place to stay in Gomera is the government-run parador on the cliffs above San Sebastian. No expense was spared to make it an outstanding work of architecture and landscaping.

CHAPTER THIRTY-ONE

1981 – A Tour of Canada, Land of the Maple Leaf

In 1982, as a guest of a Canadian resident, my tour began in Ottawa, the capital. Ottawa was chosen as Canada's capital by Queen Victoria in 1857; it is a meeting point between English and French cultures in a natural setting of great beauty. Ottawa is the anglicised form of 'Outaoue' or 'Outaouaia', an Indian tribe trading with the French on the Ottawa river in the seventeenth century.

On my first morning in Canada I was dropped off in town by Margot, my hostess. 'There you are, Jane,' she said. 'You are on your own now for the day. See you tonight!' With a wave and a smile she was off. I was left to find my way around Ottawa. With Margot's address tucked away in my bag, I set off to explore the city.

'Where can I find a coffee house?' I enquired of a passer-by. 'Over there, at the National Arts Centre; if you take the elevator to the top, you'll find one, and with a lovely view,' she said, pointing to a large building. It was a fantastic outlook on a new world below me and from the eighth floor I walked down the various levels. Among them was the Board Room, galleries of contemporary art and the development of Canadian art from the eighteenth to the twentieth centuries. The ground floor contained an impressive Hiroshima video film.

On Parliament Hill is the Peace Tower, 302 feet high, but it was closed to visitors. Within the tower are the Memorial Chambers, a 53-bell carillon, a four face clock and observation platforms. On the well-manicured lawns in front of the tower, Mounties were marching in a traditional pageantry of colour and military precision of guards with pipes, drums, bear-skin head-dress and flashing red coats, known as the Governor General's Foot Guards and the Canadian Guard of Montreal. After a fine display, the full contingent marched smartly to the drill hall.

The Centennial Flame, marking the end of Canada's first century and the beginning of the second, was lit by Prime Minister Pearson on new year's eve 1967. Alberta natural gas feeds the flame amid the shields of the ten provinces and two territories that make up Canada today.

A snake-like queue had formed at the House of Commons; I was privileged to go to the front. The Senate of Canada is the Upper House of Parliament through which all legislation must pass before it becomes law. Its members, chosen in all ten provinces and the two territories, are appointed by the governor-general on the recommendation of the prime minister. The Senate is a vast edifice; the interior is colourful with the walls adorned with Canadian scenes and from the ceiling hangs a massive candelabra. At the back of the chamber is the Speaker's Gallery.

Ottawa in spring is a blaze of flowers, thanks to the Dutch people. As a token of appreciation for Canada's hospitality to the Dutch royal family during World War II, the government of Holland sends annually millions of flower bulbs to adorn parts of Canada.

After a week I left for Toronto railway station for my grand tour of Canada. The Canadian Pacific Railway train, known as *Via,* arrived from Montreal at midnight. This trans-continental train is Canada's most famous, with over twenty coaches, each with different names. Bound for Vancouver, in three days it covers 3,000 miles through Quebec, Ontario, Manitoba, Saskatchewan, Alberta and British Columbia. From the observation dome car I had awe-inspiring views of the Rocky Mountains, the ever-changing countryside, great lakes, vast prairies and vivid sunsets as the train threaded its way around hair-pin bends and sneaked through vast tunnels of rock. With the aid of my *Scenic Guide,* published by Bill Coe, and ex-conductor, I assessed the mileage and timing of the stations through which i passed – names like Medicine Hat, White River and Thunder Bay. My roomette in *Enterprise* coach had a pull-out bed and toilet facilities.

Going west, a three-hour stop was made at the historic prairie metropolis of Winnipeg, capital of Manitoba. On a walk-about in this important industrial and agricultural city where water melons grow in abundance, I found the shopping area, the museum, planetarium, legislative buildings and art gallery which are close to Grand Central Station. In grand style I toured the city on an authentic red double-decker London bus with Piccadilly proudly displayed on the front. We drove through the heart of a thriving and elegant part of Winnipeg with six thousand souls, pioneered by hardy settlers two hundred years ago. It is now a major financial centre and a vibrant and sophisticated friendly city. Flowing through it are the Red and Assoinboine rivers. We lunched on mv *River Rouge* which has been patronised by Princess Margaret.

Reboarding *Via,* we passed Moose Jaw and on through Saskatchewan to Calgary in Alberta. There we had a two-hour stop with a chance to see one of southern Alberta's major cities in the foothills of the Rockies. Calgary is Gaelic for 'clear running water' and is named after a bay on the Scottish Isle of Mull. Calgary was founded in 1883 when a contingent of North West Mounted Police, now called the Mounties, set up camp near the river junction. In 1894 it became a city and with the CPR opening, settlers were lured by cheap land. In 1914 oil was discovered in Turner Valley thirty miles south-west of the city.

One of Calgary's greatest attractions in July is the incredible Western Exhibition and Stampede billed as 'The Greatest Outside Show in the World', attracting visitors from everywhere.

From Calgary Tower near the station there were fabulous views and I had breakfast there in the restaurant. A walk to the down-town area led me to the centre of things.

Centre Street and the River Bow divide the city into quarters. Streets run north to south and avenues are east to west.

We were on our way again and in less than a hundred miles we pulled into Banff, a picturesque town in the Rockies and a favourite of Agatha Christie. It has only four thousand inhabitants and was to be my base for the next few days as recommended to me by a theatre-goer in London. Enclosed in a national park of great beauty, the town was overrun with curio gift shops. There were many old stone buildings. In the distance was the Banff Springs Hotel looking like a baronial-style castle in the trees, and I enjoyed lunch there; its predecessor, the first hotel came into being in 1888 as a five-storey wooden structure. The 1920s saw its expansion.

The history of the hotel is tightly linked with that of the Canadian Pacific Railway. Originally known as Siding Twenty, Banff was named by senior CPR director Lord Strathoona. The landscape reminded him greatly of his birthplace and homeland in Banffshire, Scotland. The hotel, however, was the brainchild of CPR president, William Cornelius Van Horne who saw the great potential of the area as a tourist resort to royal calibre guests who were travelling on the railway. The clientele would thus have the opportunity to rest and enjoy in style this mountain playground. The result of his dreams was the Banff Springs Hotel. The hotel had a ghost bell boy even when he was employed as an old man. When guests rang for service the old man would appear in uniform. The guests assumed he worked in the hotel. The story goes that a couple were locked in their room and the old man unlocked their door, but the real bell boy came to give service! At sundown a Scottish piper appears on the lawns playing his bagpipes before the lowering of the Canadian flag.

From down-town Banff I headed for 7,500 feet high Sulphur Mountain and took a gondola to the top, riding well above the tree tops. From the observation terraces there was a panoramic view all round.

The Upper National Springs are the beginning of Banff National Park and the springs are supposed to have cured Agatha Christie's arthritis.

Banff National Park is known as 'Bear Country'. It has been the home of the grizzly and black bears for thousands of years. We were the visitors! Looking for the bears was a novelty for us, but we were warned not to go near a bear, especially a cub. Their mothers, great hairy creatures, are dangerous to humans. They spend most of their time searching for food and they will eat almost anything. Campers' garbage bins have to be kept tightly closed as the bears associate food with humans. Black bears are in the park, but sanctuary for the grizzly is limited to western and northern ranges.

We made a tour of Banff and Lake Louise areas, taking in Johnston Canyon and Moraine Lake before arriving at Lake Louise via Kicking Horse Pass. Lake Louise is steeped in history; it was first seen many years ago by an Indian out hunting. From the top of a gondola, Lake Louise appears as an emerald in a gigantic setting of rock and ice. Overlooking the lake is a chateau set in these magnificent surroundings. This gracious chateau used to be patronised by long-term visitors who dined in style and always in evening dress. The chateau is now a haven for coach tours. To endeavour to retain some of its past glory, afternoon tea is served 'Victorian style' in the great drawing room, accompanied by a harpist. We lunched at the hotel. it was late August, but the restaurant and staff were dressed up for Christmas! Garlands hung around adding to the festive spirit. The hotel closes at the end of August for the winter months.

Leaving Banff, I booked a one-way bus ticket to the town of Jasper, which came into being when the Grand Trunk Pacific Railway was laying steel up the Athabasca River valley toward Yellowhead Pass. on the Jasper to Banff highway it lies astride the British Columbia/Alberta boundary between Banff and Jasper. It is famous for the Waoutik Columbia ice fields which are fascinating. With other adventurous tourists I booked a hair-raising ride on a snowcoach over the great ice fields – a priceless arctic experience on an ancient river of ice. Our driver manoevred his snocoach almost at a snail's pace along the treacherous icy road and on to the glacier. At one point there was over a thousand feet of ice under me! This is one of the most accessible ice fields in North America. With its glaciers the Columbia Ice Fields cover an area of over a hundred square miles, reaching down to two thousand feet above sea level.

Taking the Skenna train, I travelled to Prince Rupert on Kalen Island, facing one of the world's great natural harbours and the gateway to the north. On the train i met Marion from Santiago and we travelled together as far as Vancouver.

Prince Rupert was designed as the west coast terminus for the Canadian National Railway and it is now serving the most rapidly expanding port of the Pacific coast. The down-town area has beautiful parks, a museum housing a collection of minerals and marine life, and the traditional totem poles. A chairlift took me up two thousand feet in seven minutes and I saw rugged and fine stretches of the British Columbia coastline, as far as Queen Charlotte Islands which I was to pass en route to Vancouver.

It was while Marion and I had put up for the night at Prince Rupert Hotel that we discussed our itinerary. I was in the bathroom next morning when Marion called out, 'Jane, would you like to go to Alaska today?' I jumped at the idea and within minutes we were being rushed by taxi to the harbour. The steamer was about to sail, but was held up for us. I had to obtain some American dollars for the fare and promised to return the same day as I had no visa.

We docked at Ketchikan; with twelve hundred inhabitants it was reckoned to be the fourth largest town in Alaska. The longest day of the year begins at 5.05 a.m. and ends at 10.25 p.m. the shortest day has seven hours and ten minutes of daylight. Ketchikan is notorious for its rain though we did not see any. The average annual rainfall is 130 inches making it the wettest town on the North American continent.

'Five miles long, four blocks wide and two blocks up Dear Mountain' is how the Alaskans describe Ketchikan, the southernmost Alaskan city, and claimed it to be the salmon capital of the world.

Fishing, canning, cold storage, tourism, a lumber industry and mineral exploration are Alaska's economical backbone. Alaska is over twice the size of Texas and considered to be even more friendly! The word Ketchikan evolves from the name of an early Tingit Indian named Kitache who settled along the fish-rich shores of what is now Ketchikan Creek. Mining first lured folks to the town.

A bus took us from the docks around the town; the streets wound round historic and cultural layers of Ketchikan's past with old and new native arts works. A salmon hatchery was full of king and sobo salmon. A salmon dies after mating. Crossing Ketchikan Creek we came to unique Greek Street, a relic of a rough and tumble past, a wooden boulevard on pilings, once supporting a thriving red-light district where Madame, known as Dolly Arthur, had her sessions. Marion and I peered in the window as the show house, now a museum, was closed.

Edmund Street, the street of stairs, has 127 steps with a rewarding view at the top over the town and to Spruce Hill. Lamp-posts were adorned with floral baskets and along the thoroughfare were shops and eating houses, one of which we sampled. When the time came to leave Ketchikan we found our sailing had been cancelled due to a collision at sea. We left next morning by *Queen of the South* for Port Hardy, via the beautiful Queen Charlotte Islands, through the Hecate Strait and the Queen Charlotte Sound. The archipelago is also referred to as the Misty Islands as so much mist prevails over them added to their isolation and climate.

From Port Hardy, the most northern town of Vancouver Island where fishing is excellent, Marion and I booked a coach to Campbell River on the Strait of Georgia, hugging the coastline. Over to Vancouver City on the mainland, I said goodbye to my delightful travelling companion who left for Santiago. With a few days in hand I booked at an hotel where I met Helen, a Canadian resident, who gave me hospitality in her home. Leaving Vancouver, I ferried across to the regal city of Victoria which is known as a bit of old England. On Sunday afternoons, tea is served in the elegant CPR Empress Hotel with an orchestra playing old time tunes as in bygone days.

My last highlight before flying back to England was a visit to Butchart Gardens, one of Victoria's loveliest attractions. They were landscaped by Robert Butchart and his wife who donated the gardens to the nation. They occupy thirty-five acres of a 130 acre estate and are made out of the bleakness of an abandoned quarry, becoming one of the world's greatest horticultural triumphs. The gardens began as a hobby by the Butcharts who constantly expanded and improved them. They named their estate *Ben Venuto* and for half a century hundreds of thousands of visitors have found the true meaning of 'welcome'.

Robert Butchart was a pioneer in the manufacture of Portland cement in Canada and president of a cement company nearby. The quarry, its limestone exhausted, offended Mrs Butchart's sensitive feeling for beauty. She resolved to include it in her plans for landscaping their home grounds. Through the skilful mixture of rare and exotic shrubs, trees and plants, often collected by the Butcharts when abroad, the now world-famous sunken garden was created, together with English, Japanese and Italian gardens. It takes a whole day to explore the gardens. In 1953 floodlighting was installed to commemorate the fiftieth anniversary of the gardens.

CHAPTER THIRTY-TWO

1983 – South Africa re-visited

In 1983 I was back in South Africa, this time on a family visit, meeting up with my friend Ena, who lived previously in Cape Town, staying at the small township of Amanzimtoti, Toti for short, twenty-five kilometres from Durban.

Toti is situated on an elevated position off the beaten track and is a popular seaside resort of Natal. The beach stretches for miles but to reach it steep inclines have to be tackled. Coastguards guard the beaches as it is a dangerous coastline with very rough seas most of the year.

Apart from the beach, there is little of interest in Toti for the visitor, beyond a collection of small village-like shops and the odd hotel which cater for the moving population. For bird enthusiasts a sanctuary is the home for water fowl, domesticated peacocks and small animals such as the blue ulker, rabbits and tortoises.

My next venue was east of the Drakensberg Mountains, in Underberg, situated forty kilometres east of the Natal-Lesotho border, set in magnificent scenery. Joining a party in Durban, we set off by road early one morning to the Underberg for five days at the Bushmen's Nek Hotel, a time-share family complex some 240 kilometres from Durban and about 620 kilometres from Johannesburg.

We travelled via Botha Hill, the viewpoint of the impressive Valley of a Thousand Hills, and reached the provincial capital of Natal, Pietermaritzburg, named after two Voortrekker leaders, Piet Retiep and Gert Maritz. We drove via the spectacular Howick Falls and, taking the Merrivale Road, we reached the historic town of Bulwer, where the first settler arrived in 1866. Turning off the highway, we entered a side road on to a very rough and bumpy track, the only part of the entire route which was not tarmacked.

At Bushmen's Nek Hotel we were welcomed by our host and hostess, and porters were lined up to take charge of our cases. From my window I had a superb view of the Underberg area. From sunrise to sunset the mountains all around and so close to us took on varied hues of browns, greys and gold with a touch of red. There are very few mountains to match the charm of the Natal Drakensberg country.

The countryside, with its invigorating climate, is a walker's paradise, with grasslands, tumbling waterfalls and gurgling streams. The broad Ngwangwe river close to the hotel was full of trout skimming the waters. Apart from the local walks with members of our party, the management organised excursions to places of interest.

The High Adventure Tour, for four well shod adults, was a six-hour round trip in a four-wheel drive Land Rover and partly by foot to Bushmen's Nek Pass to see the bushmen's paintings. The drive was through the Sani Pass to the highest hotel in Africa at 9,400 feet and on to the mountain chalet for a picnic lunch. I did not participate!

Alternatively there were trips into Lesotho or to Himeville, or by the hotel jeep to the local stores for souvenirs. The children enjoyed the entertainment facilities laid on for them in the grounds. Especially popular was pony trekking.

The following verses were displayed on our breakfast tables on the day we left. They were written by Ada Krysiak for Bushmen's Nek Hotel and express the charm of the Underberg region, sentimentally known as The Berg.

THE BERG

The mist is settling on the mount,
The air is quiet and still;
A soft cloth forms upon its head,
So white serenely filled.
The rainy droplets dance around
Like fairies in the sun,
Their trail of silver beckons on
To join them in their fun.

The tall green mountains that I see,
As giants in the sky,
All rule the earth and sea below,
Their reign can never die.
It makes me think how great God is,
The Lord who made it all,
And the winding Berg with all its charms,
Re-echoes with its call.

I climb the slopes so fresh and green,
And step by step I see,
The marks of other men who've trod
This path of destiny.
And as I look from my high stand,
On earth and life below,
I feel as great as a mighty king,
Who's crushed his deadly foe.

The birds are hovering round my head,
A pretty sight to see,
Their silver wings a halo brings,
As bright as eternity.
The sunset peeps from its golden bed,
With colours all divine,
In shades of pastel, blue and red,
This heaven is only mine.

The mountains whisper in my ear,
I must return to earth,
And as I breathe the magic air,
I know just what it's worth.
And then I stand and look once more
At my faithful mountain friend;
Before I go, I breathe a prayer,
And then my steps descend.

CHAPTER THIRTY-THREE

1983 – By Ferry to Iceland

In June 1983 a high class ferry service began between Bremerhaven, Newcastle-upon-Tyne and Iceland's capital, Reykjavik. The vessel carried nine hundred passengers, was capable of sailing at twenty knots and was fitted with stabilisers. One of the chief attractions was the buffet which served a large variety of international dishes.

From Tyneside I boarded the mv *Edda* of 7,800 GRT on her maiden voyage from Bremerhaven to Reykjavik with two days at sea – a mini cruise in itself and one of the chief attractions. On board I met a charming Icelander on her way home. I visited her (Margaret) in her mother's bric-a-brac shop in the town.

Iceland, a small republic in the North Atlantic, was a new experience, an island of many contrasts with massive glaciers and ice-caps, rivers and lakes, mile after mile of fiords backed by majestic snow-capped mountains, spouting geysers, volcanoes and thermal activity.

There are no railways in Iceland. Coaches cater for the casual visitor along the 7,500 miles of roads, some of which were very bumpy.

Characteristics of the landscape are the many impressive waterfalls. Foremost is the Golden Waterfall at Gullfoss, which cascades down the hillside to the waters below, one of the most beautiful sights in the country.

A few miles from Gullfoss is a fascinating geyser area with numerous hot springs. Among them is the old geyser renowned for seven hundred years, but now dormant. The most active is the Great Geyser, which gave its name to hot springs all over the world; it erupts up to seventy feet every few minutes – a fantastic sight!

Thingvellir is the historical seat of the Icelandic Parliament, the Althing, established in 930 A.D., now an ancient ruin. Thingvellir is of special interest to geologists as two plates of the earth's crust are drifting apart on the site. The present parliament house is in Reykjavik's principal square, Austur Vellur.

Opposite the Althing is the statue of Jon Sigurosson, one of Iceland's national heroes (1811-79) who played an important part in helping the country to secure its own constitution. Also in the square is the nineteenth century Lutheran cathedral. There is only one Roman Catholic church in Iceland.

There are many types of places to stay in Iceland, from good hotels to sleeping bags in hostels. I stayed with a local family; the wife was an Icelander, the husband German.

A modern fleet of comfortable buses provide frequent service to every corner of the city, but most of the local sights can be reached on foot. There are no posters or hoardings to mar the town.

The National Museum and Art Gallery features Icelandic history and culture, and the Einar Jonsson Museum houses a collection of interesting sculpture with an Icelandic and mystical background. For lovers of art, the Asgrimur Jonsson Gallery has a excellent exhibition of paintings by one of Iceland's former leading artists, which he bequeathed to the nation.

A lift took me up to the look-out platform of the city's largest and most decorated church, Haligrimakirkja, where I had fine views from the tall steeple, a landmark for miles around.

A drive to the Kryauvik hot springs, twenty-two miles south of Reykjavik, was through extensive lava fields. This area makes it easy to understand why American astronauts trained here for the first landing on the moon.

The sandy coastline is the playground of seals, flanked by steep bird cliffs, where puffins and other sea birds were nesting. Bird life is prolific in Iceland; every year, millions of Arctic terns flock to the island from the South Pole. There is an absence of trees everywhere but, in sheltered places, there are low birchwoods. The highlands are mainly deserts of sand, stone and lava.

On a peninsula fifteen kilometres from the capital, stands the whitewashed, brown-roofed residence of the President of Iceland, Vigdis Finnbogadottir, the first woman to be elected president of a democratic country. Dotted around Bessastadir are whitewashed smaller houses and a church.

Taking an island trip by ferry from Reykjavik, we docked at picturesque small ports; during the eight-day voyage, the ferry stops at twenty-five ports. Other ferry excursions are from Reykjavik to the nearby island of Videy, once the residence of the Danish governor. A service also operates to Akranes, about one hour's sailing time, on the opposite side of the bay.

The Icelanders, most of whom speak English, are mainly descendants of settlers who arrived from Norway in 870-950 with their families and slaves. A sophisticated, industrious, honest, hospitable and friendly race, they are fond of social life and are welcoming to strangers. I received many kindnesses during my stay on the island. They are great readers and have a flair for languages. Bookshops were stacked with overseas literature and every home has its library. The population of Reykjavik has increased from three hundred in 1801 to over 76,000 in 1983.

Iceland is one of the cleanest countries in the world. The air is fresh and clear. Reykjavic is now a smokeless city. There are no polluting factory chimneys. The streets are free from garbage. The people are proud of their island and cultural heritage, especially the medieval sagas.

By tradition, a husband and wife have different surnames, because Iceland retains an old Nordic custom whereby when a woman marries she does not change her name.

Sons and daughters are given their father's christian name with the addition of *son* or *dottir* as their surname.

Eighty per cent of the homes are owner-occupied and some are like replicas of *Ideal Home* magazine. First they acquire a building site and when they have saved enough money they start to build their house. Geothermal heat is widely used for home heating in towns as well as for schools, swimming pools and greenhouses in rural areas.

The children are delightful and much prized by their parents. Educational standards have been high in Iceland since early times. There is compulsory education between the ages of seven and fifteen. Most continue their schooling after this, some reaching university standard. The university was founded in 1911 and has added several new languages to its curriculum by the building of new sites. The university also has students reading theology, law and commerce, medicine, philosophy, Icelandic studies and other subjects.

In their summer holidays the twelve to fifteen year-olds help with tourism. In the streets of the town boys were cheerfully calling out newspapers for sale. With six publications, more newsprint per had of population is sold than anywhere in the world. Six smiling newsboys posed for me to take a picture. Girls were busy keeping the parks and ornamental gardens in order, and planting sapling trees, while others sold ice cream. The four and five-year-olds spend their holidays on farms learning animal welfare.

Eating out in Iceland is costly and it is wise to shop around. For traditional Icelandic dishes, Hotel Borg in Parliament Square, served excellent smoked lamb (hangkjot) as the main course and much relished by Icelanders on Christmas Eve. The dairy product sayr, which is related to yoghurt and not unlike curdled milk, is refreshing. It is Iceland's most popular natural speciality and said to be good for the brain! An outsize bowl of this froth-like mixture was set before me in Hotel Borg and it was delicious. Tipping has always been frowned upon; a service charge is added to the bill which is sufficient.

Iceland's main industry is fishing, although tourism is not far behind. For a fishy meal I was recommended to the busy Kaffivagninn restaurant by the fishing harbour, open before sunrise till midnight. One of the restaurant's specialities is the nourishing seafood soup, the ingredients for which come fresh from the ocean every day. During the summer months freshly-caught lake trout is much prized on the menu.

A cheaper type of eating house, and much frequented by families, is the Svarta Pannan, by the waterfront. Here I enjoyed a snack lunch from a dainty basket of fish (or chicken) and chips. Wafers or small pancakes with whipped cream are often served with tea or coffee. Dried fish called hardfiskur or ryrlinger is available from stalls in the town.

Liquor is served in licensed houses. By law the island's brewed beer is weak. Those in the know used to bring their quota of eight tins of foreign beer from the mainland; since then this is not necessary as foreign brands are now imported. Home-brewed beer is banned in Iceland.

In the old town a liquor store stocked the popular local drink, Brennivin, known as Black Death; it was very potent! There are no public houses on the island but Friday night is drink night!

In the summer months when everyone is out of doors, television viewing is for three hours only, from eight to eleven o'clock at night. Thursday is church night when there is no viewing at all.

Icelandic woollen goods made up on the island are an important industry but they are expensive. The most popular were the hand-knitted sweaters in traditional patterns and colours, knitted up in mohair and New Zealand merino wool, very soft, lightweight and water-repellent. Sheepskin coats are especially in demand. For most of the summer sheep are grazed on the extensive meadows.

Among local souvenirs were lava ceramics and hand-made jewellery. My last purchase before boarding the ferry for England was a gift-package of Icelandic fish.

The oceanic climate has a mild temperature due to the Gulf Stream, but it can be humid and stormy, averaging 55 degrees Fahrenheit in the summer but dropping to 30 degrees in January, the coldest month. There are about eleven hundred hours of sunshine annually with rain on 216 days. The people laugh at the rain; they say that one minute they put up their umbrellas, the next they put them down. During the month of June when I was there, the weather was exceptionally mild.

Daylight is practically round the clock in June; I had no need to switch on the electric light in my room. Up to midnight during the summer months, the children take advantage of the long daylight hours. Close to my guest house little ones were playing happily outside their homes at midnight. At two o'clock in the morning I could read a newspaper without artificial light. But the winter nights are long with daylight in December only for three hours around noon. There is little crime on the island, but Iceland is said to have a high suicide rate.

Before I left Reykjavik, I was recommended to take a dip in one of the three geothermal open-air swimming pools. It was invigorating. Every child has to learn to swim and there was a school party with me, splashing around and learning to swim.

My return ferry to Newcastle-upon Tyne included a number of Icelandic wives, and some husbands, bound for Newcastle on a shopping spree.

CHAPTER THIRTY-FOUR

1984 – Island Hopping in the North Atlantic

In the summer of 1984, I ferried through the North Atlantic. From Aberdeen I booked a round trip of seven days to the Shetlands, Faroes, East Iceland and back via Denmark. Boarding the car/passenger P&O ferry to Lerwick, capital of the Shetlands, meant changing ferries for the Atlantic route, with a two or three hours stopover at each port. Passengers could island-hop and explore whichever island took their fancy.

The Shetlands

With five hundred square miles of rugged scenic countryside and coastline, the Shetland Islands are ideal for the seafarer who wants to be away from it all, especially appealing to fishermen and bird-watchers. For animal lovers, roaming the Shetland hills are herds of Shetland ponies, while on the beaches seals collect in large numbers.

Shetland's history goes back some three thousand five hundred years to the Stone Age. Evidence of this was at the Stone Age settlement and archaeological site of Jarlshof at Sumburgh Head, near Lerwick airport. This is one of the most important settlements in Britain where layer upon layer of remains date from the Bronze and Stone Ages.

At my first port of call, Lerwick, with its fine harbour, I had a day in hand before boarding the midnight ferry for the North Atlantic route. After parking my luggage at the sea terminal, I set off for my twenty-minute stretch along the docks and the fish market. On reaching the quaint little narrow streets and shops in the town, I sauntered down Commercial Street, the main thoroughfare.

At the top of Charlotte Street stands the elegant town hall, built in 1882. In the entrance hall colourful stained-glass windows depict scenes from Shetland's Viking past. In the magnificent and ornate ballroom the Scottish Women's Rural Institute display their handicrafts during the summer. Members were busily engaged in making up Shetland woollen garments by hand, demonstrating carding, spinning and knitting. The Shetlands are the islands of the knitting needle, a tradition going back decades and today the industry flourishes still. On the sales tables were finished woollens, books and Shetland-designed aprons. I was welcomed with refreshments and I met several of the organisers.

On the lower hill-head a modern building houses the library and museum which has a fine layout of a Viking settlement. Before oil came to the islands, Shetland was famous for fishing, knitwear and tweeds. Now the chief industries are agriculture, fish catching and pressing, knitwear and oil.

During World War II Shetland was a base for the Bus Operation, when small Norwegian fishing boats frequently crossed to occupied Norway to carry out sabotage on land, often returning with refugees. A memorial plaque on the slipway commemorates this.

Six miles from Lerwick is the picturesque village of Scalloway where stands the ruins of an old seventeenth century castle, which has memories for the islanders; it was from this fort that Earl Patrick Stewart operated his tyrannical rule over Shetland during the late sixteenth and early seventeenth centuries. In the nineteenth century, Scalloway grew into a thriving centre for fishing and is now popular with tourists. I was hoping to stay at Scalloway Hotel, but it was fully booked.

The Shetlands are Great Britain's furthest north islands but still controlled by Westminster and with English currency accepted in addition to Scotland's own notes. The oil industry accounts for almost a third of Shetland's economic activity.

The Faroe Islands

These islands consist of a cluster of some eighteen small islands. Occupation dates back to the Viking period when the first Scandinavians, in search of fresh fields, arrived and settled there and formed one of Europe's oldest parliaments. It is now a self-governing community under the Danish crown. Torshavn, the capital, is a small town with a few shops and a hotel, the Hafhis. A new one, Forayar, was due to open.

The Faroe Islands have a prohibition law regarding the consumption of spirits. It does not allow the serving of alcoholic drinks on public premises nor in restaurants. Guests are, however, permitted to take wine and beer into special rooms for consumption. Hotel Hafhis had several special rooms for rent for this purpose where guests were welcome to enjoy dinner with friends and business associates. There is a youth hostel in the town.

The sea birds are an integral part of the Faroe landscape, with thousands of gannets, puffins, guillemots and other species breeding on the steep mountain slopes.

The national bird is the oyster catcher, a tiny bird with a red beak and red feet. Sheep play an important part in the islands' industry, the wool being made up into the traditional Faroe sweaters that have become so popular down the generations.

Eastern Iceland

Sailing north-westwards we eventually reached the east coast of Iceland and the tiny fishing port with the long name of Seydisfjordur, the traffic centre in Eastern Iceland. Walking round this little hamlet, I came to a store with a large assortment of

Icelandic pullovers; I could not resist buying one. A bus service operates around the island and down to the city of Reykjavik.

Returning, mv *Norrona* called again at Torshavn in the Faroes, sailing down to Northern Denmark and the fishing village of Hanstholm. I went into a restaurant on the quay and found puffin as the main course on the menu – which I did not order! By the time we reboarded the ferry, the wind had increased, making it difficult to climb the gang-plank for the journey back to Aberdeen.

CHAPTER THIRTY-FIVE

1985 – Discovering Egypt

Ah, my beloved, fill the cup that cheers
Today, of past regrets and future fears –
Tomorrow, why tomorrow, I may be myself
With yesterday's sev'n thousand years.

Rubaiyat of Omar Khayyam

At Christmas 1985 I set off for a nine-day tour of Egypt with fifty travellers and an English guide to learn something of its seven thousand years of history.

After landing at Cairo we drove fifty miles to the Mena House Oberoi Hotel which stands in extensive grounds and has a view of the pyramids. It was built a hundred years ago as a royal lodge where kings and queens were entertained and was once a retreat for Sir Winston Churchill. The hotel has since been modernised and it is difficult to imagine that camels once trod past its portals. En route, we learned our first Arabic phrase – *Alsha Allah,* meaning 'If God so wills.'

Our journey through history began with a visit to the Egyptian Museum of Antiquities, containing the finest collection of Egyptian treasures, including those of King Tutankhamun.

The plateau of Giza, where I was pestered to take camel rides and to buy postcards, was dominated by the largest and most famous of Egypt's many pyramids built by King Cheops, 450 feet high and said to be built of a million blocks of limestone. Clutching torches visitors enter the eerie interior. Nearby I gazed at the enigmatic figure of the sphinx with a lion's body and human face, said to resemble King Chefhren, builder of the second temple; his son built the third temple. The sphinx and three pyramids are one of the seven wonders of the ancient world.

Near the pyramids is Papyrus House where we had a demonstration of papyrus reeds manufactured into paper – hence our word paper. In the adjoining gallery, I chose a hand painted papyrus picture, but found I had no Egyptian pounds. Between changing travellers' cheques in the hotel and visiting the museum, the money had vanished! An amusing incident at the hotel concerned Rona, one of our party, who gave the cloakroom attendant a twenty pound Egyptian note (£10) as a tip!

Victory Day is marked on 23rd December when everyone celebrates the seizure of the Suez Canal by Colonel Nasser in 1956. His sudden decision to take the canal came in the wake of the refusal by Britain and the USA to finance the building of the Aswan high dam. To avoid heavy traffic we made an early start to Islamic Cairo and the twelfth century Citadel of Saladin which dominates Cairo from the Mokattan Hills. The roads were already blocked with cars which the police were trying to control. At one point a flower-seller threaded his way in and out of the cars peddling his wares. On the northern heights of the citadel is the Alabaster Mosque whence every part of Cairo can be seen, distinguished by its fifty-two metre high dome and two minarets eighty-four metres from the courtyard.

As a contrast we visited the Khan al Khalili bazaar, one of the greatest of oriental bazaars. We strolled through its precincts where a great variety of brassware was for sale.

Through old Cairo, we reached the Roman Fortress of Babylon with the Coptic Cross which resembles the Maltese Cross, symbol of the Trinity.

Seventy per cent of Cairo's population are fellaheen, or peasants, who have resettled from the countryside. In rural areas the fellaheen live like their ancestors did centuries ago, amidst ramshackle donkey carts and ancient water wheels. Scattered throughout the country are the Copts, direct descendants of the ancient Egyptians. Today the Copts, who make up about fourteen per cent of the country's population, practise a form of Christianity established by St Mark in Alexandria, and use their own language for liturgical purposes. About eighty-five per cent of the people are Sunni Muslim. The European, Levantine, Turkish and Jewish minorities, that played a significant commercial and political role in medieval times, now constitute less than one per cent of Egypt's population.

A picturesque sight along the Nile banks was women squatting close to the water's edge washing clothes as centuries ago. Others were drawing water from the Nile, irrespective of pollution.

The old ways of keeping houses cool and private was by means of screens which covered windows and balconies from strong sun; owners could see out without being seen from outside. Some screens still exist on older types of houses. In the streets, women jostled along in full-length colourful gowns with swishing skirts, while others wore the traditional long gowns with the lower part of their faces covered. The men sauntered in long white or blue gowns.

Leaving Mena House Oberoi Hotel we boarded the overnight train for Luxor, one of Egypt's delightful winter resorts. We stayed for two days at the Jolie Fille Hotel in lush surroundings.

Historical Luxor, with its two great temples, Luxor and Karnak, is at the heart of the fertile Nile Valley on the east bank of the Nile. Karnak is the more important temple, but Luxor has a unique collection of Egyptian temples and tombs of the Pharaonic kings and nobles. The walls of the monuments of the ancient Egyptians have given expression to their great talent and skill in inscriptions, sculptures and portraits which have become museum pieces.

At the Nile quay, we were shown the markings indicating the level of the Nile floods. A road led to Karnak Temple flanked on each side by an avenue of rams and the figure of Rameses II. On the left was a courtyard with a small three-roomed temple, the first ever example of the basilica-shape. Beneath the temple was housed the sacred boats of the Thebian Trinity.

Reaching the Karnak Temple and passing through two pylons, we came to the great hall with 132 columns. One of the obelisks was erected by Queen Hatshepsut; this remarkable woman set the obelisk, a monolithic shaft, in honour of Amun, god of Thebes. The inscription read that the queen covered the obelisk top with gold. Standing two metres high, its estimated weight is thirty-two tons.

A great spectacle of Karnak Temple is the presentation of the Son et Lumiere which produces an inspiring and romantic atmosphere and recalls events of ancient history. On a moonlit night we followed the crowds shuffle-fashion into the interior, gazing in awe at the illuminated sections of the temple with its gigantic pillars – a dramatic experience under such magnificent conditions. We were welcomed by loudspeaker and, as we followed the lights, a voice related the story of this great edifice. Gradually we reached the vantage point facing the auditorium and the sacred lake. From total darkness the area was again floodlit, casting shadows on the skyline.

Travelling a hundred and twenty miles by road we arrived at Aswan and the Aman Sheraton Village Hotel. Aswan is an ideal winter resort, a haven of peace in a delightful climate and popular with invalids. Lying at the north of Lake Nasser, Aswan is the gateway to Africa and an important trading centre, combining the past with the present. Once called Swana, meaning market, it was an important ivory centre. It was also known as Abwa, Greek for elephant.

We set sail by felucca to the west bank of the Nile to the burial place of the Aga Khan. The mausoleum has a shrine of solid marble. A bronze door revealed the tomb open to the sky. The white sarcophagus was covered with Arabic script. At the head was a small vase holding one red rose. When the Begum is in residence at her white villa, she places a red rose every day on the tomb. Sailing on we came to Kitchener's Island, once the property of Lord Kitchener. The island is now a botanical public garden. It is also named Elephantine and is the longest-inhabited island in Aswan, with an abundance of flora and relics of ancient temples.

We viewed the old dam which was constructed 1898 to 1902, and then continued to the high dam. Construction here started in 1960 and some 35,000 Egyptian workmen laboured on this site until completion some ten years later. When it was finished it became the largest rock-filled dam in the world. The dam is two miles across the top and 364 feet high. In addition to regulating the flow of the Nile, the dam has increased Egypt's arable land and her output from quarries that produced stone for the temples, obelisks and shrines. We were to see these quarries later.

The 27th December was a special day when I flew with some of our party to Abu Simbel to see the temples of Rameses II and his Hittite wife. The monuments were built during his long reign from 1292 to 1225 B.C. The reader will recall the lifting of the two temples in 1962 when they were threatened by the rising waters of Lake Nasser. The United Nations helped with funding the £58 million that it cost to move the temples two hundred metres to higher ground. The temples had been hewn into the solid rock and the moving operation involved cutting and numbering two thousand pieces of rock each weighing up to forty tons before rebuilding at a higher level. The temples still retain the old watermark where the flooded Nile seeped up. It was a magnificent feat of engineering. Eventually eleven temples were moved. The smaller Temple of Nefrere, north of the Great Temple, was built in homage to the Hathor, goddess of love and beauty. On the site is a plaque relating the removal of the temples.

Back in Aswan, I relaxed on a sunset sail while boatmen tended their boats. After an overnight stop at the El Salam Hyatt Hotel we flew back to Heathrow.

CHAPTER THIRTY-SIX

1986 – The Norwegian Fiords

Cruising three thousand miles on P&O's *Canberra* from Southampton in June 1986 to Oslo, Andalsnes, Trondheim, Narvik and Bergen, was a leisurely experience with impressive scenery, from rugged North Cape to the sunny south. In between are many islands and skerries protecting the sailing channel. My companion was Freda, of *Strathnavar* days.

For sixty miles before the ship reached Oslo her path led through the beautiful Oslo fiord, much prized by the Norwegians, though it does not compare in grandeur with other fiords on the western coast, although it has a special charm of its own.

In Oslo Harbour, backed by green hills, a string of yachts added colour to the scene. On the water, boat owners spouted water cannons to welcome us. The Norwegian merchant fleet is one of the biggest and most modern in the world with an average age of the vessels of less than five years. A large percentage is tankers. The fleet, although manned by only about forty-five thousand seamen, accounts for a substantial part of the national income. The Norwegians call themselves the freightermen of the world.

Oslo is a widely spread capital, much of it in forests. In winter it is partially covered with snow when sledges and dogs are used to get about.

With a day in port a tour was arranged to Bygdoy to see the Viking ships and Kon Tiki, of particular interest to marine enthusiasts. Leaving the quayside, we drove through the city centre with its wide cedar-lined streets, passing the parliament building, the national theatre and the elegant royal palace. We continued through the suburban villa areas to Frogner Park which contains a mass of sculptures by Gustav Vigeland, before reaching the Bygdoy peninsula, originally owned by the king. The attractive houses, partially laid out as a museum area, were picturesque and there were three original Viking ships about 1100 years old on view at their moorings. The Oseburg was used in the funeral of a queen and the Gokstad ship was built to cross the Atlantic. Balconies surround the area so we were able to admire at close quarters the amazing craftsmanship of the early boatbuilders and seafarers.

The Kon Tiki Museum, in complete contrast, holds the raft of bales which Thor Heyerdahl and five companions sailed 4,300 miles across the Pacific Ocean from Peru to Polynesia. Also on show was the papyrus boat, Ra II, in which Thor crossed the Atlantic in 1970.

Cruising on we anchored off Andalsnes, a popular resort with painted houses giving a picture postcard charm, enhanced by the backdrop of the surrounding mountains. The air is pure, clean and invigorating.

A thirty-five mile coach tour took us up the Trollstigheim Pass and back through the Romsdalen Valley. As we ascended higher and higher past such mountains as the 5,000 foot Romsdalshorn and by a series of eleven stupendous hairpin bends, we reached the land of glaciers and eternal ice and the Trollstigheim Restaurant for refreshments. Nearby was the magnificent giant's cauldron. We returned past a hydroelectric power station, built three hundred metres into the mountain, and some of the world's most difficult climbing routes. On one side of the River Rauma lies the farm *Fiva* owned by the English Davenport family for several generations.

Sailing on to Trondheim, one of Norway's oldest and most delightful cities, we reached the quay by launch. It was a very cold and rainy day but hot snacks awaited us. Remarking on the weather, a local sailor said, 'It's red 'ot in Narvik!' We drove through the main business section to the cathedral, a twelfth century Gothic edifice, the second largest medieval building in Europe. Here seven kings and three queens were crowned and ten kings and most archbishops are buried. The Folk Museum in Syverresborg is Trondheim's museum of urban and rural culture.

Crossing the Arctic Circle was a special day for me, my eightieth birthday. As is traditional in Norwegian waters, King Neptune and his court appeared on board to welcome *Canberra* into the Arctic Circle, when there was much laughter and splashing into the pool from the greasy pole. The area north of the Arctic Circle is known as the Land of the Midnight Sun, a great attraction for the visitor. At midnight we all appeared on deck to see the phenomenon of the sunset and sunrise following each other almost simultaneously.

Narvik harbour, built in 1901, owes its existence, and the bombardment during the last war, to the fact that it is the port for the iron ore brought by rail across the border from Sweden. It has been rebuilt and is now a busy place with cargo ships of many nations loading their holds with the essential ore.

Passing through Narvik, a modern and distinctive town, we visited the iron ore shipping plant and the war museum. The city park contained rows of white crosses marking the graves of British, French, Polish and Norwegian servicemen who fell when the allies recaptured the town briefly in 1940 in the first major setback of the war for the Germans.

On 23rd June I joined a tour to Abisko in Swedish Lapland, by special train, on the ore-carrying Ofoten railway system, a project which required great skill to design and carry through. Many workmen died through accidents. The cook for the railway builders, the Black Bear as she was affectionately called, was noted for her excellent cooking; through her beauty and charm she became a legend. She died at the age of twenty-two, through a fight with a man. She was buried not far from the spot.

Setting off with macs and umbrellas, we boarded the train with already a splendid view of the mountains. Climbing up to the plateau, 1600 feet up, we reached the last station on the Norwegian side and crossed the border into Sweden for Lapland. A rocky, barren area, it is noted specially for salmon fishing, shooting and skiing. The line ran along by a lake and to the tourist station, our venue for lunch of reindeer meat. Abisko is one of the most popular resorts in Lapland and we had time to survey the surroundings.

Our return journey was by coach. A stop was made close to where Yugoslavians were shot by the Germans. A cemetery contained thirty-four British servicemen among eighteen hundred graves, including those of forty aircraft women and a hundred French.

The most beautiful section of the Norwegian fiords is undoubtedly the scenic Geiranger Fiord, along which *Canberra* slowly steamed. From the deck ships looked like toy boats on the water. Sunlight played on tumbling waterfalls, like the Seven Sisters and Bridal Veil, with fine spray in all the colours of the rainbow.

Through this great waterway there were times when *Canberra* was almost hemmed in a channel with little space for this great liner to turn round. Hanging precariously on the steep mountain slopes were little hamlets and farms, now mostly deserted, in this stunningly beautiful part of the fiords. Many tales are told of a life of toil when the people were cut off from the outside world for most of the year. Built close to the water's edge, the remaining occupied hamlets and farms still cultivate their tiny plots, assisted by children who have to be tethered, like animals, to prevent them from falling into the fiords.

Bergen is a city which seems for ever perched on the edge of adventure; it was once an oil haven, but this industry declined over the years and the image of Bergen has changed to fish farming. Bergen sits in the crook between the mountains and the sea, a fascinating mixture of old and new, a city set at the head of Norway's glorious fiord country. The people call themselves Bergeneres and, although Oslo is the capital, they like to think Bergen is the most important city in Norway.

In a temperature of 81 degrees Fahrenheit, though Bergen is noted for its rain, we set out on a tour of the city, the second largest city of Norway, and an important commercial and shopping centre. Some of its buildings date from the thirteenth century. Driving along the waterfront we passed the fishmarket and flower stalls, and on to the old and new parts of the city on our way to Teoldhaugen five miles distant.

The Hill of Trolls was the home of Norway's most distinguished composer, Edward Grieg, where he lived and worked. Nina, his wife, assisted him with his manuscripts and died at the age of ninety-two. Among the musician's meticulously preserved possessions are his spectacles, lying just where he left them, together with an open book. In the hall hangs his hat and coat.

In the neighbouring village of Fantfitt is a superb example of a stave church, dating from the middle of the twelfth century. It looked rather like a Chinese pagoda and contains no metal of any sort, not even a nail. In the grounds was an early medieval stone cross from Tjora Sols, Rogaland, possibly erected in the early years of Christianity in Norway before churches were built.

On the return voyage *Canberra* passed through the North Sea east of the Ekofisk oil field before entering the Strait of Dover for Southampton.

CHAPTER THIRTY-SEVEN

1987 – On Board Queen Elizabeth II to New York, Bermuda and Martha's Vineyard

Sunday, 24th July was embarkation day for Cunard's *QE2* at Southampton. Due to a technical hitch with propellors, the liner had been delayed in Gibraltar so we did not leave until the following day. The cruise to New York, Bermuda and Martha's Vineyard Island was shortened by a day. About 1750 passengers had their sailing times delayed, with overnight stays in and around Southampton.

At the terminal next morning there was chaos until we were all sorted out. As we boarded the liner each passenger was caught by the ship's photographer for a 'welcome on board' photograph.

At exactly 4.45 pm 'the hotel left town', as *QE2* put it, to the accompaniment of the ship's band.

My first day out was spent wandering around this vast 65,000 ton liner after unpacking. My cabin was adorned with flowers from Thomas Cook. For four days I lapped up the luxury of this floating hotel with entertainment round the clock for all ages. At the fancy dress parade I came away with a prize for *My Fair Lady QE2!*

As we neared New York, we prepared to disembark, while the ship's personnel were busy arranging to take on more passengers for Bermuda and Martha's Vineyard.

At 7 am *QE2* was in the Hudson River and sailed by the Statue of Liberty. Slowly we manouvred off Pier 90 with three tugs escorting us into the berth. On the small television in my cabin, I was able to watch this procedure. Half an hour elapsed before the liner turned round to enter her berth, a two-storey building that juts out more than a thousand feet into the Hudson River. I then saw the flag hoisted aft.

A Tour of New York

Skipping breakfast, I joined a party for a complimentary tour of Manhatten by coach, escorted by the Cunard ATI tour director. As we left the passenger terminal we made for the harbour to view the 152 foot figure of the Statue of Liberty on Liberty Island and now a national monument.

West of Broadway, from 14th Street, we arrived at Greenwich Village to take pictures of the quaint old houses which sheltered many noted artists and writers over the years. The streets around Broadway are now lined with craft and curio shops and restaurants. ΔNew York's Chinatown, which has been in existence for over a hundred years, was a hive of activity, resembling the side streets of Hong Kong. Shop windows were packed with Chinese junk.

From 47th Street, close to Fifth Avenue, we strolled by the Rockefeller Centre which was a mass of flowers making a photographic scene with the flags of all nations. The world's largest privately owned business and entertainment complex, its sunken plaza was full of coloured umbrellas under which people had gathered for refreshments.

We stopped at Times Square, intersected by Broadway, known as the 'Great White Way' on account of the brilliantly illuminated neon signs at night, the centre of the theatrical world with numerous theatres and night clubs.

Several landmarks were familiar to me from my previous visit while my Greek freighter was in port for a day en route for Japan in 1970. The fare on the Staten Island ferry was five cents; now it had gone up to twenty-five cents. As we neared Manhatten, I remembered seeing the Chase Manhatten Bank on fire on the previous occasion.

I well remember ascending the Empire State Building in 1970. By 1987, the twin tours of the World Trade Centre had overtaken it with one hundred and ten storeys. I also remembered Macy's, the great department store with one hundred and fifty departments under one roof. Walking round Manhattan in earlier days created no problem. Today, it is unwise to go on foot.

To wind up the morning, lunch had been booked for us at the Waldorf Astoria Hotel in Park Avenue. A luxury buffet was laid on for us before we had to return to the ship.

Bermuda, the English Isle

Sailing by a bunch of straggling islands, some uninhabited, we entered Bermuda, so very English, yet the archipelago is a neighbour of the USA. Lying less than six hundred miles off the coast of the state of North Carolina, the islands have a total area of less than twenty-one square miles.

In 1501 the Spanish explorer Juan Bermude was shipwrecked on these unknown islands in the Atlantic Ocean; he could not have been impressed with what he saw as he did not claim them as Spanish. In 1609 British Admiral Sir George Somers, shipwrecked on the reefs in his ship *Sea Venture* while on a discovery mission, saw the islands' potential. Staking his claim, he hoisted the British flag and called the islands Bermuda after the Spanish explorer though they are also known as Somers Islands. Today, Bermuda is Great Britain's oldest colony.

In the early 1900s Bermuda traded in farming. Onions and potatoes were sent to New York markets in small boats in heavy seas. On the return voyage the people of New York were encouraged to act as ballast, and so tourism came into being. Today these sub-tropical islands have half a million visitors each year.

Through market trading the onion was much prized and became a status symbol, one of the islands' important vegetables extensively used in cooking and depicted on tourists' souvenirs.

Much evidence of the British influence in Bermuda is in its churches with an Anglican church in every one of the nine parishes; there are also a Methodist church, two Presbyterian and a church of Scotland. As our liner *QE2* anchored off Hamilton Harbour, I could see the square tower of the Gothic Roman Catholic Cathedral.

The Bermuda Regiment parades on formal occasions during the year in ceremonial dress. The smiling bobbies, with their shiny helmets, have an English air; they also have a traditional style of their own with their navy-blue Bermudan shorts. At the corner of Front and Queen Streets, a traffic cop stands directing traffic from a cage-like covered platform.

Shopping in Hamilton is a pleasure, with helpful assistants, but the prices are high. The best bargains are English woollens, Irish and Scottish tweeds, Italian silks, French perfumes, Swiss watches, Danish silver and, of course, Bermudan shorts which have crept into the dress of residents and visitors. The Bermudan dollar is pegged to the US dollar on an equal basis.

Growing in both quality and quantity are the genuine Bermudan products, identified by a designed sticker sign. In the jewellery line, the island bird emblem, the longtail, is outstanding in a fourteen carat pendant made in Bermuda. Longtails are seen flying around the island. On the restaurant tables Outerbridge's sherry peppers are popular; a few drops in soups and drinks add flavour. Shops sell gift packs of four sauces – sherry peppers, hot mustard sauce, rum peppers and Bloody Mary fix, which is a Bermudan tradition made to a secret recipe. A gold liqueur as an after dinner drink is made from ripe loquats. The smooth, full-flavoured Black Seal Rum is the only authentic Bermuda black rum. Bermuda is also noted for its cedarware, shell jewellery, pottery, fashions, record players and paintings by local artists.

Outstanding in the perfume line are the lily perfumes made from tropical flowers. Natural essences include oleander, Easter lily, jasmine, sweet pea, passion flower and frangipani. there are after-shave perfumes for men. On the Harrington Sound tour we were taken to the lily perfume factory set in a charming cedar-beamed cottage standing in six acres of garden.

For a look at Bermuda's night life, we were driven along dark, quiet country lanes to Devonshire parish. The only sound of life was the orchestration of Bermuda's tiny whistling tree frogs; the only visible lights were from the country houses. Our destination was Clay House Inn, which was decked out in coloured lights. The stage set contained a steel Trinidadian band. On shining red-painted garbage bins, men in red and white costumes rapped away lively numbers on these 'drums' producing fantastic excerpts from well-known shows. Artists, in dashing outfits, twisted and turned in a snake-like fashion. The audience was invited to join in. As a volunteer, I was carried away with the atmosphere, and came away with a record of the steel band show. The Hamilton people rise early with shops doing a brisk trade, while the young at heart career around the island on hired tiny mopeds or scooters. Until 1948 the only cars allowed were those used by the government or municipalities. Even now, only one car is allowed to each family. The horse-drawn carriages, topped with a white canopy, are popular with visitors. Bermudans drive on the left.

With an American passenger, Betty Sheldon of New Jersey, I boarded an eleven-foot motor sailing boat for a three-hour aquatic tour. The highlight was Hartley's Underworld of deep-sea fish and coral, from a glass-bottomed boat.

We cruised into tranquil seaweed waters, swaying palms, white-washed houses and striking pink coral beaches; the most famous of all Bermuda's beaches is Horseshoe Bay, a sweeping sandy stretch in the shape of its name. The island has an equable climate, annually averaging 70 degrees Fahrenheit. Rain is spread spasmodically over the year, but the island is subject to high humidity.

Passing Spanish Point, we reached Ireland Island, and the British naval base, entering Sandys Parish with the Maritime Museum, once the governor's residence, the Arts Centre, the old prison, Fort Scour and Mangrove Bay. We transferred into a glass-bottomed boat anchored in deep waters. Shoals of fish were visible – bream, red-snapper, angel and parrot fish, and large lumps of coral. We passed the smallest drawbridge in the world, possibly the most photographed, just wide enough to let the spar of a sailboat pass through.

We re-crossed the Great Sound as we cruised back to Hamilton Harbour. Ashore there were many eating houses. The Lobster Pot looked inviting; inside was a tank full of live lobsters. I settled for the local hearty broth-like dish of chowday soup, laced with the traditional black rum, to which had been added sherry pepper sauce.

Our visit to Bermuda was brief and we set sail for the slow calm atmosphere of Martha's Vineyard, one of America's vacation spots.

Martha's Vineyard

Stepping ashore on this island of peace and tranquillity, it is hard to visualise it was once a busy whaling station, but is now the home of artists, writers and musicians. It is at the western side of Nantucket Sound off southern Massachusetts.

In 1602, the queen of England sent Bartholomew Gosnold to survey this unknown island; he named it Martha after his youngest daughter, and Vineyard for the wild grapes growing there.

Three hundred and fifty years ago, white settlers claimed the island but they had not reckoned with a Wampanong Indian community they found living there. An ordained pastor saw to it that no land was taken from the Indians without fair payment and consent. In exchange, the Indians taught the settlers the whaling industry, but the American Civil War put an end to the golden age of whaling. Ships on the high seas were captured by the Confederate navy. Others were caught up in the harbour. Either way it was financial ruin for the shipowners and the island.

With the disappearance of the whaling economy, Martha's Vineyard became a summer resort and a vacation campaign was promoted far and wide so that soon liners were docking regularly there.

On an August morning in 1987, the *QE2* docked off Oak Bluff's harbour which was once a swamp and was opened up at the turn of the century; it is now a great yachting centre. Dockside Market Place was thronged with visitors roaming the distinctive little shops. Before I explored this unique township, Mad Martha's Ice Cream Parlour caught my eye.

On the island of Martha's Vineyard, visitors can choose from a selection of Christmas-orientated activities beginning at the weekend nearest to 12th December. It seemed odd in the summer to be wandering around a store called *Christmas Cottage* crammed with festive decorations and novelties.

One of the chief town attractions are the Gothic gingerbread cottages in avenues. The owner of the Pearl Lagoon store, selling prairie oysters in attractive shells, directed me, 'One block and a half away, through the arcade building and under the archway,' he said.

In the middle of a great arena stood an old wrought iron, roofed in open-air auditorium, known as the Tabernacle, the focal point of past worshippers and now an open shell. Standing a hundred feet high, 130 feet across, it seats three thousand spectators. In 1835 a small band of Edgartown Methodists held a camp meeting in an oak grove high on the bluffs at the northern end of the town. This was just one of the hundreds of revivals that were being held in outdoor settings at the time. The worshippers and their preachers lived in improvised tents and the speakers' platform was made of driftwood. The camp meeting became a yearly affair and one of rapidly growing popularity.

By 1880 the gathering had grown to a thousand wooden framed tents, the gingerbread cottages replacing them. The area is known as Cottage City of America, with the addition of hotels, restaurants and stores attracting people from Cape Cod and beyond. Today the site is used for community singing. On 6th August each year. Thousands of people congregate around the tabernacle to sing and to witness the glow of hundreds of Japanese lanterns hanging from the framework of the tabernacle and eaves of the gingerbread cottages.

The original owners of the cottages modelled their summer houses on Victorian lines and competed with each other, adding unique filigree work to the exteriors.

A stroll around Oak Bluffs through the camp meeting ground led me to the quaint and colourful Victorian gingerbread cottages. One of them, *Over the Rainbow,* attracted my attention as it was a mass of vividly-coloured flowers. At the garden gate was the owner, who introduced himself as William Lane. He invited me in to look around and meet his wife. Before I left I enjoyed a chat and coffee on the terrace. It was the day before the island's yearly great illumination night when thousands of Japanese lanterns adorn the town and up to sixty thousand revellers celebrate.

Oak Bluffs, derived from the first commercial building of Oak Bluffs Land and Wharf Company, which was responsible for most of the layout of the town.

The Europeans of New England divided the island into six townships, each with an historical interest of its own, and a tourist attraction. Gay Head Cliffs was originally called Dover Cliffs by Bartholomew Gosnold, but British sailors preferred the more colourful name. Like a sentry, the lighthouse stands above all, a guiding light to passing ships. The Wampanong Indians still live on Gay Head, preserving their culture.

CHAPTER THIRTY-EIGHT

1987 – A Concorde Crossing

There she was on the tarmac. I could see her from the window of the first-class British Airways lounge at John F. Kennedy International Airport, New York.

Her elegant slim lines resembled a white bird about to take flight. At the age of eighty-one, I was about to take my first supersonic flight on Concorde across the North Atlantic ocean in three hours and twenty minutes.

I gazed at her with interest as I nibbled dainty canapes and sipped my Moet and Chandon champagne; it was champagne all the way! As I photographed her, I wondered how such a small aeroplane could possibly travel at up to 1400 miles an hour, eleven miles up, across an ocean.

At the entrance to the aircraft, I was handed a souvenir, a boxed plastic model of Concorde before being escorted to a front non-smoking seat in the second section of the plane by an attractive hostess wearing a red, white and blue striped suit. I sank into a leather armchair next to a charming Canadian, John G., from Niagara-on-the-Lake in Canada. From my window I was able to watch the quick take-off of Concorde.

She taxied along the runway and suddenly rose, almost perpendicular it seemed, into the sky like a bird on the wing but with a supersonic sound. Cameras clicked and the eighty-nine passengers chatted to each other as we soared over the skyscrapers of Manhatten. Captain Colin Morris gave a running commentary on height and speed. To reduce noise over the city, the power of the four Rolls Royce Sneema Olympus 593 engines was lowered; once over the Atlantic Ocean, power was increased.

Meanwhile, I sipped more champagne and nibbled more canapes. The usual aircraft safety precautions were demonstrated and the menu was produced. The cover displayed gorgeous pink orchids named *Mad Hatter,* descended from species originating in the tropics of the Far East.

There was a varied assortment of drinks to whet my appetite on the drinks side of the menu and the lunch menu contained delightful alternatives for a luscious meal.

Each passenger received a folder with information on Concorde, some magazines and a souvenir certificate of the flight signed by Sir Colin Marshall, chief executive, and Captain Brian Walpole, general manager of the Concorde division, to prove that we had flown supersonically on Concorde.

Some passengers passed the time by listening to the entertainment by audio programmes which were detailed in the in-flight guide. As we climbed up into the sky, breaking the sound barrier, our watches were synchronised with London by advancing five hours to six o'clock.

On the bulk-head in front of me was the in-flight display board which gave air-speed readings in miles per hour as well as other information such as air temperature, altitude, etc.

Passengers were invited for a brief visit to the flight deck. As a novice, I thought the control panel was a massive collection of knobs and buttons. At the controls were Captain Colin Morris and Captain Neil Rannell who kindly signed my notebook, and the flight engineer added his signature.

To fly Concorde (I have been given permission to quote) is granted to very few skilled and dedicated professional airmen. To command is a distinction given to even fewer. The engine flight crew strength of the British Airways Concorde fleet numbers less than one hundred pilots and flight engineers. Only about two dozen of them hold the rank of captain. They have reached their coveted position after long years of experience at the control of subsonic jets, followed by rigorous selection and meticulous training. Every six months they undergo medical checks. Every six months they return to the flight simulator to rehearse their skills under the appraising eyes of instructors. The pattern of training and examination never ceases throughout their working lives. The standard demanded of them never wavers.

As we neared Heathrow Airport, gradually Concorde descended to earth. Below I could see cotton wool clouds; then tiny specks of land, trees and buildings. Like a graceful lady, Concorde reached the tarmac at Heathrow and glided swiftly along the runway until she came to a halt and her engines were switched off.

No jet lag was experienced on Concorde, which travels at twenty-three miles a minute, faster than a bullet, at twice the height of Mount Everest and with more than three thousand hours of test flying behind her.

Concorde is unprecedented in the level of excellence. Since its inaugural commercial flight on 21st January, 1976, more than a million passengers have flown on Concorde.

To some people, flying Concorde is a way of life; to me it was a fantastic and memorable transatlantic experience.

CHAPTER THIRTY-NINE

1988 – Canada Again

In 1988 my base was Richmond, South Vancouver, a thriving, straggling, dynamic community set in natural surroundings of parks, farms and leisure centres. I was the guest of my niece Gerry, whose beautiful home was built like many Canadian houses as an open plan rancher, on one level with bedrooms one end, dining and domestic quarters the other, front door in the middle and garden front and back, with a large patio. The grass is kept cut and free of weeds by a weed-man who contracts to the householder to keep the turf in good order for a nominal fee. What makes these Ranchers so special is that they can actually be transferred to another site by House Moving Ltd, who jack up the building and move it by lorry.

The Ranchers are parked on land four feet below sea level. A dyke separates the town from the sea, controlling the incoming waters. A favourite walk is along the rough track bordering the dyke, backed on one side by houses, on the other by marshes. This is Lulu Island which is in the delta of the Fraser River. To the south of the island is the rustic and historical village of Steveston, a splendid fishing area with great depth of water. I fell for the charm of Steveston.

The history of Steveston dates back to the first settlers of 1877 when a farmer from Ontario settled in the north-east part of Lulu Island. The 1880s saw the introduction of canneries and the importation of the first herd of Holstein cows for dairy farming. Founded in 1889, the little hamlet had already some laid-out streets but a William Steves saw the potential for the layout of the whole town. He had ideas of rivalling the then young Vancouver city with Steveston becoming a major seaport. It became a boom town, but there was much drinking, gambling and prostitution in the taverns among the ten thousand inhabitants. In 1893, the first hospital was founded by a Japanese fishermen's association which also served the whites. Steveston is home to a large commercial fishing fleet with fish sold straight from the boats.

From a little hamlet in the 1880s, once known as the Blueberry Capital of Canada and the Cranberry Capital of the World, Steveston has developed into a first-class residential town with modern shopping facilities. But it still retains some of its old character, including Hiro's Grocery in Moncton Street which dates back to 1911, one of several small stores, with unique architecture, operated by Japanese merchants. The tiny Steveston museum is an example of early pre-fab construction. Built in four sections, it was shipped down the Fraser River and assembled on site. Located in the original Royal Bank building of 1906, it houses a fully operational post office and school. It gives informative displays of historical items and photographs reflecting Steveston's unique heritage.

In a small park off Moncton Street, Byng's School Band was giving a lively performance by young scholars. The school stands on the site of the old Steveston School which was damaged by one of the many fires suffered by the town. It was rebuilt and named after Lord Byng who was Governor-general of Canada 1921-6.

Art is much to the fore with galleries of outstanding maritime art. Local artists sell their oils and water-colours in the town streets and studios. In the Gulf of Georgia Galleries I was shown works by internationally acclaimed artists.

Browsing around a gift shop run by Norman Boycott, I came across tiny pieces of jade carved into animal figures. Jade is a stone of good fortune; precious nephrite jade has been supplied to the Orient in quantities for years from the Canadian mountains. In British Columbia a Canadian industry has developed with talented artists and craftsmen working their native Canadian jade, one of the toughest materials in nature. Jade requires long hours of work, mostly with diamond tools, to produce finished goods durable for hundreds of years.

On downtown waterfront is the birthplace of Vancouver which saw phenomenal growth after the arrival of the Canadian Pacific Railway in 1885. In 1867, 'Gassy' Jack Deighton canoed in with a couple of barrels of whiskey and opened a saloon in Maple Street Square. A statue to his memory marks the spot where Vancouver began. A community and then a city grew around it, flourishing with commerce, and it had become the liveliest part of the west coast of Canada when the great fire of 1886 burned it to the ground. Immediately this town of Gassy's, shortened to Gastown, rose from the ashes to become the new city centre.

Gastown thrives in an unusual setting with a collection of Victorian architectural buildings enhanced by cobbled streets full of character with street musicians and outdoor festivals.

The city is famous for its ornate clock, the first steam-powered clock weighing over two tons. Standing on the corner of Gambie and Water Streets, it was designed by R. H. Saunders and erected for people's enjoyment. It has four dials highlighted by hand-made enamelled copper dogwood flowers. The clock plays Westminster chimes. The downtown night lights attract the shoppers and the promiscuous girls on the street corners in their tight jeans or mini skirts hoping for customers.

One of downtown's great attractions is the classical Chinese Garden on an acre site, the first authentic garden of the Ming dynasty to be built outside China. It is a replica of one of the gardens at Suzhou outside Shanghai which I visited on my Chinese tour in 1980.

Connecting Vancouver with North Vancouver is the Capilano suspension bridge, considered by some to be the eighth wonder of the world. It is 450 feet long and 230 feet above the sea. The bridge sways in the wind, sometimes causing it to be a hazard to visitors.

Back in 1980 I took the little steam train for a scenic run up to Sqamish. The first white settlers arrived in 1886 from Manitoba Province. A store and post office were established and the logging of the giant fir trees has become the life-blood of Sqamish ever since. Sqamish means Mother of the Winds. This time I travelled up by road with my niece with views of rich green isles and majestic mountain peaks – a natural panorama. The population of Sqamish is only eleven thousand, a tiny township set all alone, yet self-sufficient, with representation of the Royal Canadian Mounties and other services.

My niece took me over to Vancouver Island by car, a short ferry crossing from the mainland of Vancouver to Victoria which has castles, gardens and totem poles, but with English traditions. Of special mention is the elegant CPR Empress Hotel, an enormous castle-like structure overlooking the inner harbour. Part French chateau and part English manor house, the Empress is noted for its superb cuisine and known to heads of state the world over. In lush surroundings we relished an olde English tea served in the beautiful restaurant to the soothing background of piano and cello music.

The Butchart Gardens were as lovely as on my previous visit and maintained so well by the Butchart family.

Tucked away down a drive in Victoria is the picturesque replica of the ten-roomed cottage of Ann Hathaway, wife of William Shakespeare. The building resembles a bit of Olde England transferred from Stratford-on-Avon and is a perfect reproduction of the Elizabethan period. The cottage is correct right down to the furnishings of the sixteenth and seventeenth centuries. They seem to be identical to those in the original cottage in Stratford.

Niagara's Thundering Falls

Through a special offer of a cheap ticket in Vancouver, I flew three thousand miles for a weekend visit to see Niagara Falls, having managed to book en route by road from Toronto three nights at Blackstone Motel, within walking distance of the falls.

The Niagara Falls began with one fall seven miles downstream from the present location but the water has gradually worn the rocks away. Described as the Land of the Rainbow, Niagara meant to the ancient Indians 'thunder of water' or in their own language, *ongola amra.* Wandering Indian hunters left their mark with stone tools which have been tentatively dated as 7,000 B.C.

Legend has it that two Indians battled a life and death struggle for a beautiful Indian maiden on an island at a precipice of the Canadian Horseshoe Falls. Seeing the man she loved struck dead, she leaped into her canoe and was at once swept over a cataract and was drowned. According to the legend, this Indian maiden may still be seen with her arms reaching upwards to her lover.

Moored on the great crest of the American Falls is a small red steel scow, a fixture since 1918 when it broke its tow line as it was being brought in by a tug. William Red Hill helped to rescue two men.

Niagara is a great go-ahead town with a population of seventy-three thousand.

Every year some fifteen million visitors gaze in awe at the mighty falls as they thunder down into the Niagara river below. The water drains from Lakes Michigan, Superior, Huron and Erie and goes on through Lake Ontario into the St Lawrence River. At Niagara the water flows over hard limestone twenty feet thick; beneath the limestone are layers of soft shale and more limestone. The falling waters drop into a plunge pool below the falls.

The American Falls are 167 feet high and the Canadian Horseshoe Falls, where the Niagara River plunges over the Niagara Escarpment, are 158 feet high.

At the base of Clifton Hill is the boarding dock for two ferryboats taking visitors, in protective clothing, for a two-hour cruise by the Niagara Falls and the Canadian Horseshoe Falls – one of the oldest tourist attractions in North America.

Over the years, many people have attempted to go over the falls in a barrel. One was in 1901 when Anna Edmos Taylor, a forty-five year old schoolteacher from Manitoba, braved the ordeal in a 260lb sealed steel-bound barrel; she was set adrift near the Canadian Horseshoe Falls accompanied by a black kitten for luck. She returned safely but shaken and lived for many years before she died, forgotten, in poverty. The kitten is said to have survived the barrel ride, but her coat turned white!

On many occasions the Hill family braved the rapids with William Red Hill, not only a Niagara enthusiast, but also a rescuer of those other dare-devils at risk in the rapids. In 1889 Jean Francois Gravelet, known as Blondin, actually walked over the falls on a high-wire, performing tricks as he went across.

Niagara is known as Honeymoon Capital or Niagara Honeymoon Land. It is a favourtite place for newly-weds ever since Napoleon Bonaparte's brother sailed up to Niagara from New Orleans with his bride.

While Niagara is impressive at any time of the year, it celebrates the Blossom Festival in spring, the Peach Festival in summer and the Festival of Light in Winter when the falls, with their white snow mantle, have an air of wonderland. At night, the falls are a magnificent sight with a *Son et Lumiere* effect in a rainbow of light.

Before leaving for Vancouver I sat spellbound in a theatre adjacent to the Skylon Tower as I watched on a screen, ten times the size of a normal screen, legendary episodes of the falls, its ancient history of myths and magic, and a glimpse of the Indian settlers of 12,000 years ago when they worshipped the thunder beings thousands of years before the first European discovered the falls. The Indian maiden was shown setting out in her canoe to rescue her lover, and we saw the many dare-devils who challenged the Niagara Falls.

CHAPTER FORTY

1988 – In Search of Skye

In mid September 1988, I had the urge to see the Isle of Skye in the Inner Hebrides off the west coast of Scotland. It was a long haul from the south-east coast of England, by rail and ferry, but worth the effort for the scenic beauty of the Western Highlands.

Known as the Mystic Isle, or in Gaelic *Eilean a Chao,* the Island of the Mist, Skye is also referred to as the Rainbow Isle for its vivid rainbows and the Winged Island as it is shaped like wings.

On the last lap of my rail journey to Mallaig on the extreme west coast of Scotland, I passed by towering mountain peaks, with a view of Ben Nevis, rugged coastlines, rivers and lochs, with Loch Lomond threading its way through sheltered waters.

It was a twenty-five minute crossing over the sea to Armadale across the Sound of Sleat. From the pier I could see Armadale Castle in the distance. The castle stands on the lovely Sleat Peninsula in lush vegetation and a profusion of trees. Although it is no longer inhabited, the castle is still the focal point of the clans, with parts restored to house the Clan Donald Centre and a museum with an historical collection of 1300 years of Clan Macdonald history. In 1986 the exhibition won eight major awards as the Scottish museum of the year.

At the pier head I caught the bus for the forty-five mile drive to Portree, the island capital and a good base for touring Skye. On the road to Broadford and Portree, I had my first glimpse of the Cuillins, a range of mountains with twenty-five peaks shrouded in mist but well-known to mountaineers, some of whom have successfully climbed the peaks.

Portree, from the Gaelic *Port Righ,* the king's port, is the largest village on the island and is the administrative centre. Built around the natural harbour of Portree Loch, it is a busy fishing port, providing a safe harbour for local fishing boats and yachts. Skye is especially noted for its salmon and trout fisheries and prawn and shrimp hatcheries. A picture postcard scene, the harbour is partly surrounded by colourful houses and shops. In the village is a tiny police station, a bank, a tea-house and bakery, library, Lutheran church, and on a high ridge, the old jail, now used as a tourist office. The Royal Hotel was once a thatched building called MacNab's Inn.

The island is steeped in folklore. The 1988 Skye Folk Festival took place in August with events centred on Portree's Skye Gathering Hall. As Peter Turner, area officer of *The Visitor,* says, and I quote, 'Skye is undoubtedly one of the most romantic islands of the Hebrides.' The tourist office in Portree was very helpful on the island generally and bookshops have a number of informative books which chronicle part of the folklore of the island.

I was fortunate in booking the last room in Portree Hotel in the Square and I feasted on wild salmon, common in that area. It was also the last week of the season. I took advantage of the tours and my history books came to life with tales of Bonnie Prince Charlie, who, at the outbreak of war in 1743 between Britain and France where he was living, was inspired to secure for himself the Scottish throne. Aided by the intrepid Flora Macdonald, living on the island of Uist, he reached the Hebrides, went into hiding and became a fugitive. Dressed as Betty Burke, Flora's companion, he moved from place to place chased by his enemies and with a £30,000 ransom on his head.

Skye is mainly agricultural, with cattle and sheep. Sixty thousand sheep roam the moors and highways. The moors are covered with purple heather and peat bogs. Peat, an organic material and the remains of plants, is normally cut in spring so that it is ready for winter fuel.

Touring the north circular route, from Portree we drove via Loch Fada with a view of the Isle of Raasay, and by the Storr Loch, with the Black Storr rock rising to a height of 2,300 feet and visible for miles. The Old Man of Storr, a crumbling pinnacle 165 feet high, remained unconquered until the summer of 1965 when three men climbed to the summit, descending on rope suspended from a metal peg hammered into the Old Man's crown.

Heading for Kilmuir, we came to the old Skye Crofter's House Folk Museum containing a unique collection of highland and island relics gathered together in several thatched cottages by an island crofter. The museum features a typical crofter's holding of a hundred years ago, with a weaving shed, smithy, barn, outbuildings and tools. Near the museum was a craft shop specialising in sheepskin products. A few yards away was Dame Flora Macdonald's grave and an imposing monument to the memory of this heroic woman.

A westwards tour, via the Cuillins, road was to the imposing Dunvegan Castle, the jewel in the crown of the Isle of Skye, opened to the public forty years ago. A fortress stronghold in an idyllic loch-side setting, it is surrounded by dramatic scenery where seals play and eagles soar. From the ramparts I could see the hills of Harris and the flat-topped MacLeod Tables range of mountains.

Dunvegan is the only fortress in the Hebrides to have remained intact and in the hands of one family for seven hundred and fifty years of recorded history. It is now the ancestral home of the twenty-ninth chief, John MacLeod of Macleod and his family. The oldest part of the castle dates from the fifteenth century with additions in the nineteenth century when a Fairy Tower was added.

The castle's interior contains many historical clan objects and relics, including family portraits, antiques, silver and a library of rare books. Walking through the rooms it was evident it was a much lived-in castle full of ancestors' treasures in use when the family is in residence. The Business Room, as it is now known, was once Flora's study where she entertained many contemporary visitors including Sir Walter Scott, Dr Samuel Johnson, whose portrait hangs on the wall, and James Boswell. In glass cases in the drawing room was a yellow silk fairy flag or crusader's banner, somewhat tattered over the years but still definable. Also on display was the ancestral clan drinking vessel, the Rory Mor's Horn. It was decreed that the chief's heir at his coming of age must take a full horn of claret and drain it at one draught 'without setting down or falling down'. Within six feet of the drawing room was the eerie dungeon where, down a small aperture, I could see a pit thirteen feet below where prisoners were lowered or thrown to end their days. The pit has since been cleared.

Visitors can purchase an enjoyable reminder of their tour of the castle. John MacLeod of Macleod, the twenty-ninth chief, has prepared a video film outlining the history of the castle stretching back nearly eight hundred years.

From Portree it was a bus ride to the pretty village of Carbost to visit the modern Tallisker whisky distillery, situated on the shore of Loch Harport within sight of the Cuillins in a setting of unspoilt beauty. It was founded in 1830 by Hugh and Kenneth Macaskill of the Isle of Eigg where their father had been the island doctor. The Reverend Roderick MacLeod, a former minister of this parish and an eminent evangelical preacher, described the 'erection and establishment of a whisky distillery at Carbost as one of the greatest curses that in the ordinary course of Providence could befall it or any other place'. At one time the whisky distillery employed thirty local men but, due to the depressed state of the trade, the number had decreased and the distillery now operates only four days a week. The day I was there, it was a non-productive day but visitors could tour the works. Our guide, Liz, provided tots of malt whisky for us all before we climbed four flights of winding stairs. This whisky has a great reputation for blending. It is also available as a single malt and has a distinct flavour all of its own, different from whisky made from peat moor water. The water used for this whisky comes over fourteen waterfalls. Scotch whisky is known as the 'Water of Life'.

Skye is a hikers' and campers' paradise. Within a short distance of Portree village on the Dunvegan road, I walked to the Skye Woollen Mill where, in a large complex, there was an ossortment of pullovers, jumpers, tweeds, tartans, Pringles and the like for sale.

Returning south I took with me lovely memories of when I went in search of Skye.

This chapter was published in The Guild of St. Helena Magazine, *London.*

CHAPTER FORTY-ONE

1988 – Christmas on the Mexican Riviera

I had to fly to Los Angeles to join the P&O *Sun Princess* for an eleven day cruise along the Mexican Riviera. After boarding the liner for my 3397 miles rendezvous with the sun, one of the first priorities was a mock-bomb exercise for the ship's company and passengers.

Through the San Pedro Channel we sailed for three days by some of Mexico's rugged but beautiful coastline. Off the west coast of Baja California we made a landfall off the rocky and barren Cedros Islands, of particular interest as the seas around there are abundant with marine life – four species of whale, porpoises, sealions and turtles.

At the southern tip of Baja we cruised past the resort of Cabo San Lucas before clearing the peninsula and crossing the Sea of Cortes for Puerto Vallarta.

Puerto Vallarta is a picturesque seaside resort embraced by the beautiful Bay of Banderas on one side, with mountains behind. A former fishing village turned into a vacation paradise with six to nine liners docking each week. People from all walks of life flocked to the area in search of metals as it is rich in tin and copper.

The city, with its cobblestone streets and red-roofed little houses, dates back to pre-Columbus civilisation. Evidence of this is seen in skills for the local handicrafts handed down by generations of artisans.

The first explorer to land on the east coast of Mexico was a notorious thirty-year old, Herman Cortez, with his army of several hundred men. A great leader, a man adept with the knife and a great womaniser, he fought many duels for a maiden he cherished.

More than three centuries later a family settled north of the Cualo River, the area being known as Puerto las Penas. In 1918 it was designated a municipality and renamed Puerto Vallarta.

About twenty-five years ago, it began to be promoted for tourism but it was a slow process. For years it remained a backwater of Mexico; it now has a population of some two thousand.

A tour began with a drive along the Mallecon Promenade. The waterfront runs along by the bay lined with first-class shops and restaurants. Along the quaint cobblestone streets we came to the town's most distinctive landmark, the Cathedral of Our Lady of Guadalupe. The brilliant gold crown atop its steeple doubles as a navigation aid for ships. A short distance away is Gringo Gulch where beautiful holiday homes of numerous celebrities cling to the cliff edges above the River Cualo. Before crossing the bridge over the river, we explored the tropical grounds. Travelling southwards along the scenic coastal highway there were magnificent vistas of lush tropical vegetation on one side and the azure Pacific Ocean on the other. Past the exclusive Gold Coast section were rows of lovely white stucco and red tile roofed homes and luxury hotels to Mismaloya Beach where *Night of the Iguana,* the film that made Puerto Vallarta famous, was made. At the quaint Bay of Boca di Tomatlan is the charming Chee Chee hillside restaurant where refreshing drinks were served in coconut shells.

Shopping in the artisan quarter was fun, with tempting fine silver jewellery. In a workshop I watched rings being made. At the quayside, among the laden stalls of handicrafts were large wooden painted parrots and I was offered an outsize live iguana!

Acapulco – Epitome of the Mexican Riviera

Acapulco, the glittering treasure coast of Mexico, the millionaires' playground of the jet-set, the rich and the famous, and now I was there! An all-round-the-clock resort, there's no place like it in the world. For over forty years it's been drawing millions of people to its sunny shores.

It is a city of over a million people and is blessed with spectacular and fabulous facilities. The towering Sierra Madre mountains lie behind one of the most beautiful harbours in the world, rimmed with golden sands and high-rise flats. You have only to view Acapulco Bay from the Scenic Highway, skirting one of the nearby hills, to sense that there is something special in its panorama.

To set foot in this flesh-pot of the Mexican Riviera is to know that a certain amount of permissiveness is in the air but there are few rules to spoil the fun. Anything goes, if within the law. Acapulco reeks of sensuality; its sexiness is part of its legend. The locals are frequently flaunting their bodies in a natural sort of way. Dress is casual in the extreme all through the twenty-four hours, but in a very style-conscious way. In the evening, the ladies follow their favourite fantasy, provocative or conservative. No-one will bat an eyelid at what they wear, within reason. Men don a fresh cotton shirt and slacks as formal wear; for dinner dates, a light blazer or tropical white jacket, will suffice at a first-class restaurant, but ties and even socks, can be left behind.

Acapulco has plenty of Mexican flavour. In many ways, life goes on as it has for centuries, though the city is a jet-set resort. Fishermen leave at dawn with giant nets, cooks prepare ancient recipes, workers mould clay and paint pottery as their forefathers have before them. But the three open-air colourful markets are as varied and as vital to every day life as any others in Mexico. This sophisticated international playground is as Mexican as other parts of the Mexican Riviera.

Mexico's Acapulco is endowed with a magnificent bay and twenty golden beaches.

One of the most colourful landmarks that distinguishes this part of the coast from all other Mexican resorts is illustrated by the Al Quebrada rugged cliffs or the Breakers.

The attractiveness of the Quebrada is not just the rock cliffs themselves, but their peculiar contours and formation, and the water currents in the area. The sea breaks against these rocks with unusual violence. A grandstand view is from the Hotel el Mirador in the Las Brisas area and the Bar la Perla at the highest point.

La Quebrada is also famous for the extraordinary death-defying divers. Young men who are familiar with the movements of the sea, climb with bare hands and feet up the sheer cliff wall to more than 130 feet above the sea. Carefully studying the movement of the water and tide, they must select the precise moment when an entering wave will fill the tiny crevice with water deep enough for them to dive safely. Their dive must have enough horizontal impulse to carry them far away from the sides of the cliff to enter the very centre of the water below. The divers perform daily, free of charge. At our session four dripping divers lined up; they certainly deserved their tips. When not diving, they plunge below the waters in search of oysters.

By way of variation, cruise liners come regularly to Acapulco, once a fishing village and almost unknown to the outside world. In the early days the hotels were built high up on the hills of the Caleta area to catch the ocean breezes and for the views of the bay.

The bright white cathedral of Acapulco presides over the Zocaldo (Coronation) Square where the traditional Mexican bandstand sits on one of the town's oldest restaurants. The main street, La Cottera Miguel Aleman, begins in the old part of the town. Heading towards the highway an underpass divides old Acapulco from the sea.

Along the Cottera are many high-rise hotels, beaches, restaurants and excellent shopping complexes. The major hotel, La Condesa del Mar, is the most popular in Acapulco and is set in the glamorous and busy part of the town, with its discoes. The Convention Centre stages one of the best folklore shows in all Acapulco.

Eastwards we came to the small Icacos naval base and headed up the hills to an exclusive area where American celebrities have their homes. A short drive away, sprawling over a mountainside and covering both sides of the road, is the most exclusive resort in Acapulco, Las Brisas. We passed by the calm Puerto Marques Bay, virtually water-logged and said to be the location of Acapulco's best period of growth and expansion.

Two of the finest and most sought-after hotels, both under the same management, are the Pierre Marques and next door the Hotel Acapulco Princess, known as the Disneyland of hotels. These two beautiful hotels are magnificently sited on lovely Revolcadero Beach with the Sierra Madre mountains as a backdrop; a world of luxury and pleasure! The distinctive and special architecture of the Acapulco Princess, built in the shape of three pyramids, reflects the design built in the great Mayan culture of early Mexico. The landscaped Princess estate covers 240 acres. The grounds contained strolling peacocks, a Tarzan rope bridge and waterfalls, an ocean view restaurant and on the beach a native market. The day was hot, and it was pleasant relaxing in a deckchair in such fantastic surroundings, backed by the majestic Acapulco Princess Hotel with 720 rooms. There are three championship golf courses and a full range of resort facilities. Many guests are loath to leave the premises during their stay. Driving on the Scenic Highway, we lunched Mexican style at Hotel Miramar in peaceful and elegant style.

Mazatlan, the Pearl of the Pacific

Mazatlan was originally inhabited by indigenous groups of Indians who hunted deer and gathered seed and fruits. In the language of these Nahuati Indians, Mazatlan means Place of the Deer.

Originally founded in 1531 by the Spanish conquistador, Nuno de Guzman, by the early 1800s a permanent Spanish colony was established in Mazatlan, based on a flourishing and growing shipping industry. The city became known as the Athens of the West Coast. In 1827, the first municipal government was formed. The war-like defences along the coastline are an indication of the French mistake of trying to put Emperor Maximilian on the throne of Mexico in 1864.

Mazatlan is the home of the country's largest shrimp-fishing fleet. It is a major Pacific port, a picturesque scene with some eight hundred boats operating. It is also one of the few resorts where hunting still goes on, though I do not know what there is to hunt there. Mazatlan is surely a sportsman's paradise with every kind of outdoor sport to suit the visitor from water sports to bull-fighting for the blood-thirsty ones.

On the horizon of Mazatlan's ocean front is the world's second highest lighthouse, Gibraltar being the highest. There are also off-shore islands and a scenic shore-line.

Mazatlan is spread out. The major area stretches from the lighthouse to the condominiums on the northern beaches. The strip of seaside highway contains some sparkling hotels; beginning in the old part of Mazatlan it winds north to the Golden Zone. In old downtown there is a busy market and the cathedral which lies behind the older section of Highway 15.

Winding into the rugged foothills of the Sierra Madre, we arrived at the quaint town of Concordia with its beautiful colonial church, furniture factory and potter's shed with its kiln which produces jugs, jars, flowerpots and dishes typical of this region.

Continuing on into the mountains we came to the ghost town of Copala, once a flourishing Spanish gold mining town, founded in 1565. We wandered through the town's cobblestone streets which were lined either side with colonial-style houses; people at their doors greeted us and a man with a van-load of oranges cut one in half and gave it to me to quench my thirst. We passed the jail and imposing church which dated back to the time of the conquista. It's a peaceful little world all of its own; the children go to school by donkey and chickens and pigs wander at will. At the top end of the street was Daniel's restaurant, a white-washed building where a traditional Mexican meal was laid out for our party – tortilla pastry wrapped around shredded hot meat, seasoned with garlic, chilli and onion, accompanied by a seasonal sauce and followed by banana cream pie.

Browsing around a gift shop, I came across a delightful black and white illustrated booklet on Mazatlan by a well-known artist and writer, Paul Hodlin, dedicated to his wife and friends. Paul describes his love of Copala, the Island Paradise in the Sky, which is the name of the restaurant in Copala owned by his friend, Dan, which we visited. Paul depicts Copala through the ages, his present reflections and his hopes for the future of the town. He tells us that the name Copala is derived from copal, a resin-like substance found in abundance there, which when burned produces an aromatic smoke used in homes and for religious ceremonies. It is believed to be a connecting point to the umbilical cord and thus like a navel to heaven. Paul describes the smiling people as firm devotees of the town and the church and lovers of their children and animals, with pride in their homes and heritage; their sense of humour makes the people of Copala delightful to meet, an hospitable and kindly area with a population of 25,000.

Some youths are first-class divers. In Old Mazatlan spectators gather at the rocky look-out, El Mirador, on Paseo Clauses, to watch these dare-devils take off from the high rocks, as in Acapulco, to plunge gracefully into the ocean below.

Shopping in Mazatlan is not so good as in other parts of the Pacific coast, but there are many stores and boutiques. Leather is an excellent buy, made into wallets, fashionable skirts and jackets.

To get around there are fascinating open-air palainias, motorised carts, which are more fun and less expensive than taxis, and picturesque two-wheeled horse-drawn carriages, called aranas, which trot along the streets.

The climate of Mazatlan is fantastic. The sun was so hot on Christmas Day, that I bought a pair of shorts to wear instead of slacks.

Like all other Mexican towns, Mazatlan has a continual round of fiestas. In the square, Indian male dancers in full and colourful regalia performed a spectacular ritual dance, followed by the Flying Pole Dance, Los Valadoras. This courageous band of men fly through the air around a hundred-foot pole, while a couple on top give a musical display. Thousands of visitors flock into Mazatlan to enjoy the fiestas.

Cabo San Lucas

On to Cabo San Lucas which lies at the southern tip of the six hundred mile long Baja peninsula, once a hideaway for pirates, who plundered the Mexican coast. It took the Spanish a hundred and fifty years to establish the first settlement in this rugged and hostile land. Today, it is a much sought-after resort, one of Mexico's fastest-growing communities and a mecca for sport-fishing, snorkelling, diving and water sports in general. De luxe hotels provide all the amenities for what is rapidly becoming a world-class resort.

The scenic beauty of 'Land's End' cannot be exaggerated. Its dramatic rocks jut out of the ocean from the Sea of Cortes, an enormous fish trap. From our glass-bottomed boat we gazed into clean and unpolluted water with an abundance of sea life for birds and sealions. The Sea of Cortes is famous for blue and striped marlin, the type most sought after by anglers. About 40,000 marlin are hauled out of 'Marlin Alley' waters every year.

Sailing around the cape, a dramatic rugged rock, called Los Arcos, reached starkly out of the sea, a natural formation called the Arches. Rounding this window, the Pacific Ocean meets the Sea of Cortes. Lovers' Beach (Playa del Amor) faces it and the Pacific. Locals cynically call its turbulent, unswimmable Pacific side, Divorcee Beach. High on the rocks were masses of pelicans; these strange birds, with their great long pouched beaks and six-foot wing span, are abundant along the Mexican coast. They fly over the sea in search of fish for their young and can travel in long lines before dive-bombing with folded wings into the water, creating a terrific splash, often coming up with their bills full of live fish. On the rocks, sealions were resting. Our boatman called out to them, and they answered him with a strange call.

Shopping in the duty-free town consisted chiefly of American goods which were of major interest to Mexican consumers. There were no chic shops. Popular items were sportswear advertising Cabo San Lucas on the shirt fronts. We then headed back to Los Angeles for a last day.

Back to L.A.

At the end of December, *Sun Princess* was back at her berth in LA. Los Angeles is a sprawling city of many faces in Southern California and one of the largest in the world. Many families have three cars. English is the main language but there are many Spanish speakers. Most people are protestants by religion, although all major religions are represented.

Spaniards from Mexico took over the Indian settlement of Yang-na in 1769 and named it Nuestra Senora la Reina de los Angeles. The Stars and Stripes were raised over the city in 1846.

After driving over Vincent Thomas harbour bridge we went along the palm-lined avenues, through the industrial area to Long Beach harbour to see, permanently berthed, the old British liner *Queen Mary* which takes half a day to go over. Also there is the *Spruce Goose* complex.

Los Angeles' Spanish heritage is for ever enshrined in the rustic charm of downtown Olvera Street. The original block-long El Pueblo still retains a latin flavour with traditional Spanish costumes and the aroma of Mexican food. This colourful and festive street reflects days of long ago when L.A. was a scruffy, sleepy, 'pebble'. Now there is a two-way 'strip' known as Sunset Boulevard, with lavish homes, theatrical agencies and night clubs; it is a setting between Hollywood and Beverley Hills, with modern facilities, an area for the elite and curious visitor. Rolls, Mercedes and Jags line the streets while the famous, and not so famous, stroll along Sunset Boulevard hoping to be recognised among the fashion trendies. Stores with luxury names like Gucci, Pucci and Giorgia's add a modern touch of glamour to the scene.

Just around the corner, announced by the hillside signwriting, Hollywood thrives on the creative energies of film directors and the like. Universal Studios is now the world's largest motion picture complex, stretching over 420 acres, a make-believe world of film sets; since my visit a fire devastated a large portion of the studios. Over the hill is Disneyland.

In the this 'City of Angels' one of the great downtown sights is the super decorated high-rise hotels. The Bonaventure, a thirty-six storey block, has 1420 rooms. There are modern condominiums and high-rise office blocks. The crown jewel is the exquisite Music Centre for the Performing Arts.

One of the tourist spots we visited was Farmer's Market at Third Street – a conglomeration of Spanish and Mexican stalls, shops and restaurants fit for the gourmet or the fish-and-chips enthusiast.

On the Hollywood Pacific Highway is the Chinese Theatre, resembling an enormous pagoda. The foot and hand prints of celebrities embedded in the courtyard pavement squares were of special interest. Wherever I walked there was an imprint of a personality. Little Tokyo, with its gaily-decorated streets, nestled in the vast metropolis which has the largest Japanese community in the United States. As we travelled along we were shown the old city jail for terrorists where Patty Hearst was serving her sentence.

It is impossible to see the city in one day but, while awaiting a flight home, it gives one an insight to this vast and up-to-the-minute city.

CHAPTER FORTY-TWO

1989 – Staying on an American Marines Base

A Tar Hell Toast to North Carolina:

Here's to the land of the long leaf pine.
The summerland where the sun doth shine,
Where the weak grow strong, and strong grow great,
Here's to the 'down home', the Old North State.

It was a brilliant day in May 1989 when I boarded the Piedmont Boeing 787-200 expanded range jet at Gatwick. The first leg of my journey was an eight-hour flight to Charlotte, North Carolina, where I changed planes for Jacksonville. I was on my way to stay with a family on a Marine Base. I met the wife, Frances, when I was in Tangier in 1979. Readers may recall that I was robbed after boarding the train to Marrakesh. My good Samaritan helped me with hotel expenses when our flight to Gibraltar was cancelled leaving me penniless and without a passport in Tangier. We have been staunch friends ever since.

My night flight at Charlotte meant a four-hour wait, but once on the little plane for the fifty minute hop to Jacksonville, I was soon flying over the roof-tops of the brightly-coloured illuminated towns, a fairy-like scene. On arrival at Jacksonville I was whisked off by my hostess to her home on the Marine Base, my host being a member of the Marine Corps. Here, in peaceful surroundings, partly enclosed by the long leaf pine where squirrels abound, I met the family, including the two boisterous boys.

My first introduction to Jacksonville was a tour of the vast Marine Base, set in woodland, with a helicopter site, truck depots and rifle ranges. About 50,000 marines live on the base. Tree-lined avenues lead on to the highways and to the coast. Jacksonville is a coastal resort with sandy beaches, one of which is reserved for the marines.

Baseball is a great sporting event for the young at heart. Youngsters, boys and girls, start playing at about five years old, taking the game seriously, especially the elder boy of the family with whom I stayed. Fathers act as coaches and see that the rules are kept. Mothers are called upon to act as umpires and to provide refreshments to the players. The children are dressed in long white pants, caps, stout shoes and tops with their name and team printed on the back.

Just off the highway is an impressive memorial, honouring the Marines who gave their lives in Beirut in 1982. Their names are recorded on a roll of honour. An inscription reads, 'They came in Peace. May we always remember them who are ready to protect our freedom.' On a nearby plinth is a striking bronze figure of a marine by a well-known scupltress, commissioned by the people of Jacksonville and dedicated on 23rd October, 1986.

About twenty miles from the base is the quaint rustic fishing village of Swansboro, nestled on the south of the White Rock River. It was Arts and Crafts Day when we visited Swansboro, an annual exhibitionm of the arts by the sea, sponsored by the Swansboro Chamber of Commerce in conjunction with the Onslow Council for the Arts.

More than fifty artists, artizans and craftsmen of different disciplines were displaying their wares on stalls up and down historic Front Street, to the accompaniment of the local band. High quality and original handicrafts included lapidary (the art of cutting and polishing gems and stones), woodcraft, lace-making, quilting, basket-weaving, pottery, ceramics, jewellery, brightly coloured stuffed dolls, appliques, balloon sculptures and handicrafted ducks, geese and swan decoys. Attractive were the notelets sold loose or in packs, with views of the Eastern Carolina coast, including eighteenth century towns, resort areas, farmlands, pine forests and fishing villages. Also on display was an original oil-painting of the scene by Jeanne Isenhart.

The Marine Corps was formed on 10th November, 1770. Thursday, 25th May, was graduation day for the marines for 1989 and my host, Bob, was one of the graduates to receive his award. As I read through the printer's proof of this chapter, I heard that Bob had been posted to Saudi Arabia to help to settle the Gulf crisis. The ceremony and exercise were to be held in Virginia by invitation of the Commanding General, Marine Corps Combat Development Command.

We set off early for the six-hour drive to the Academy in Virginia on the Quantico Marine Base, a journey of some 350 miles. The route was through miles of pine forests and towns like Petersburg, Richmond and Fredericksburg. There was a strong aroma of tobacco, once the farmers' salvation, as we passed through Jamestown. Spanish tobacco leaf was grown in the Caribbean and was all the rage in London. In 1612 a farmer brought some seeds to Jamestown and planted them. For a while tobacco was their only means of support apart from the fishing industry. Today Jamestown has grown into a modern town, but it still retains its colonial flavour with seventeenth and eighteenth century historic mansions. Broad rolling fields of wheat and rye sweep rich and golden to the sharp curl of the Atlantic Ocean, where seas pound against a rugged coastline.

The graduation exercises were held in the FBI (Federal Bureau of Investigation) Academy of Quantico Marine Base. In this great edifice dozens of marines were already seated, smartly turned out in white uniforms with crew-cut hair. Flags decked the stage, the Marine Band struck up the national anthem, readings and an address were given, followed by the presentation of individual awards. With *Anchors Away* and the *Mariners' Hymn,* the ceremony ended.

Back in Northern Carolina we drove to Wilmington to tour the US battleship *North Carolina,* with its eight decks and levels, situated across the Cape Fear River. The permanently-berthed battleship is open daily and attracts thousands of visitors.

The temperature was in the nineties, but it did not deter us from exploring the main and lower decks. Commissioned in 1941, the *North Carolina* was considered the greatest sea weapon in the world at the time. It was turbine driven, developing a total of 121,000 horse-power, driving four propellors to give the vessel a speed of twenty-seven knots. Since 1961, the *North Carolina* has been dedicated to the men and women who died defending their country during World War II, and to nearly 10,000 North Carolinians who gave their lives in that war.

There were notices around the battleship: 'Do not feed the alligators'. One monster could be seen resting on a platform close to the water.

I left North Carolina on Memorial Weekend, special to marines, sailors and Americans in all walks of life in the USA. The official day was Monday, 28th May, for reflection and re-dedication through a remembrance of comrades in arms. It is a solemn occasion all over the country, to honour and remember the hundreds of thousands of patriotic Americans who have been killed in battle since the Civil War. It also a national holiday, though not a celebration as such.

Memorial Day started by being called Decoration Day, first observed on 30th May, 1868 with various states declaring it a holiday from 1874 onwards. It later became a memorial holiday observed in all states. Today the recognition of Memorial Day includes parades, wreath-laying ceremonies at commemorative sites and monuments, drum and bugle corps presentations, speeches and exhibitions featuring military and national guard units. On Memorial Day the flag is flown at half mast from sunrise to noon, and at full mast from noon to sunset.

Americans from coast to coast and in Hawaii and Alaska pause and remember their dead relatives and friends on this Monday Memorial Day.

CHAPTER FORTY-THREE

1989 – Tailed by a Hurricane

Prior to Christmas 1989, I joined the Russian ship mv *Kareilya,* built on the lines of a cross-channel ferry, for a tour to Gibraltar, Morocco, the Canaries and Portugal.

The weather forecast for the English Channel were poor; in the Bay of Biscay the weather worsened with tremendous seas, a force eleven hurricane and wind speeds of seventy knots tailing us to Gibraltar. We were the only vessel to go through the Bay; others sought shelter. Many on board were seasick and terrified at the thought of the return passage. An elderly man died of a heart attack. Deck sports were cancelled but indoor entertainment carried on with traditional Russian folkdancing and a dainty Russian tea party.

We were not fully bunkered at Tibury and had to go slowly. Scheduled to arrive at Gibraltar at 1800 hours, we were twenty hours late. Owing to adverse weather conditions in Gibraltar the port authorities closed the port till the next morning. It was imperative that we docked in Gibraltar as we were short of fuel. Passengers were allowed ashore.

As distances between ports were short, it was decided to cancel our calls at Agadir and Lanzarote and head for the remaining ports.

La Palma was bathed in sunshine; it is the highest island in the world relative to its small area of 280 square miles. It is a pretty, leaf-shaped patch in the ocean and known as 'La Verid'. From Santa Cruz, the capital, we toured part of the island, including the southernmost tip of Fuencaliente, to the small hamlet of Las Caletas, the home of wine-making and where we did some wine-tasting. Up north, we stopped at the enormous crater, Caldera de Taburiente, declared a national park, with impressive landscapes and pine forests.

In Tenerife it rained and there was no prospect of driving up Mount Teide with friends Freda and Donald as it was shrouded with mist.

Madeira was all agog for New Year's Eve festivities with a grand firework display illuminating Funchal and the surrounding area. Next day it was traditional to take tea at Reid's Hotel, once the rendezvous of aristocrats; still a member of the Leading Hotels in the World, it retains its popularity with the visitor. To have tea in this exclusive hotel is considered a top priority when visiting Madeira. A fellow passenger, Lilian, and I enjoyed tea on the balcony and the view along the coast to the port of Funchal. Afterwards we walked around the lovely clifftop garden with its wide range of sub-tropical flowers.

Due to the island's geographical position in the Gulf Stream, it has a mild temperature generally varying only between 65 and 75 degrees Fahrenheit throughout the year. In Funchal the wicker sledges from Monte still scurry down the steep slopes carrying passengers for fun and frolic. In the wine vaults of an old Franciscan monastery we joined the tourists for free wine-tasting, before purchasing some genuine Madeira.

Our last port of call was Lisbon, the city on seven hills; the streets are so steep that lifts have been constructed. A half-day tour took us to Cintra Palace, now a museum, housing a varied collection of furniture and paintings dating back to the fifteenth century.

With fears of a rough passage back to Tilbury, eighty passengers flew home from Lisbon; the rest of us sailed home to Tilbury over calmer seas.

Epilogue

As this book goes to press I am planning more travelling around our lovely world. I shall never run out of places I want to see and there are many that I would like to see again.

Among the places which I have not recorded are Switzerland, Majorca, the Italian Lakes, France, the Channel Isles, Isle of Man, Isle of Capri and the Isles of Scilly.

I have already booked trips to take me back to the Caribbean islands and a two month Italian round cargo voyage to Brazil and West Africa where it will be interesting to compare Lagos now with what I remember of the capital when we lived there forty years ago.

Perhaps my Itchy Feet will take me to enough new places so that I can write about more of my roamings for the pleasure of the armchair traveller.